YOU NEED A BIGGER SWORD

YOU NEED A BIGGER SWORD

METAMORPHOSIS ONLINE™ BOOK ONE

NATALIE GREY

MICHAEL ANDERLE

DISRUPTIVE IMAGINATION

YOU NEED A BIGGER SWORD TEAM

Thanks to our Beta Team

John Ashmore, Bree Buras, Crystal Wren, Nicole Emens,
Mary Morris, Kelly O'Donnell

Thanks to our JIT Readers

Jeff Eaton
John Raisor
Angel LaVey
Larry Omans
Misty Roa

If We've missed anyone, please let us know!

Editor
The Skyhunter Editing Team

From Natalie

For M and T

From Michael

*To Family, Friends and
Those Who Love
To Read.
May We All Enjoy Grace
To Live The Life We Are
Called.*

CHAPTER ONE

"Fifteen. Dealer has eighteen." Gracie King smiled at the man sitting in front of her. At 2AM on a Tuesday, the tables at the Torrino were not filled with either the high-rollers or anyone massively successful. This man was wearing a watch a few links too big and a jacket that had not been tailored for him, and he was clearly on the wrong side of tipsy.

Bad start.

He looked at the card, confusion wrinkling his brow, and she saw him trying to do the math in his head.

She resisted the urge to sigh. She had seen all of this play out before—dozens of times tonight alone. It began with someone looking around until their eyes focused on her table. Then they'd come sit down and give her a happy, hearty greeting. Reality would start to intrude as they considered their bet, and she could get a sense of how things would go from whether they bothered to consider the amounts before tossing the chips onto the table.

Sometimes there was a spark, a shared confidence in

the way they smiled. They were here for Las Vegas, not the cards. They loved the city like she did: the absolute, unabashed opulence of it. Some of them were even good blackjack players, accepting the whims of the cards with a smile. Playing the long game.

Those patrons brightened a whole shift. It was like being back in high school, having someone you liked smile at you as they passed in the hall. It wasn't much, but it gave you a high that lasted all day.

But most of the people who came here weren't like that. They were like this man.

Gracie would deal and the player would go through the stages of the game, as predictable as clockwork. They would try to consider what the odds of getting the card they needed were. They would be blinded by the idea of winning. They would want to *do* something, not just sit and wait. They would fall prey to any number of logical fallacies, and she would watch while they lost and lost again, and kept losing until they eventually went away to try another table.

As if that would help them.

She kept the annoyance from her face, but it pulsed through her. She didn't like people who didn't even *try* to make good decisions. They came to her table, terrified of losing the money represented by those brightly-colored chips, and they almost *always* lost it. Then they were sad, and there was no way for her to make that better. Some days, she resented all of it.

Then again, she worked in a casino. These people paid her bills.

The man at the table looked up at her and searched her

eyes for the answer. Gracie kept her smile fixed firmly on her face. After a year of working here, she knew how to make herself smile like a robot, perfectly friendly with absolutely no hints or clues. She couldn't help him. She couldn't make his choice for him.

They were coming to the last stage of the process, the one where people would get reckless.

"Hit me," the guy said at last, right on schedule. He flashed Gracie a smile.

Her own did not waver as she flipped one more card over and slid it into place in front of him.

Eight of clubs, giving him twenty-three.

His smile faltered for a moment as he stared at it, then he shrugged and his smile came back, bright and now divorced from reality.

"What can you do, eh?"

"Bad luck," Gracie said. She hated the sound of the words coming out of her mouth. She couldn't do any more for him, not without angering the gods who watched through the security cameras on the ceiling. She couldn't take the time to tell him that it had been the right choice, all things considered. That with so many cards in play, and partial decks, he could never assess the *exact* odds, but that asking for another card at fifteen had been the right call statistically.

It was just a fluke, genuinely bad luck. She swallowed.

This guy didn't get angry, though. He tried to hide the disappointment. "Absolutely. Can't have a bad streak forever, right?" He brought his martini glass up to drain it, realized it was already empty, and stood. "Clearly it's time for another drink." He winked and headed off, weaving slightly.

Gracie didn't tell him that the nearest bar was in the other direction. He had probably just been trying to get away from the woman who'd seen him lose, and in any case, he didn't need more alcohol. His judgment was impaired enough already.

There was a tap on her shoulder and she turned to see Matt, the manager on duty. Tim was standing next to him, ready to take the table.

"Your shift's done," Matt told her.

Gracie nodded. Casinos existed in a sort of endless evening, with soft, golden lighting, waitresses in sparkly costumes, and jazz playing over the speakers. There was no way to know what time it really was, and the casinos liked that. There were no clocks. Dealers weren't allowed to wear watches, and she had learned not to try to anticipate what time it was. She simply existed until someone came to get her for a break or the end of her shift.

She cleared her hands for the cameras, took the tips from her lockbox, and made her way quickly through the tables to the end of the room, Matt at her side.

"Have you thought about it?" he asked her.

Gracie tensed slightly. "No."

"You should," Matt insisted. Tall and relatively good-looking, he wore his dark hair just on the edge of being too messy for a dealer. "I know you'd make a ton in tips. We never get complaints about you."

She hated this. Gracie swiped her card at the door to the back hallways as she gathered her courage. "I meant, I did think about it. No."

Matt tipped his head back and sighed. "Come *on*, Gracie. You'd be making so much more, and we're short-staffed—"

"I know, and I'm sorry. I just...don't want to." Gracie gave him a nod and ended the conversation by force, slipping through the door and leaving him behind.

She walked quickly to her locker, annoyed. A few weeks ago, Matt had come to her to ask if she would consider taking some shifts as a cocktail waitress. *Nicer uniform*, he'd said with a laugh. He gestured at the white shirts and silk vests the dealers wore. *Better than this atrocity.*

It was hard to argue with that. Sparkly and glamorous, the dresses the cocktail waitresses wore were quintessentially Vegas, part of the glamor that had drawn Gracie here after she finished college. She wanted to wear a sparkly dress as a patron, though, not as a waitress. When she was working, she *liked* the relative anonymity of her mandated plain hairstyle, understated makeup, and distinctly un-sexy uniform.

She didn't want to be bringing overpriced cocktails to already-drunk patrons, not with all the comments and catcalls she could expect.

It was late, and she should go straight home, but after that last client and Matt's disappointment, she decided to head to one of her favorite places on the strip: the Bellagio fountains.

Even this late, the air was warm. She'd stripped off her white shirt and vest, leaving the tank top underneath, replaced the black slacks with jeans, and swapped her black work shoes for flip flops. She looked up at the lights and listened to the music and laughter and the wind rustling in the trees, and felt her tension melt away.

She stood and watched the fountains for a while. This was what she liked most about Vegas: stately grandeur mixed with unabashed glitz. *I know it's too much,* the whole Vegas Strip seemed to say. *That's the point.*

Gracie had chosen Vegas on a whim, moving here after she finished college while her parents demanded to know exactly what she was planning to do with a statistics degree in Las Vegas, of all places. Gracie had told them she'd figure it out. Then, after interviewing at a bunch of soulless offices where they murmured things about "depreciation" and "client experience," she'd taken a job as a dealer on a lark.

Okay, and a *little* bit to piss off her parents.

Whatever, it was working out fine. Mostly fine. Not entirely fine, but she'd find a way to make more money that *didn't* involve calling them and admitting she'd been wrong. She gave one last smile at the fountains, smiled, and headed back to her car.

Her apartment building was one of the first in a planned development, so it was a jarring mix of a fairly nice building on an empty, dusty lot with a lot of construction vehicles and steel girders. Gracie parked in an unoccupied patch of dirt near the building and headed up, taking the stairs two at a time.

She smelled Vietnamese food as she came into the apartment. "Alex?"

"In the living room," Alex called back. Thirty-five, he had moved to Vegas three years ago to get over a divorce and had been fully committed to the bachelor lifestyle ever since, eating mac and cheese directly out of the saucepan and playing video games until he passed out in front of the tv. When Grace poked her head into the living room, he waved her over. "I got a ton of food. You hungry?"

"Always." Gracie kicked off her flip flops and came to sit cross-legged on the couch with him, pulling a container of spicy noodles toward her. "Why do you always get chopsticks? We don't *use* chopsticks."

Alex shrugged, his mouth full of food. "How was work?" he asked a moment later.

"Shit, same as always."

"Your job is shit because you're such a bleeding heart that you want to *help* all the people who suck at playing blackjack."

"I am *not* a bleeding heart, and they're not *playing* black-jack," Gracie said, annoyed. She took a bite, barely chewed, and gulped it down. "They're *playing* 'casinos.' They just *think* they're playing blackjack. That's why they lose."

Alex nodded contemplatively.

"This is good," Gracie said after a moment. "New place?"

"Opened near my work," Alex said. He was employed at an upscale accounting firm, helping the rising stars of the casinos to hide their wealth every April. "Hey, so I was thinking about the VR headset."

Gracie groaned.

"It would be so fun," Alex cajoled. "Come on! It'd be *so* fun."

"If it's that fun, you'll be playing it all the time, and I'll never get a shot."

"Aha! I thought you might say that." Alex looked triumphant.

Gracie froze, her fork halfway to her mouth. "Oh, no. That was a trap, wasn't it?"

"One hundred percent," he agreed cheerfully. "Metamorphosis Online is sponsoring a buy-one-get-one-fifty-percent-off deal right now. I figure if we went halfsies on *that...*"

"So, now instead of paying fifty percent for a VR headset I didn't want, I'm paying seventy-five percent for a VR headset I don't want?" Gracie raised an eyebrow and finished the piece of chicken. "No way."

"I always forget you can do math."

"Dude, it's why you chose me to be your roommate." Gracie and Alex had both gone to Harvey Mudd College and majored in mathematics, although several years apart. That connection had gotten her a room here when Alex had a list of applicants as long as his arm. Despite the twelve years between them, they got along well. Gracie never harped on him not to put his socks on the floor, and he didn't give her crap for preferring to spend her days in sweats rather than dresses.

They also had a mutual agreement never to ask each other where their lives were going or what their aspirations were. It was too depressing a topic, and they both got enough of that from their parents.

Alex grinned. "Okay, tell you what. I'll front the money, and if you *like* the headset, *then* you'll pay your seventy-five percent."

"Deal." Grace reached over and shook on it. "What's *Metamorphosis Online*?"

"The game I was telling you about."

"You tell me about a lot of games. Give me paper and dice any day."

"You say that, but how long has it been since you actually played D&D?"

"I haven't found a good group here." Not that she hadn't tried, of course, but it was hard to find one where she could just be one of the guys. Eventually, Gracie had given up.

"*Metamorphosis Online* is the one where they pay you to play it," Alex reminded her.

"Oh, right." Gracie took another bite and gave him a look. "They pay you *if* you get to a high enough rank."

Alex shook his head, holding his fork up to make a point. "Or if you do a first-clear—you know, when your guild is the first one to clear the new content each month —*or* when you—"

"Alex, you *know* this is a trap." Gracie groaned and let her head thump back on the couch. "It's not real! They've got all these finicky little rules, and they make it super-complicated to figure out how much you make. You *know* you're not going to make your money back."

"Whatever." He gave her a look of great dignity and began sorting through his container, pushing the vegetables aside with his fork. "Man, this stuff is tasty, but they *really* stiffed me on the chicken. Anyway, it's still a fun game."

"Uh-huh." Gracie gestured meaningfully to the racks of game discs. "And it's such a shame you don't have any of *those*."

"I am telling you." Alex jabbed a fork at her. "You will

love the VR headset, and you will love *Metamorphosis Online*. I'll pay for the first month of that, too."

"Eh, why the hell not? We're down the rabbit hole anyway." Gracie settled back on the couch and harrumphed, staring down at her food. "I don't want to go back to work tomorrow."

"I feel ya." Alex took a mouthful of food. "Hey, maybe you'll make enough at this game that you don't have to."

"Maybe I'll sprout wings and fly up your butt."

"Gross."

"Yeah, I didn't think that one through." Gracie grinned and downed the last of the noodles. "Okay, *Call of Duty*. Come on."

"You hate *Call of Duty*."

"Yeah, but now that I've started learning it, I *have* to get good. It's my pathology."

"You have a long way to go," Alex quipped.

"Yeah, well, I'm calling it." Gracie gestured broadly as if she were a presenter. "Tonight's the night I don't get stuck in any corners."

"Good luck," Alex said doubtfully.

CHAPTER TWO

The headset was there when Gracie got home from work a few days later. So was Alex, and he was practically vibrating with excitement.

"Don't you have *work?*" Gracie called to him as she stuffed her work clothes in the washer and started it. She swore and fished out her silk vest just in time. "Son of a— that would have sucked to buy again." She caught sight of Alex in the corner of her vision. "Did you know they charge a *hundred fucking bucks* for one of those if you— You're not listening, are you?"

"The *game,*" Alex said. His hands were palm-up, fingers cupped as though he were offering a prayer up to some god of pixels and game mechanics. He gave her a pleading look. "Come on, you have *got* to roll your character.

"I have got to *eat,*" Gracie said, using the tone she would use for a stubborn toddler. "If I do not, I will kill you violently."

"It would be worth it to know I've brought another fine soul to the world of *Metamorphosis Online.*"

"Are you…did you get a job with their marketing team?" Gracie shook her head at him as she went to the kitchen. "I smell pizza."

"Yeah, yeah. Look, you get into the game, and I'll feed you pizza while you roll a character."

"That's a hard no from me, chief." Gracie grabbed a slice, saw the look on his face, and sighed. "Okay, how about this? I'll come eat in the living room, and you can play so I can see the game."

"No," Alex moaned softly, although he chuckled when Gracie grabbed the whole pizza box. "I swear, one of these days, science will discover a portal in your stomach."

"If they could fix it, I'd save a lot of money," Gracie said around a mouthful of cheese. She chewed and swallowed. "Okay, so what's so important about *me* playing the game?"

"It's just…" Alex flopped on the couch and gazed up at the ceiling. "It's *so cool.* I can't even tell you." He rolled his head to look at her. "I did the whole starting zone, and now I want to do *more.* But I also want to hang out there to help *you* because I want *you* to see it because it's so freaking *cool.*"

"Well, hold up there, I haven't even made an account." Gracie stuffed the rest of the slice in her mouth, wiped her fingers off on a paper towel, and grabbed her laptop.

"I…might have set one up for you. You left your wallet, so I had your credit card info."

"You—" She shook her head, laughing. "What's a day without a little light credit card fraud?"

"Yeah, yeah. No jokes about that where my boss could hear, though."

"Oh, solid point." Gracie took another slice, rolled it up,

and stuffed the whole thing in her mouth, nodding at the VR headset. "Oh-hay. Hoo me uh."

"Women," Alex said whimsically. "Such graceful, delicate creatures." He brought up his phone and took a picture. "I'm sending you this for posterity. Seriously, I swear your jaw unhinges when you eat."

Gracie chewed and swallowed. "And don't you forget it." She guffawed when the picture came through. "All right, I'm banking this. The next time Matt gets on my case about being a cocktail waitress, I'm sending him this pic." She wiped her fingers again. "How do I put this stuff on?"

"Ah, right." Alex began searching through boxes. "So, here are the undergloves. Watch the dangling bits, those go on your arms. Oh, crap, forgot the belt. Arms up."

Gracie pulled on the gloves as Alex fastened the belt and got out the actual headset. The gloves tracked the movements of her hands and the rig attached to her elbow and shoulders, connecting across the back and hooking up to a piece that came up from the belt. Similar connections went down both legs, hooking up at the knees and ankles.

"Well, *this* isn't going to be quick to get into and out of," she commented. "Couldn't they just do one of those things like the dance games, where it tracks your movements?"

"You *can* do that," Alex said dismissively. "But the suit is more accurate, *and* it has haptics."

"Sure, sure. Having my elbow buzz really puts me into a game."

"You're joking, but it actually does. Just you wait. Ready for the headset?" At her nod, Alex settled it over her head and strapped it in place. It was shiny and white and had elegantly sculpted edges, and it cocooned her in silence.

"Uh…Alex? Is the game on?"

She could feel the faint tremors in the floor from him walking around, and then his voice popped up in her ear. "Turning it on now. If you link the headsets, you get a voice chat even in-game. Okay. You ready?"

His voice had taken on an almost awed tone.

"Yeah." Gracie was laughing. "I'm ready for this crazy, *mystical—*"

Her voice broke off as blue burst into her vision. A ripple of harp music sounded, and she felt her jaw hanging open. She was formless, floating in the middle of a void filled with swirls of light. The music came from all around her.

"Okay," she managed after a moment, "I get it."

"Yeah." The voice came from beside her, and she turned to see Alex "walking" toward her. He'd made a character that looked a lot like him in real life: tall, with very close-cropped brown hair, only he was a lot more muscular in the game, and his eyes were brilliant blue instead of their actual brown. "Yeah," he repeated. "It's really something, isn't it?"

Gracie could only nod. Then she looked around and down at herself. She didn't seem to exist. "Wait, what do *I* look like?"

"That's the first thing to tackle. You open a systems menu by holding three fingers out and then tipping them up, like this." He demonstrated. "They wanted something you wouldn't do by accident."

"Right." Gracie brought up the menu. "New character. All right. Female, yeah. Ooh, okay. Do I want to be a human? I'm not sure I do. What are all of these?" She scrolled through the races, first bringing up Aosi.

A woman sprang into being in front of her. Tall and stately, she had an unearthly purple sheen to her skin, and her long white hair flowed behind her, twisting and swirling as though it were underwater.

Gracie scrolled to Ocru and jumped when her character shrank, becoming much more human-sized. The figure had defined muscles and tiny tusks at the corners of her mouth. Her hair was black now, and her eyes blazed gold. Her skin had a greenish sheen.

"Where do I see my stats bonuses?" Gracie asked Alex. She was scrolling along the side.

"Race doesn't affect stats in this game."

"What the hell? What kind of lawless fantasy wasteland is this? Society has *rules*."

Alex was laughing. "Think of it as a nice blank slate. Try Piskies; they're hilarious."

Gracie selected Piskie and started laughing when her character became knee-high. The miniature humanoid was bouncing on her feet and looking around, her hair bright pink and piled into an elaborate gravity-defying hairdo.

Human was the only race that Gracie hadn't tried, and she sighed and shrugged when she saw a fairly standard human woman pop up. As with the other races, sliders on the right-hand side of the screen could adjust colors, hairstyle, and other features, but all of the ones for humans were normal, boring human colors.

Gracie went back to the Aosi and grinned. "Yeah. I'm gonna be a tall...I don't know. Tall. Let's start there. Height slider *up*."

"What class are you playing?" Alex asked her.

"I don't know. Probably a tank; that's what I usually play. What are the tank classes?" She looked at his leather armor. "What do you play?"

"There are three classes at the start," Alex explained. He watched as Gracie picked a shade of purple for her skin and began scrolling through eye colors. "They grouped them sort of oddly. So you have Fighter—that's probably easiest to explain. That's anyone who fights up close, and then you'd spec into DPS or tank, rogue or warrior, et cetera, right?"

"Weird, but I guess I can see it. What's DPS? Melee?"

"Nah, it's…DPS means Damage Per Second. In that context, it's someone who isn't a tank and isn't a healer. So they do damage, right?"

"Okay. I'll learn all the lingo sometime, it's just *slightly* different from D&D and that's going to fuck with me. Should I go with my face? Yeah, I'll go with my face."

"It works," Alex commented. "Sometimes it looks super weird, though. Especially Piskies, but I looked *weird* as an Aosi. Anyway, I'm a Summoner. That's anyone who fights with a companion—that's hunters, warlocks, and necro-mancers."

"Ooh, 'kay." Gracie settled on pale purplish skin with deep blue hair and eyes. Now her fingers were hovering over the three icons on the bottom: a sword, a wolf, and a stylized explosion.

"Yeah. Then there's Senders—anyone who does ranged damage or healing. Mages, clerics, that sort of thing. So what happens is you pick one, you get this basic starter pack of some magic and some non-magic abilities, and then you evolve according to your play style."

"Huh. Okay." Gracie considered. "Fighter it is, then." She double-tapped the sword icon in the lower right corner and her Aosi female changed from plain white pants and a shirt to basic leather armor. There was a stick in one hand. "Good to go. What about you? Got any pets yet? A wolf? A demon? A...zombie wolf-demon?"

"Well, I *did* have a panther, but my new goal is having a zombie wolf-demon."

"I support this goal." Gracie double-tapped the name field and typed in Callista. That had been the name of her first character in D&D, and it had stuck. It was her tag in every game she played.

At least it made some sense in this world.

She clicked through to accept her character, and her pointer hovered above the LOAD button. "All right, can I just...go?"

"Yep. I'll make sure I'm near your starting point. Enjoy the intro." Alex disappeared.

Gracie pressed the LOAD button and jumped when everything went black. The music vanished, leaving behind a ringing silence—and a growing growl.

"*Ten thousand years ago, the gods created Elakara.*" The voice was female, low and oddly persuasive. In the black, color rushed to a single point and a chunk of land appeared, spinning slowly. Boulders had broken off from its sides, and they tumbled one over end in the void beyond the land's borders.

Ocru appeared, running in groups with dogs at their sides and spears in their hands. "The first to walk the land were the Ocru, mystics and shamans who subdued the beasts of the wilds."

Then there were humans, their spears set aside as they sat around campfires with the Ocru. Some held balls of magic. Others held books. *"Next came the humans. Together, the humans and the Ocru learned the mysteries of magic. Together, they molded the Piskies."*

Now there were cities, smaller buildings in the alleys with Piskies emerging from half-sized doors. The camera panned through the city, and Gracie saw taverns, fighting rings, auction houses, and more.

"But war broke out," the woman told her, and a flaming boulder shattered the building beside Gracie.

"Fuck!" Gracie threw up her hands instinctively. The haptics on that side of her suit buzzed, and the picture careened away as if she'd been thrown by the explosion. A moment later, the haptics on the other side simulated the landing. Though it was nowhere near as painful as it would have been, Alex was right. It *did* put her in the story.

Armed soldiers rushed through the streets, people fled, and screams rang out. Smoke filled the air, and when it cleared, there were armies facing one another on the battlefield. A group of animals and others—wolves, bears, panthers, and shambling undead—surged across the open land toward their enemies, fighting their way through arrows and raining ice.

"Desperate to end the fighting, the gods created the Aosi," the narrator told Gracie. The battle froze into slow motion and two figures stood in beams of light between the advancing armies, their heads thrown back to look at heaven. *"They were made to be more—smarter, faster, wiser. In the end, however..."*

Again, the picture shifted, showing two new armies, this time with Aosi on both sides.

"The Aosi were no different," the narrator said sadly. *"They picked sides in the wars between and among the races, and in a last attempt to make peace, the gods flung the four races to the far corners of Elakara."* A maelstrom was shown, ripping people from their homes, dragging them away as indistinct figures stood in the middle of the storm, guiding the winds. *"Now the races have found their way together once more. In the city of Kithara, they mingle, astonished to find that the beings from their myths truly exist, unaware that all of this has happened before..."*

The picture soared above a city and then descended, dizzyingly, below the ground. Blackness surrounded Gracie.

"You have come to Kithara to see this new world," the narrator told her softly. *"But there are many trials to pass before you may enter the city. Good luck, adventurer."*

The world brightened. Gracie was underground, a rough stone ceiling above, the walls of the cave stretching away into the darkness. She could hear water dripping somewhere nearby and she took a few steps in the real world before controls popped up on the screen to show her how to move. A very faint glow around her showed her where she was within the VR area, showing her where it was safe to move. She heard the faint scuff of her character's shoes as she moved. Something was glowing nearby on the ground.

She came around a corner and gasped. This path had led to a pool of water, shining faintly from within. Gracie knelt entirely by instinct, and the view of the water drew closer. She reached out trembling fingers and dragged them through it, the haptics buzzing slightly.

It was beautiful. After all of those years imagining a magical world, now she was truly *in* one.

That was when she heard the growl.

CHAPTER THREE

That sound was unmistakable—it was something that wanted to kill her, rip her to shreds. Gracie spun and ducked at the same time, throwing herself sideways. She didn't care about anything but surviving right now. She had completely forgotten that she was standing in the middle of the living room, and she only just managed to stay within the VR area.

"*Fuck* me!" She rolled and came to her feet, hands up. There was a jolt of pure adrenaline as she stared down the thing in front of her.

"Shit." Alex's voice echoed in her headset. "Are you already fighting?"

"*Yeah*. Fucking…wolf-beast thing."

She had never seen anything like it. It wasn't quite a wolf, nor was it a fox or even a bigger cat. It had similarities to all of them, though.

Mainly its giant claws and curved, blood-covered teeth.

Its fur rippled with the same luminescence as the pool of water. The coat was thick, but there was no mistaking the ripple of muscles or the graceful way it had sunk into a crouch. As Gracie watched, it growled again and tilted its head to the side, sinking lower.

She waited, forcing herself to stillness. You weren't supposed to run from a predator, but she couldn't see how it would be a better idea to attack.

Blood dripped from one of the teeth as she watched, then it sprang at her.

It probably would have been smart to duck, but Gracie had always been more angry than smart when something like this happened. As soon as she saw the muscles bunch, she felt an absolute wave of fury. This thing had cornered her here, and now it was going to attack her?

Oh, *hell* no.

She felt her face settle into a snarl and she stepped back with one foot, wound up a punch, and slammed her fist forward with all her might.

A red four burst into the air over the beast's head and the haptics in her hand shuddered, but they could only do so much. There wasn't, after all, a real wolf there to punch, and Gracie nearly overbalanced. She would have laughed at herself—except that wolf was still there, now circling warily away. A health bar had appeared over its head, showing that she'd chewed up about a quarter of its life.

"Come on," Gracie taunted it. "Come on, bitch! I got three more punches in me. Fucking try it!"

"Glad to hear you're doing well." Alex sounded annoyed. "I'm sorry, it's taking longer to get to you than I thought it—"

The beast crouched to leap again.

"Busy!" Gracie yelled in what she guessed was Alex's

general direction before swooping out of the way and turning to lash out with her elbow. She wound back up and shot her fist outwards, only to have a faint red wall appear close to where her fingers were. Glowing words appeared: EDGE OF VR AREA.

At this precise moment, Gracie didn't care much. She'd punch the TV if she had to in order to win. What was taking her attention was the wolf's pained whine as it circled. She'd hit it three times, and it should be close to dead.

Unfortunately, its eyes were now glowing red, and as she watched, it threw its head back and gave an unearthly shriek—which was answered from the other tunnels.

"You just *know* that's not good," Gracie muttered.

It was still growling, and reckless energy filled her. It hadn't crouched or given any indication that it was going to move, so she had her character charge it, and she landed a flurry of punches on its face and sides. It collapsed into a heap, went rigid, and disappeared in a shower of pixels, leaving two glowing gold coins and a blue jewel that shimmered beautifully. She knelt to pick them up, and they rose into the air and zoomed to the bottom of the screen, where a coin purse icon had appeared. The haptics at her right hip buzzed to show her that something had gone into her inventory.

It was a cool mechanic, and she would have admired it a lot more if she couldn't hear the sounds of running animals. More wolf-beasts, she was sure, and she thought to check if she was injured.

She was. Her life bar was at half.

A tutorial for how to drink something called a vitality

potion appeared, and she drank it down. The glug of the liquid was so realistic that she found herself swallowing out of reflex. She looked around, wondering if there was a weapon stashed anywhere, and saw a rock lying on the ground nearby.

The only problem was that she was going to have to wade into the water, and she had no idea if that would be a problem.

"What the hell. I can always reload, right?" She directed her character into the water and was amused to see her health bar start to fill up and pulse. "So, glowing water refills your health. Good to know." She made her way slowly through the water, which sloshed slightly, and grabbed the rock. She couldn't pick it up, but now that she was here, she could see an old staff that had been hidden from her vantage point leaning against the wall in the alcove. "Mine," she said, snatching it.

Then she had another idea. She waited, frozen in the water as the beasts' footsteps drew closer. *Don't move,* she told herself. *Not an inch.* She even held her breath until she remembered that wasn't going to do anything in-game.

It worked. The wolves paused nearby, but then the clicking of their nails moved away again.

Slowly, carefully, Gracie eased out of the pool of water. The game had astounding attention to detail. She now left wet footprints and dripped water on the ground as she crept forward.

She peeked into the hall and saw two wolf-beasts sniffing their way toward her.

"I'm close," Alex said in her ear, making her jump.

"Jesus! Forgot you existed there for a moment. There are two wolves between you and me."

"They're not attacking you?"

"Did you hear me swearing?" she retorted.

"No."

"Then I'm not fighting anything."

"Right." He was laughing. "Well, stay back, and I'll zap them. I barely got through that fight."

"Nuh-uh. I found a stick, and I'm gonna use it." Gracie pondered how best to sneak up on the wolves. "I bet I could take two. Just, you know, hang out in case I can't—"

"Shit!" Alex's voice rose sharply.

"What? Did you trip over something? I swear, it's only a matter of time until we run into each other while playing—"

"Bear! There's a bear! This was not here when I was here before! Oh, *shit*, it has a lot of health!"

"Do your best, and I'll be there in a second!" Gracie told him. Apparently, there was no point in preparing a best plan of attack for these two wolves. The name of the game now was speed; get through the wolves and get to Alex.

Gracie burst out of cover and pushed her character to a sprint. It was hardly quiet, and the wolves wheeled around, but they still weren't ready to attack by the time she bowled into them.

"Hi-yah!" Gracie yelled. She brought the stick down on one of their heads and turned quickly to swipe at the other one, catching Alex's arm as she did so. "Sorry, sorry! *Oof!* Look, I said I was sorry!"

"Sorry!" Alex echoed back. "Christ, this thing just took Teef down to half-health with one swipe! What *is* this?"

"Think you should run?" Gracie asked him as she whacked one wolf with the stick and directed a kick and a punch at the other. "Off. I said *geroff*! Ha! And *stay* down!" She turned to the remaining beast and settled into a crouch. "Just you and me, bucko, and you're standing between a friend in trouble and me."

"Shit shit shit shit," Alex was chanting in her ear.

Gracie didn't wait for the wolf-thing to attack. She lunged at it and landed a flurry of blows on its head. It collapsed, and she swiped her hand around herself to pick up the loot before scrambling up and taking off along the corridor. She could hear the snarls of two animals fighting, and the twang of a bow.

As she ran, she noticed a strange notch in the stick, and a thought occurred to her. Swiping to open her inventory, she grabbed the glowing blue stone and pressed it into place. It flared and the staff split at the end, tendrils of wood grabbing the stone to hold it in place.

"*Nice,*" she said in satisfaction.

Then she came around the corner and bowled directly into the bear—just straight into its ass. All of her haptics shuddered and her character staggered back, clearly shaking her head in a daze from the way the camera swung and the headset shuddered.

"Oof. That can't have smelled good," Gracie joked. Then the bear turned, eyes glowing faintly red and a snarl coming from its throat. "Oh, shit."

There was something primal about staring down a bear; that was the thing. Bears were freaking *huge*, and this one had a deranged look to it, at once hulking and ravenous. Its teeth were stained with age and blood.

"Gracie? *Gracie!*" Alex sounded a bit panicked. "This thing is *way* too strong for a Level 1."

"I'm not saying I should fight it on my own, donut brain. I'm saying maybe attack it while it's not paying attention!"

"Oh! Right." There was a twang, then a cat snarled and the bear howled in pain. "What now, bear?" Alex asked.

The bear wheeled around.

"Okay, I didn't have a good plan, here!"

"Oh, for—" Gracie whipped her staff around and slammed it down on the bear's butt. An arc of blue light trailed away from the gem as it flew through the air, and there was a burst of light when it hit the bear's fur. The health bar, which had been creeping down, acquired a purple tinge. "What's the purple?"

"No idea! Wait, maybe it's a DOT?"

"What?"

"Damage over time."

"No, I know DOT, just didn't catch what you said. Seems right." Gracie wound up and, as the bear turned once more, whacked it on the nose. "What now, fang-face? All right, Alex, time to sic the cat on it again!"

"Yup, got it. Operation Yo-yo is in full swing!" There was a louder bow twang this time, and the bear gave a shriek. Its health bar went down a significant chunk.

It still swiped at Gracie.

"Not enough yo-yo!" she yelled as she threw herself sideways. "Ow, dammit! Listen, *bear*, you are just asking for a blue jewel up the nose!"

"What the hell does that even mean?" She could hear

Alex shooting and pulling out more arrows, and the snarls and snapping of the two animals fighting.

"I'll show you in a sec." Gracie pushed herself up, readied the staff, and swiped at the bear's legs. Then she brought the staff up and over, slamming it down on the bear again and again. As it wheeled back to her, she jabbed the staff straight into its face.

The haptics shuddered, and the bear collapsed. Its life had been eaten away by the Damage Over Time spell, layered every time Gracie hit it, and between her, Alex, and his pet, the bear hadn't stood a chance. The corpse trailed away into pixels as they watched, and then the air around Gracie filled with gold sparkles and a glowing 2 appeared.

"Level 2 achieved," a female voice told her. "You have learned a new skill: Accelerate." The air filled with sparkles again. "Level 3 achieved. You have learned a new skill: Shock Blast."

"Oooh." Gracie watched as the two icons zoomed to the bottom bar.

Alex was kneeling over his pet. A bandage appeared in his hand from nowhere, and then flared and disappeared, with an answering flare on the panther's deep purple fur. Alex stood, shaking his head.

"Whew, *that* was something. I think that's to punish me for trying to help you in the starting zone. Wait, are you Level 3 now?"

"Yeah, this thing must've been worth a lot of XP, so thanks for that. Got two shiny new skills to try out." Gracie hefted her staff. "How do I holster this thing?"

"Swing it up over your back. Hey, that's a pretty jewel. I just sold mine. Should've kept it."

"Hell, yeah, you should have. Don't you know the rule? Always keep shiny things." Gracie holstered her staff and crossed her arms.

"Also, there's a filter that makes your voice all echoey and cool. I think it's an Aosi thing."

"Whoa, really?"

"Yeah, they made this big deal out of it when they launched the game. Your voice gets fed through these filters so you sound like your character 'should' sound." He made finger quotes, which was surprisingly jarring considering his fantasy garb.

"Huh." Gracie considered. "So if I'd made a male character…"

"I think it would deepen your voice or something? No idea."

"That's insane. You can actually be anyone you want here." She brightened. "Hey, I could be a grizzled old dude yelling at kids to get off my lawn!"

Alex guffawed.

"But before we get too caught up in this, how about we get out of here before more bears show up?"

"You got it." Alex gave her a thumbs-up. "Huh, wait a sec." His character's hand came up to its ear, and its head cocked very strangely to the side. "Yep," Gracie heard. "No, not—just hanging out with my roommate. Why? *What*? I'll be right there." The head rotated back, and she realized he must have tipped his headset up to get the phone to his ear. "Look, I gotta go," he told her. "One of our clients is getting audited, apparently. And, uh…how do I put this delicately…"

"They have a lot to hide?" Gracie asked sweetly.

"I didn't say it," Alex said innocently. "Okay, looks like you're on track. I'll catch up with you later."

"Later," Gracie called.

"Wait, forgot to ask. You enjoying the game?"

"Hell, yeah, I am! I get to whack things with a stick!" Gracie waved. "Have fun doing accounting all night."

"I cannot *believe* I just got this game and I'm going to spend all night at the office," Alex grumbled. "Okay, I'll see you in a bit. Have fun for me, will you?"

"Will do."

CHAPTER FOUR

"Guess I'm on my own," Gracie murmured as Alex's character disappeared into pixelated dust. "That's not so bad, though. World can't be *full* of bears, right?"

She gave a nervous look over her shoulder, but the hallway remained empty. After testing that she knew how to get her staff off her back, she trotted down the corridor, going in the direction that sloped vaguely up. There were other caverns, one with a few blue pebbles, but she didn't find anything else, and she soon emerged onto a path that led between two grass-covered hills.

It was nighttime in this world—perhaps they took their time of day from the player's location—and a band of stars was scattered across the sky. It was curved instead of being a straight line like the Milky Way, and Gracie stared at it in awe as she walked.

"A beautiful night," said a voice nearby.

Gracie jumped and swore. She whirled to find a man in pale robes, his hands linked behind his back. He appeared to be unarmed.

"My apologies," he told her. "I did not mean to startle you."

"No, it's…it's okay." Gracie tilted her head. "Are you a player or an NPC?"

"I am the warden of these hills," he said after a moment. "Perhaps you mean, am I one of the ones who has come to visit this new city?" He pointed now, and Gracie looked over to see the city shining faintly on a nearby hill. "No," the man told her. "No, I keep my vigil here."

"What vigil?" She was curious now.

"I make sure that those who cross these hills are safe… and that these lands are safe from *them*, as well." There was a warning in his tone.

"What does that mean?" Gracie asked.

"It means that these lands hold many secrets and treasures, things valuable to the…" His voice trailed off as he eyed her. "Well, *your* kind would call them the 'lower races.' The fae, the kobolds. I am their warden."

"I won't hurt them." Gracie looked around. "Unless… well, *they* won't hurt *me*, will they?"

"If you do not disturb them, they will not." The man smiled, although there was little humor in his expression.

"Right." Gracie felt a chill and had to remind herself that none of this was real. She wasn't *really* in the middle of nowhere being warned about bloodthirsty creatures. "Um. So, I just walk to the city, on the road, and…that's it?"

The man's lips curved. Again, there was no amusement to it.

"What's back there?" Gracie gestured behind them. They were on the downslope of a hill, so she could not see what lay in the other direction. She considered. "Can you *show* me what's back there? That way—"

She broke off, telling herself not to be stupid. She didn't need to assure this man that she wasn't going to hurt the kobolds.

He wasn't *real.*

"I could show you," he said. "To be clear, you wish to see the lands to the east?"

"I, uh… I don't suppose you'd know if there's a compass interface in this thing, would you?" Gracie joked. Either she'd said a keyword or the NPC was programmed to help because a compass appeared in the top of her view. She rotated until she was facing east, the direction opposite the city. "Yes, east was what I meant."

The man turned and walked away silently, and Gracie hurried after him.

"That is a fine stone on your staff," he commented as he walked.

"Yes, I, uh, I found it in the caves. And the staff, actually." Gracie felt a sudden surge of humor. "That's the problem with adventurers, right? They come in, kill everyone, and steal their stuff." The man shot a glance at her, and she felt another chill before reminding herself, for what felt like the eightieth time that he wasn't *real.* Still, she found herself saying, "It's a…joke."

"Is it?" He did not sound amused. *"Treasure you see and treasure you take / goodness you are, or goodness you wake / blue is the sky, and power, and sea / ancestors' power, captured for me."* He kept walking, not looking at her.

Gracie paused, but when he did not stop, she had to hurry after him. "What was that? What did you just recite?"

"It is a kobold riddle, or so I'm told." He reached the crest of the hill and stopped, his hands once again linked behind his back.

He had said there were lower races here, but Gracie saw almost no sign of them. While the city of Kithara glimmered with lamplight, these plains had neither lamps nor fires and only one structure, which was somehow jarring. It was constructed of dark stone and starkly illuminated where it sat on the swell of a hill perhaps a half a mile away.

"What's that?" Gracie asked.

"A tomb."

"*One* person's tomb? Who was it, a king?"

"Whose? That is lost to us. The kobolds built it, but the fae live there now." There was a wealth of history in those words. Stories hinted at but not spelled out.

Gracie blinked.

"I offer travelers a quest to get to know these lands if they want it." The warden NPC looked at her.

"I, uh...yeah, that sounds good." It wasn't like she was *really* out alone at night, after all. She could play around now and go see the city later.

"In the hills behind us, a path leads to a glowing pool. Go to it, and slay three of the beasts nearby."

"Like the wolf at the glowing pool in the caves?" Gracie asked.

He paused. "Yes," he said, after a moment. "The beasts are drawn to the magic here. They cannot use it, but they sense its power. The kobolds and the fae have been driven from the sacred pools."

"Oh." Gracie looked back down the hill. "Can I…go see the tomb?"

"I told you that the lower races will not bother you if you do not bother them."

"I don't want to disturb it," Gracie assured him. "I just want to see it. Can I?"

"It is not my choice to make." His voice was calm.

Nothing ventured, nothing gained, Gracie told herself. She squared her shoulders. "I'll come back if anyone seems irritated."

He said nothing.

"Fine," Gracie said. "Uh, good night." She headed down the hill before turning back. "Thanks for showing me around."

The NPC nodded slightly.

"Stupid," Gracie muttered to herself. "You're being polite to a robot, Gracie." Still, as she always kidded with Alex, when the robots eventually *did* rise up, she wanted to be on their good side.

Jay watched the Aosi walk away, her rounded hips swaying under the plain armor, her dark hair shining deep blue under the starlight. She'd done a good job with the character creator.

Well, they all had. Jay had gotten in on the ground floor of Dragon Soul Productions right when they were first starting to develop *Metamorphosis Online*, and after years of work, the past month had been a giddy process of launching the game and fine-tuning as people began to trickle into the world.

The project meant a lot to him. Fed up with years of trying to prove his worth in the "real" world, he'd sunk almost all of his spare time into MMOs—the only place where he was valued for his quick thinking and accomplishments without anyone caring what he looked like or whether he was awkward sometimes when he talked. He could lead raids, guide his party through dungeons, and respec as often as he liked (a feature the real world was sorely lacking).

The world of *Metamorphosis Online* was like nothing ever played before, and much had been made of the fact that players could interact with the NPCs to learn about the world. While that wasn't *exactly* a lie, the fact was that many NPCs had a human working behind the scenes to answer out-of-scope questions and file tickets to add those answers to the NPCs' playlist.

Most players didn't ask the hill warden for much. Most took the quest, although a lot of them never returned to collect the reward. Some ran off into the hills to kill kobolds and fae and found out the hard way that the lower races could summon minor demons.

This player, Callista, *might* be intending to do that, but Jay doubted it. He found himself curious about where she was going. There were Easter eggs scattered around, in this part of the game in particular, to reward curious players— and punish some of them—and he wondered which ones she might stumble across.

He activated a party chat. "Andrew."

"Hey."

"Could you take over for me with the hill warden? I'm going to roll a character and follow that player."

There was a pause, during which he imagined Andrew bringing up a live feed of the game. Then his employee laughed. Andrew was famously good-tempered. He found everything funny, but never in a mean way.

"Uh, Jay?"

"Yes?"

"You know that's probably a dude, right?"

Jay started laughing as well. "Yeah, yeah, I get it. It's not *that.*"

"Uh-huh. Sure. Just thank Mike on the way out the door." Mike headed the graphics team, and he had been instrumental in creating the character models.

Jay laughed, exited out of the GM controls, and headed into the character screen. His fighter, Anders, was already built, and he used his controls to drop himself into the game right next to the hill warden. He gave Andrew a two-fingered salute and ran off, hugging the side of one hill.

He didn't want to interfere. He wanted to watch and see what she was going to do.

Gracie trudged through the grass, periodically reaching out her hands to brush through it, and then remembering the grass wasn't real. She wanted to take out her staff to reassure herself, but she didn't want the kobolds to think she was getting aggressive.

"You're overthinking this, Gracie," she muttered.

She thought she saw something out of the side of her

eyes and turned her head quickly, but there was nothing there. She must have imagined it. Then she heard a high-voiced mutter, hastily cut off, and knew *something* was here with her.

She stopped and looked around herself. "Hello?"

There was a long pause. Whoever they were, they didn't trust her.

"Hello?" Gracie asked again.

The grass in front of her rustled, and a kobold hopped out onto the path in front of her. It chattered at her in a language Gracie didn't know, then pointed at her head and shrieked.

"Rude," Gracie said. "There's nothing wrong with my face." She was grinning, though. She was having fun making up what it said.

It hopped and chattered, moving its hands strangely.

Then she had a thought. She swung the staff over her head and put it down hastily when the kobold took off.

"Wait! Wait. I'm not going to hurt you." She looked up to see it peeping out of the grass. "Was this what you were pointing at?" Gracie asked. She tapped the blue stone.

It crept closer, wiggling its whiskers.

"Yeah, I thought so." Gracie thought of the hill warden's rhyme and wished she could remember it better. She looked over her shoulder and saw the warden still watching her. "Creepy. Hey! Hey, can you come over here?"

He didn't move.

"Typical," Gracie muttered. She tapped the stone. "Is this a kobold thing?"

The kobold darted forward and touched the stone, then ran away and hid again.

Gracie laughed. "Come on. I'm going to take it to that tomb, okay?" She picked up the staff and walked carefully around the kobold, giving it a wide berth and looking over her shoulder to beckon to it. "Come on. Come with me."

It chattered at her but followed as she headed off. Unseen, the fighter in the hills muttered a soft "aha" to himself and followed them.

CHAPTER FIVE

G racie hadn't gone very far before she realized she was accumulating kobolds. First, it was just one more. It hopped along beside the other one, waving around a flower of some sort. The two of them chattered to one another and gave a few shrieks.

The next time she looked back, there was a handful. The time after that, there were well over a dozen.

"I really hope you're not planning to sacrifice me to a demon," Gracie told them. They chattered back at her. "Not reassuring, guys."

By the time she arrived at the tomb, there were dozens of them swarming around her, all lit by a ghostly blue glow —which she now realized was coming from her stone. She took her staff out and stared at it.

"Whoa. Okay, so the hill warden wasn't kidding about that riddle. What'd he say? That the blue was like sky and sea? And something about ancestors? Well, rock, here's your ancestor-place."

She approached the door of the tomb cautiously. The

hill warden had said that the fae lived here now, and she was pretty sure that by returning some ancestral rock, she was going to be siding with the kobolds.

She grinned. She *loved* learning the rules and history of a new world. It was one of the things she liked best about D&D, and even though she felt a twinge of guilt as if she were betraying her roots, she had to admit it was even more fun when you had a whole world around you, completely immersive.

Her character walked up to the door, hesitated, and then rapped on it. "Hello?"

Silence.

"Hello?" Gracie asked again. "I'm here to return an artifact."

This time, something in the darkness *hissed*, and there was a rattle.

"Fuck." She adjusted her grip on the staff and rotated her shoulders, cracking her neck. "Well, I knew this wasn't going to be easy, right? Hey, all, I'm—*ow!*" A bolt of magic had whizzed out of the darkness and hit her in the head, making the haptics in her headset shudder. Her character stumbled back. "Ow! Rude!"

"*Leave!*" The voices were tiny and shrill, and there were tons of them.

Gracie chewed her lip. On the one hand, she was Level 3 now, which should mean she was well able to handle things in starting zones. On the other, she'd clearly gone a different way than the hill warden had wanted to send her.

She was probably going to get smacked down *hard*.

She glanced at the kobolds. They were peeking out from behind her, staring at the tomb, and they looked sad.

This was where their ancestors had been laid to rest, and it had been taken from them.

Fury suffused her, and Gracie squared her shoulders. She strode up to the door, and after a couple of tries of figuring out her distance, managed to kick it open. She extended the glowing blue stone into the darkness inside.

"All right, that is *enough*. This is a kobold tomb, and I'm coming to return a kobold artifact. There's no call to attack — Oh, fuck *me*."

The blue light from the staff lit the walls and ceiling, and there were hundreds of eyes glinting at her. The fae apparently slept like bats, and the effect was what Gracie would charitably call "creepy as all hell."

In various campaigns, she and her fellow adventurers had found themselves badly outmatched any number of times, only to flee, rolling desperately to evade. That was the gaming rule: you were outmatched, you ran away.

Except now she was *pissed*. Gracie tilted her head at the fae, bared her teeth in a smile they couldn't see, and said in her best ice-cold-bitch voice, "I'm going to count to three."

They might not have understood the exact words, but they seemed to realize she wasn't going away because they began charging fireballs again. Hoping the haptics couldn't shock her, Gracie said a silent prayer and began to swing her stick with wild abandon.

Keep moving, keep moving, keep moving. Maybe if she kept her character in motion, they wouldn't send magical bolts her way to avoid hitting one another. It was as good a plan as any; after all, there were hundreds of them. *Keep moving,* Gracie told herself. It was surprisingly frightening to be surrounded by angry fae who were swarming and ready to use magic. Part of her wanted to freeze. *Keep moving.*

And then the kobolds got involved. The door burst open and they swarmed in, yelling angrily and throwing things at the ceiling. The fae shrieked, the kobolds shrieked, and Gracie gave a whoop. It was a proper brawl now, and she was enjoying that. She lost count of how many fireballs she ducked, how many fae she bonked on the head with her staff, and how many she grabbed out of midair and threw out the door.

When her screen began flashing red, she realized she hadn't been paying attention to her hit points. She swiped for potions and gulped down the last one. She was going to have to get more of those, and hope that nothing worse than this crowd of fae was going to happen to her before she could.

The fae, luckily, were on the run. After some chattering in both English and their own language, they disappeared, streaming out the door into the night. Gracie and the kobolds were left inside.

Gracie looked around herself and gasped to see several of the kobolds lying on the ground, not moving. Of course, they weren't moving, she told herself. This had been a fight with weapons.

She had the feeling that she'd led an uprising without having any idea what it was going to cost. For a moment, she forgot that none of this was real and stared at the bodies with her lip trembling. She hadn't meant for this to happen.

One of the kobolds approached her and tugged on her hand, and Gracie numbly followed it farther into the tomb.

It must have been built into the side of the hill, because she was led down a much longer hallway than was possible in the part of the building she had seen. The corridor sloped down slightly, and she found herself adjusting her balance and then nearly falling over. That, at least, made her laugh a little. She felt like an idiot for crying about the dead, pixelated kobolds.

The blue stone was glowing brighter, so much so that Gracie was squinting when they emerged into a small room paneled in marble.

She blamed not immediately noticing the giant kobold on the squinting. When she did, she jumped, swore, and dropped the staff. It clattered on the floor, and Gracie muttered that apparently she could even be awkward in a virtual world.

"Er," she said after she'd recovered, "hi. Hello. I'm...Callista."

"Callista." The voice was very deep. It made her jump, even though she'd expected it. "Why are you here?"

"Oh. Right." Gracie held out the staff. "I heard a kobold riddle from the hill warden, and it seemed like maybe this stone belonged here."

The kobold nodded its head. "Yes. Take the stone from the staff, and place it here on the altar."

"Uh." Gracie set about removing the stone from the staff. The game, luckily, seemed to know what she was trying to do. After she'd taken it out, she holstered the staff on her back and approached the altar, where she found an indentation in the center. She laid the stone carefully in it and felt a jolt from the haptics. Carved lines in the white altar flared with light. "Whoa."

"The stone was stolen," the kobold explained. "It was taken from us, and without it, this place was not kept safe. Now that it is returned, we have access to many powers we had thought lost."

Gracie smiled. "I'm glad." She turned and blinked. The giant kobold was gone, as was the smaller one who had brought her here. She was alone in the room. She looked back just to make sure she hadn't imagined the stone, but it was still shimmering there.

"New quest activated," the female voice told her as cheerily as it had informed her of her last level-up. "Long May She Reign. Accept?"

"Er, yes?"

"Quest accepted."

Gracie looked around once more but still saw no one else. It could be a glitch, of course, but she didn't think so. She had the sense that the kobold had been a ghost of some sort. With a faint smile, she headed back up the hall into the main area, which was now filled with kobolds. Ceremonial fires had been lit in the corners of the room.

The kobolds hopped about, hardly paying any attention to her at all, and Gracie only faintly caught the sound of sliding stone. She turned in time to see stone doors close behind her. The effect was so seamless that if she hadn't known there was a corridor, she never would have guessed it.

"That's CGI for you, I guess," she murmured to herself, and she made her way out through the main door with a small smile. "Nothing like a little bit of hero-ing to make your day better. I— Gah!" She jumped.

"I'm sorry to startle you," the man said courteously. He

emerged from the shadow of a tree and gave a half-bow. "I was...coming to see this place."

"Oh. It's a tomb." Gracie looked over her shoulder. "For kobolds, I guess. They have some powers or something all wrapped up in it. It's cool. If you got a blue stone in the caves, you can turn it in here. I don't think there's any XP but it's interesting."

"Mmm." The man had cocked his head to the side. He was a human, even taller than Gracie's Aosi, and absolutely jacked. Muscles rippled when he moved. He was also ridiculously handsome, enough so that she felt genuinely awkward.

He wasn't real, she reminded herself. It wasn't like *she* really had dark blue hair, after all.

"I could help you go back to the caves if you didn't get the blue stone," Gracie offered. Then she remembered the bear. "Actually, that's probably not a good idea. There might be bears."

"Ran into one already?" The man seemed amused.

"Yeah. My roommate came to party up with me for the starting zone, and, well—sudden demon-bear." Gracie laughed.

"Yes. Everyone must begin on their own, proving themselves with their skills and nothing more." He sounded very sure of himself.

"Are you an NPC?" Gracie asked.

"Oh. No. Just, uh, getting into character." He shrugged and cleared his throat. "Want to make a party for the wolf quest?"

"Sounds good." Gracie stuck out a hand. "I'm Callista."

"Anders." He smiled and shook her hand. A moment

later, a party invite flashed up on the screen. Gracie accepted it.

"So, how did you hear about the game?" she asked as they made their way back up the hill.

"A friend mentioned it," he said casually. "You?"

"My roommate was going on and *on*." Gracie laughed. "He just plays shooters. I was always more into tabletop, but I have to say he was right. This game is amazing. It's so immersive."

"It's beautiful," the man agreed. He had stopped at the top of the hill and was staring at the city in the distance. "A whole world where you can be a hero and really do the things you wanted to do when you were little and reading books, you know? Make an actual difference instead of…"

He sighed, and there was something so heartfelt in it that Gracie lost any lingering doubt that he was an NPC. Even with the voice filters, there was no missing the depth of emotion, and she recognized those emotions very well.

After all, she'd had grand plans of changing the world when she graduated.

And now she was dealing blackjack. She squashed down the feeling and swallowed hard.

"Yeah," she managed, hoping he'd heard her agreement and they could just move past this without having to discuss it. She cleared her throat and looked at him. "And movies, of course. I always wanted to be a Jedi."

"Not a Sith?" He looked at her, and his character smiled. "The Aosi give me Sith vibes."

"Their costumes *were* better," Gracie said. "Let's say, Jedi morals and a Sith wardrobe. Although, the Jedi were so rigid. Chaotic good all the way."

"This is gonna be a good group," Anders said. "I can tell. Shall we go kill some wolves?"

"Fuck, yeah." Gracie hoisted her now-stoneless staff. "Let's get our hero on and save some sacred wells. Also, how do you emote like that? Facial expressions and so on."

"Ah, I'll show you. You can hotkey some of them. They're not super easy to find, but— Hey, there." He gave the hill warden a nod as they passed.

"Greetings," the hill warden said.

Gracie waved. "Super in-depth game. I almost expected him to ask how the kobold extravaganza went."

Anders laughed. "There's only so much you can expect from NPCs, right?"

CHAPTER SIX

"And your sister wanted to know everyone's plans for the 4th of July."

"Uh-huh." Gracie pinched the phone between her shoulder and her ear and hopped to push her car door closed with her foot. With her dry-cleaned vest hanging from one hand, a giant pack of paper towels clasped in the crook of that arm, and a plastic bag of takeout in the other hand, she was seriously beginning to doubt that she could get to her apartment without dropping something.

"So, dear." Her mother's voice sounded, as always, forcedly cheerful. "What *are* your plans?"

"Um…" Luckily, one of her neighbors was coming out as she was going in. The woman smiled and waved, and Gracie managed to flex her fingers and wave back.

"Gracie?"

"Sorry, a little busy right now." *Like I told you when you called.* "I, uh… Mom, the 4th is months away. I have no idea what my plans are. I'll probably be working."

"Really?"

"Yeah. Any holiday is big for people coming to gamble." Gracie made it up the first flight of stairs and hitched her hip slightly to catch the paper towels, which were beginning to slip out of her grasp. "They tend to have all the pit staff working overtime, and—"

"Oh, sweetie, you won't *still* be working there in July, will you?"

Gracie stopped dead. She was fighting the urge to hang up and not say another word. Her parents hadn't been thrilled when she had gotten her degree and run off to Vegas. They had wanted her to take her math skills and go into finance or move home and do internships, or both. Neither of those had appealed, and in any case, Gracie had always been what her mother called "relentlessly contrary."

That didn't make it any less frustrating when they got on her case about the job.

"Dear?" her mother asked. "Gracie?"

"Still here." Gracie took a deep breath and started up the second flight of stairs. "Look, I don't know where I'll be working in a few months, all right? Why does Katie even care what we're all doing?" Her sister, older than she was by three years, had graduated from MIT and immediately gotten a scholarship to a business school in New York. Apparently, Gracie's parents had liked this so much that they wanted Gracie to copy her.

"Well." Her mother drew the word out as though she were sharing a wonderful secret.

Gracie rolled her eyes but didn't play into the game. At the door of the apartment, she considered her options, then bonked her elbow into it repeatedly. She'd seen Alex's car downstairs.

Her mother gave up on waiting for her to ask for more details. "I *think* she and her *boyfriend* might have a surprise for us. Or maybe he wants to have the surprise be a family thing." Her voice was filled with excitement now. "Oh, wouldn't that be wonderful? Surrounded by family and getting engaged."

Gracie was rolling her eyes when Alex opened the door, clutching a towel around his waist. He frowned at her expression.

"My mother," Gracie mouthed at him.

He laughed silently and took the paper towels, throwing them one-handed down the corridor and neatly plucking the food out of her hands.

"Look, Mom, I gotta go." She remembered a moment later that her mother would find this far too abrupt. "Really exciting about Katie. Give her my best."

"Will do, darling. Love you."

"Love you, too." Gracie ended the call. "Ughhhh."

"What was that about your sister?" Alex asked from around a mouthful of Vietnamese food.

"That had *better* not be the spicy shrimp," Gracie warned him. "You finishing all of that would be very bad for your health. I've had a long day."

Alex looked a little like a deer in the headlights. He tipped a shrimp off his fork and put the container down on the counter, not breaking eye contact as he picked up the packet of eggrolls instead.

"Wise choice," Gracie said.

"Uh-huh." He watched her warily, like he might watch a rabid bear that had just wandered into his house. "So?"

"Oh, right." Gracie hung up her uniform on the coat tree

and kicked off her flip flops. "My sister is getting *married*." She punctuated her excessively cheerful tone with jazz hands. "Or she will be. Or something. Her boyfriend might be planning a proposal on the 4th. I had to get off the phone before my mother started asking me about my love life."

"You should get one of those," Alex said. He waved an eggroll. "I hear they're great." He paused contemplatively. "Although my own experience wasn't so good."

"Precisely." Gracie grabbed a seltzer out of the fridge.

"Ugh, you and your seltzers."

"They're tasty, you don't have to drink them, and bite me."

"Whoa, whoa." Alex ambled over to the table.

"Sorry." Gracie sighed, nabbed the shrimp, and went to sit with him. She poked at the contents of the container moodily. "It's just, I'd already put up with her harping about my job. I didn't want her to go on about my love life too. Did you see I got you cashew chicken?"

"You did? You're awesome." Alex was up like a shot. "God, I feel like I haven't eaten in days. What day *is* it?"

"It's Tuesday. And those bags under your eyes are pretty legit. Have you been home at all since the shit hit the fan?"

"Once." Alex settled back down with his own container. "I've begun to mark the passage of time by the bad pizzas they order for us."

Gracie snorted with laughter. "Sorry, man, but you know the rules: do accounting for rich douches, get stuck trying to hide their douchery."

Alex chortled. "Only way to get past that one in this town is to *be* one of the casino owners." He caught the flicker on Gracie's face. "Whoa, wait. *You* don't own a casino, do you? Because if you do, I'm gonna be *pissed* that we go halfsies on takeout, frankly."

Gracie snorted seltzer up her nose and grabbed for a paper towel while she recovered.

"No, not that. I just, uh… Oh, God. I got asked out."

"O-ho!" Alex twirled his fork. Then he set the fork down carefully and leaned in. "O-*ho*," he said more meaningfully.

"Oh, no. Don't." Gracie sometimes forgot how smart Alex was. He made the connections other people either were too lazy or didn't care to make, and he was quick about it. It probably helped in his job, but it also helped when he wanted to interrogate her about anything he could use to tease her with later.

"You got asked out by a casino…owner?" Alex raised an eyebrow. "No, that's not right. Don't tell me."

"What, you don't think I could pull a CEO?"

"Sweetie, I love you, you're great, but a CEO wants a yes-man at home."

"I do not have the equipment for that."

"You know what I mean. 'Helen, I want you to have blonder hair and lose five pounds. There's a charity dinner coming up.' 'Yes, dear.'"

"Ugh." Gracie mimed throwing up.

"Yeah. You don't have the makings of a trophy wife." Alex scratched his head. "But an up-and-comer? Your prospective suitor, I mean. Someone in the biz, or you wouldn't have thought of it."

"Yeah." Gracie hunched her shoulders. "Kyle…something. I guess he works at the Bellagio. Nice suit. Saw me by the fountains and came over to say hi."

"And asked you out."

"Yeah, after talking himself up. I laughed in his face." Gracie caught sight of Alex's raised eyebrows. "What? Come on, it's funny, right? I'm in a tank top from Old Navy, his suit probably cost as much as I pay for rent in a *year*, he's going to run a hotel or something, and I…deal blackjack." She could practically feel her mother's disappointment radiating all the way from Glencoe, and her shoulders hunched a bit. "He doesn't want someone like me," she finished, but the humor had gone out of her voice.

"Gracie." Alex put his food down. "So you have a shitty job. So do I. Only difference is, mine pays more. Do you *really* think that makes me better than you?"

Gracie blinked. She hadn't thought about it that way. "Noooo?" she said cautiously.

"Look, I know your parents wanted to raise some crazy army of preppy geniuses to 'lean in' and take over the world—" he made finger quotes "—with their preppy husbands, but if we're brutally honest, I *really* think you should aspire to more than that. Also, that guy who asked you out is a douche."

"What? We'll get back to that." Gracie waved a hand. "You want me to aspire to *more* than being a genius who takes over the world?"

"I want you to… No, no, put it this way, I don't think *you* want to wear matching monogrammed polo shirts and stay up late on your vacation in Nantucket to mediate some boardroom dispute like a kindergarten teacher so you can make a big, fat bonus and buy yourself a diamond tennis bracelet. Judging by the look on your face, I just hit close to home with that one."

Gracie was staring at him slack-jawed. She could see it all unfolding just the way her parents wanted: the house on the East Coast, the preppy holiday card with her hair long and shining and the perfect catalog smile on her face, the handsome husband with a prestigious job, the kids in whatever type of school was the current flavor of the month to turn out high-achieving offspring.

It hit so close to home, in fact, that she really didn't want to talk about it. She closed her mouth.

"So, uh, how'd you know this guy's a douche?"

Alex kindly let the matter drop and went back to his stir fry. "His name's Kyle. That's a douche name. The number of douches with that name is so high, it breaks the bounds of *all* logic."

Gracie raised an eyebrow at him.

"You're not the only one with infuriating older siblings," Alex told her. "It's not just your family that has preppy aspirations. Every year, my brother sends out Christmas cards with his whole family in matching cable-knit sweaters and LL Bean boots and plaid, and every year he breaks my sister-in-law's heart again with another mistress." He smiled humorlessly. "Usually his new secretary, after he fired the last one because 'she got clingy.' You think your sister's bad? She's just annoyingly perfect."

"Oh, you think so, do you?" Gracie grinned at him. "You wanna have a terrible-sibling-off? Because I'll bet you anything that my sister's going to be just as bad." She considered. "Of course, I don't really know her boyfriend that well. They might deserve each other."

"Better that than someone like my sister-in-law, who I swear is actually the sweetest woman you'll ever meet."

"So, why does she stay?"

"Beats me. Maybe she thinks it's better for the kids." Alex shook his head. "See, it's just full of tangles. I take back what I said about having a love life. Never have one."

"I see you're coming on board with my live-in-the-woods-like-a-hermit plan," Gracie observed. "We just gotta get high-speed internet and grocery delivery, and we're good to go." She jerked her head at the living room. "We'll have *Metamorphosis*. We can stay occupied forever."

"I like where your head's at," Alex agreed, then considered. "Enough that I'm seriously thinking about not going back to work and letting them fire me. We'll just look for cabins online, find a nice one, move…"

"Possibly get murdered…"

"Yeah, this *does* sound like the start of a horror movie, doesn't it?" He stood up. "Fine. I'll go back to work, but I'm not happy about it."

"Don't they worry that if you can't sleep, you'll make mistakes?"

"They have great faith in the power of cocaine."

"They make you take *cocaine*?" Gracie dropped her fork and stared at him.

"No, they just assume we do—which is a pretty safe assumption, actually." Alex shrugged. "I've never quite given enough of a fuck to want to do better at my job, but if I did, maybe I'd have fallen into the trap. So you see, being a shitty employee can be good for your health."

Gracie laughed as he ambled away rubbing at his scalp. For all his joking, Alex really did look exhausted, and from the near-empty coffee pot, she could tell he'd brewed and drunk a few cups on this stop at home.

Poor guy.

She shook her head and sighed, then took out the business card Kyle had given her. Part of her—the part that had come roaring to life as soon as she got into her teens—wanted to roll her eyes at anyone who gave a business card to a prospective date. He could have just given her his number for her to put into her phone, but he'd wanted to make sure she knew he was the Vice President of something.

She tapped the card on the table and took a drink of seltzer. The life Alex described—the life her parents wanted for her—was horrifying. She didn't think she knew anyone who lived that life who was actually *happy*.

It was part of why she'd come here after graduating instead of going home, although she hadn't realized it until tonight. When she thought of that life, she felt like she was drowning.

On the other hand, what *did* she have to show for her time here? She was barely making the rent, she didn't like her job as much as the *idea* of her job, and she didn't have anything going on in the way of dates except Kyle.

She'd never had, really. She'd had a couple of boyfriends, but never anyone she really fell for. She'd gone on a few dates in college and hated it.

Now she was beginning to wonder if she was just running herself into the ground to flip off her parents. They'd fly her out in July—they weren't going to take no for an answer, she knew that—and she'd see her sister building a life for herself that might not be perfect, but at least it would be something more than Gracie was doing, dicking around out here...

She pulled her phone out of her pocket, typed in Kyle's number, and sent a text: "Hi, it's Gracie."

Great. Now she was stuck with the sneaking suspicion that not only was that the stupidest thing anyone had ever texted, and that maybe he'd just asked her out as a joke, but also that she was going to wind up a Stepford wife in suburbia.

"Try not to freak out, Gracie," she muttered. She dropped her head into her hands and rubbed her eyes. It was just going to be coffee, right? It wasn't like she had to marry this guy if he was a total douche.

"Oh, I almost forgot." Alex spoke from right behind her and Gracie jumped.

"What's up?" She gave him a smile before he could notice her expression and ask what was wrong.

"How was the game the other night?"

"Oh! Super cool. You know that blue jewel thing? Turns out there was a quest to turn it in at a kobold tomb."

"Aw, dammit." Alex shook his head. "Maybe I'll let you level up ahead of me, and *you* can show *me* the ropes instead of the other way around."

Gracie grinned and saluted as he disappeared. Then she wolfed down the rest of her dinner and headed into the living room. It wasn't going to be a bad night, after all— because she had the game to play.

CHAPTER SEVEN

J ay ambled through the starting area outside the city gates. From his adventures with Callista two nights ago, his character was now Level 10 and shaping up to be a brawler.

He had played MMOs for years, and got an immense sense of satisfaction and pride out of building his gear sets meticulously and researching the best specializations. In MMOs, knowledge was absolutely power, and he did his research and put in the work to make his characters shine.

Each even had a backstory he'd honed after reading the world's lore, and a few had very bad portraits he'd drawn as a teenager, back when he thought he might go into video game art as a career.

He'd never really thought he'd end up in a game company, though. It had been drilled into him at a pretty early age that life wouldn't be like your daydreams. When he'd gotten the job at Dragon Soul, he'd spent the first few months waiting for someone to wake him up and send him back to work at some crushing, soulless job.

But no one had.

So, who cared if he still had a ton of student loans and not even the hint of a girlfriend? He had the best job on the planet, as far as he was concerned. He'd helped to build an MMO so big and so immersive that no one knew the whole thing inside and out. *No one*, not even the staff at Dragon Soul, could log in and not be surprised by some of the things they saw.

Maybe that was why he was enjoying running around in scraped-together Level 10 armor, making up his talent tree as he went along. He had gotten to the point where the game was giving him options of talents at each level up, making suggestions based on his play style. It was a system the team had worked hard on, and Jay was happy with how seamless it was.

His GM controls, hooked into his usual worldview, indicated a few life bars flickering perilously low nearby. On closer inspection, a small party of Piskies seemed to have bitten off more than they could chew on the sacred pool quest and were about to lose some of their progress.

Jay was feeling in a benevolent mood today, and he smiled as he selected the fight and adjusted a few parameters. The wolves' health pool shrank and the Piskies just managed to pull out a victory, only one of them dead. The other party members revived them, and Jay listened in as they chattered about what a close call it had been and how they were planning to pull their next set of enemies.

Confident that they had learned from the experience, he turned north to gaze at the ruined temple that overlooked Kithara. He had been there the night before in his GM character, invisible to the ghosts who roamed among the toppled columns and chipped, weathered statues. The view from there had been beautiful, and he decided to go up there again once the player load dropped a bit.

Technically, his team was just working on observation. They would respond to help requests from time to time, but their main function was to watch. What party mechanics were people using? What quests were they skipping or failing at? What aspects of the game did they bitch about when they didn't think the GMs were listening?

So far, there weren't many complaints, and Jay was feeling deeply satisfied with this state of affairs.

There was a faint ding on his screen, and his face lit up as he looked at the bottom left corner. Callista had come online, and she was at the tavern where she'd logged out the other day.

Jay resisted the urge to send a message. He had a healthy fear of coming off as creepy, and as always, his first instinct was not to engage. He'd had a great time laughing and joking around with Callista, but for him, that sort of interaction was something that could change at any moment without warning for reasons he wouldn't understand.

He had just about decided to log off when a private message popped up.

"Hey, you online?"

Jay clicked the button to activate voice chat. "Hey! Good to see you."

"Same here." She sounded emphatic—or maybe *he* sounded emphatic, Jay reminded himself. Those voice filters were really something. The dev team had been trolling one another for weeks, making female characters and trying to catfish each other. "Let me tell you, I could use a good bout of hero-ing right about now."

"Me, too. Should we party up?" He hoped he sounded casual, but his palms were now sweating, and for some reason, he was very aware of his ears.

"Sounds good. Let me figure out this invite mechanic. Hang on." A second later, she made a sound of satisfaction and the party invitation flashed up. "I have to say, this whole thing is a lot more intuitive than I thought it would be. I keep waiting to toggle maps or purge my inventory by accident or something, but it hasn't happened yet."

"Bet the devs would appreciate hearing that," Jay joked.

"Sure, sure. 'Hey, your game doesn't suck!'" She was laughing. "You hang out there. I'm coming your way."

"Roger that." After so many hours on the job, he'd been sitting—after all, one didn't really walk—but now he stood up and stretched. He felt more awake than he had in hours.

He saw her before too long, climbing the road that wound up and out of the city. When she cleared its shadow, the dawn light made her hair brilliant blue, and he waved. She waved back and jogged over.

"Sorry for the wait." She unsheathed her weapon. "I was just enjoying the scenery. It's so calm and peaceful after... well, everything."

"Bad day, huh?" He took a moment to study her face. It definitely wasn't one of the stock ones from the character creator, and while the faces people played with tended to fall into the uncanny category, this one really worked.

"You could say that." She shrugged, which made her coat ripple. "Let's go hit things with sticks. That'll probably help my feelings."

Jay cleared his throat. "Right."

This was *definitely* a dude.

They had both picked up a couple of gathering quests, some of which were specific to their races. Those quests were scattered throughout the game to stress ancient loyalties and test the various factions of the world.

The players didn't know it, but the game's creators were waiting to see if the races descended into outright war again. It could happen; it wouldn't be disallowed.

Callista covered him while he gathered a few herbs that the humans apparently turned into medicine, and he covered her while she had her character scramble up into a tree to reach some apples. She fell out more than once, which had them both in stitches by the time she was done, and she stretched out her arms to examine them.

"Lucky pixels don't get bruised, huh? And pixelated clothing doesn't rip."

"We'd all be in rough shape if so," Jay agreed. He looked around. "Say, what was that combo you used on the last three?"

"Oh." Callista's fingers moved, and he realized she must be thinking. "Um, trying to remember exactly how I do it. You can't always use the same one because shock blast decreases exponentially by distance."

Startled, Jay looked at her. "Been reading up on things online?"

"No." She sounded prickly now, and the reverb on the Aosi voice filters made her seem a bit like an aggrieved goddess. "I just happen to recognize exponential decay when I see it."

Jay tilted his head to the side. "So, when you're fighting—"

"Use AoE at regular intervals, and meanwhile, focus on the person with the highest DPS-to-hit-point ratio, all else being equal." She shrugged again. "So, with a sender and a fighter, I wouldn't bother with shock blast because I could focus fire on the fighter first and then get over to the sender. I suppose I'd play that one by ear. If the fighter was tank-specced like me, maybe I'd just go for the sender first. It all varies. It's like…" She was quiet for a moment. "Like there's a set of scales, and marbles, and the marbles are always moving, but they press one weight down at a time. That's all the factors, shifting and saying which ability to use."

"That's…" Jay couldn't think of an appropriate word. "That's insane. How do you keep moving while you're running numbers?"

She flashed him a smile; she had figured out the emotes. "The numbers run themselves, man. I just act on them."

"*Insane*," Jay muttered again.

"It's even more fun now that we're working with generating threat," she said, and there was genuine excitement in her voice. "Or whatever they call it in this game."

"Ire," Jay told her.

"Why they had to change the terminology, I don't know." She sounded grumpy. "It's just going to confuse people."

"I'll—" Jay remembered who he was talking to and broke off, but she had looked at him curiously.

"You'll…" she prompted when he didn't say anything.

"Just need to remember to make sure any groups are

clear on terminology," Jay improvised. "You know, so there isn't a bad situation in a dungeon or something."

She guffawed. "Kind of sounds like you're talking about a sex dungeon and safe words."

"Oh, crap." Thankfully, in-game characters couldn't blush. "Augh. That was embarrassing."

"Sorry, man, didn't mean to weird you out." She gave another laugh. "I'm a *bit* jaded due to… Eh, never mind."

"You can't start that sentence and then say 'never mind.'" Jay crossed his arms.

"Okay, counterpoint."

"Yes?"

"There's a pack of bears over there attacking a Piskie and a human."

"Shit!" Jay looked around and started running, Callista at his side. "Do we have a plan?"

"Of course we have a plan! I make everything hit me, and you take them down one by one while those two get healed up. Looks like the human is a healer, and that tiny Piskie looks like she might be working on summoning a demon. Oh, I like that. Itty bitty demon-summoner!"

Incongruously, she was still laughing as she smashed into the first bear at top speed. It gave an angry roar and wheeled to face her, and Callista started screaming obscenities at it as she whacked it and its friends with what looked like wild abandon.

The obscenities were Jay's favorite part. He'd ranked the finest ones, and the best so far had been an exceedingly detailed accounting of the lineage and sexual proclivities of a set of badgers that had attacked them while they were out foraging the day before.

This account of the bear's upbringing, however, was climbing in the ranks. She must *really* have had a bad day.

Callista had been right about the human. Heals started coming quickly and the summoner had regrouped a bit away, crouching as the pentagram around her feet glowed an unearthly green and shifted.

"Anders!" Callista yelled in his direction.

Anders punched a bear in the nose and felt the primal satisfaction of any man who has punched an apex predator. "Yeah?"

"Invite them to the party!"

"Ah, okay." In between punches, blocks, and buffs to make himself stronger and faster, he managed to invite the two individuals nearby.

"Fys," Callista called on party chat. "What kind of demon you summoning?"

"An amarok!" the summoner called back. The ice-furred wolves were huge and hulking, like something out of a nightmare, with fur that gave off the faint sound of chimes when it rustled.

And very, very big teeth.

"Cool beans. Send it over to the one on the far left, would you?"

"Got it!" Fys called back.

"Mirra, you just keep doing what you're doing, but save enough mana for a big group heal. Something's coming; I can feel it in my bones." She managed to grin at Jay as she said that last bit.

How she'd guessed it, he wasn't sure, but the "something" came about thirty seconds later. They'd unlocked some sort of bear berserker mode, maybe by killing one of the bears in front of the others. Callista's target went crazy, lunging at Jay's avatar and then turning to rampage through the amarok and bowl over both Mirra and Fys despite their attempts to get away.

"Mirra, now! Anders, with me! Fys, get that amarok on this one!"

Mirra threw her spell as the others piled onto the rampaging bear and burned its health down. Callista was throwing herself into her attacks with smooth grace. No auto-attacks or finger twitches for her; she was putting herself into every strike.

"Now, the other three at once," she called somewhat hoarsely. They could hear her panting. "Fys, you take the one on your far left. Anders, the one you've got. I'll take that one over there."

They brought the other three bears down in health all at once, and when they were close to dead, Callista called, "Bring them in!" Anders and the amarok lured the two bears closer to the third, and a moment later, Callista slammed her fists on the ground in a shock blast. All three bears crumpled.

There was a long silence, and then Callista started laughing.

"Holy shit," she managed. "Okay, hands up if this game is going to give you a heart attack."

All three of the others raised their hands at once. Even Jay was panting now. He jumped when he felt a tap on his shoulder and told the team to wait for him for a moment, switching off his voice chat before pulling his headset off.

The whole team was clustered around him, including his boss's boss, Chris. Each GM's interactions were streamed to a television to make sure they weren't off doing anything too random. They weren't technically supposed to get into parties, but Jay had been betting that no one was paying attention on this shift.

"What was that?" Chris asked him bluntly.

"Player called for help with some bears," Jay gasped. His lungs were on *fire*, but he felt strangely exhilarated.

Go on, try to get on my case, he wanted to tell Chris, *I just fought a bear, and I won.*

Luckily, he managed to talk sense into himself. "Let me tell you, you do not know how immersive VR can be until you're staring down a bear."

"Clearly you've never played the *Alien* game," one of them muttered. "I nearly pissed myself in that one."

Everyone was grinning as they drifted off. Chris opened his mouth to object, but Sam met Jay's eyes for one critical moment before slinging an arm around Chris's shoulders.

"This team was *such* a good idea," he said as if the whole thing had been Chris's idea to start with. "They're seeing how the game works right at the ground level, and Jay's been right there the whole time. He's developed this metric to track NPC interactions, and they have the sort of player feedback you couldn't *buy*, man."

They headed off, and Jay relaxed somewhat.

He knew he should say he had to go and drop the party. That was clearly what Sam was giving him time to do. On the other hand, they'd be occupied for a while looking over reports, and Jay could claim this was a new party, or he'd been getting critical feedback or tracking a bug.

Plus, he actually *was* getting good data on buffs and

debuffs. Dragon Soul had decided to make the system or advantages and disadvantages more complex than it was in other games. Some player buffs interacted with one another in ways that they were waiting to see if the players noticed, and some of the debuffs that enemies gave off, slowing the players or giving them Damage Over Time, linked up with other debuffs, or canceled out player spells.

It was an interesting system. They had spent months developing it, but Jay was now realizing that you could debate numbers all day and not really get a feel for something until you started playing around with it yourself.

Yeah, *that* was what he was going to say he was researching. He put his headset back on with a grin.

"Okay, who's up for more?"

"Me," Mirra chimed in. Short and slight, she had wispy blonde hair and a pointed chin.

"Me," Fys added. Her bright pink hair was piled above her head in three huge buns and she was sitting contentedly by her amarok.

Callista caught his eye and nodded. "Absolutely," she said. "I was hoping we hadn't lost you."

"Can't get rid of me that easily," Jay told her. "Now, let's go storm the castle. Metaphorically. Though, there is one at the end of the starting zone."

"We'll probably be there in a couple of nights," Mirra pointed out. "Party up for it? Fys and I could definitely use some DPS and a tank."

"Agreed," the Piskie said.

"I'm up for it," Callista said. She sounded deeply pleased. "I like your play style. You're both real intuitive. Jay?"

Oh, what the hell. "Sure. Yeah, sounds good."

"I sense the makings of another great guild," Fys joked. "We'll be the next HonorBound."

"Eh?" Callista asked. "Hey, this bear dropped a sword. Anyone else want it, or—"

"Nah, you should take it. And HonorBound is one of those…sponsored…guild thingies." The Piskie waved her hands. "You know, they get sponsorships to wear logo gear as they get up in the ranks because people watch the world first clears, and stuff? If they make one of those, they get extra bonuses beyond the game."

"Wait, you get a bonus for a world first?" Callista's words were slow, as though she were thinking hard.

"Yep," Jay said before she could answer. "Five grand to split."

"You're fucking *kidding.*"

"No way. Compared to the number of people paying in each month? That's chump change for them." He realized too late that maybe he shouldn't have said that. "It's only $500 apiece, I guess."

"*Only* $500?" She was laughing, now. "You must have a better job than me, man. All right, let's get our leveling on. What quests does everyone have?"

Jay watched for a moment as she, Mirra, and Fys bent their heads together to plan out an order of events. Callista's earlier annoyed energy had transformed into something happier as they fought. As Jay watched, she suggested a string of attacks to Fys for the amarok, and Fys excitedly agreed to try them out.

"Jay, come weigh in." Callista waved him over.

"Right." Jay smiled and had his character walk over to the rest of them.

This, he thought, was what *Metamorphosis Online* had been made for—this kind of connection. It had been worth every late night he'd put into it to see a world where things were finally determined by who you were, not all the other crap people usually judged you for.

And being able to punch a bear in the nose and live to tell about it. That, too.

CHAPTER EIGHT

Mirra and Fys were already waiting when Gracie logged in the next night, but Anders hadn't gotten there yet. She fought a stab of disappointment as she walked over to the other two.

"Fancy seeing you two here."

"Hey." Mirra gave her a nod. She was standing on a boulder, surveying the lands around them. "How was work?"

"'Bout the same as it was for you, I'm guessing." The night before, Mirra had mentioned that she worked at a restaurant chain. Gracie was guessing there was a healthy dose of corporate bullshit to put up with there, too. "What about you, Fys? Did you hit the job jackpot? Tell us it's possible."

"Eh, I get by." Fys shrugged her tiny shoulders.

Mirra snorted but said nothing more, and Gracie felt a flicker of curiosity. It seemed that the two of them knew each other outside the game. She didn't want to overstep, though. Part of the magic of this game was that you could let your personal life in…or not.

"So, are we all at the same stage of Something Went Bump in the Night?" Gracie asked. "Fys, you just picked it up, right?"

"Yeah. I thought maybe if we all went over to the Killing Fields, I could do the first stage and the rest of you could grab some herbs and stuff. Then I could make everyone potions for the bit in the temple ruins. I read up on that fight, and it looks a bit rough."

Gracie looked at the hill that held the temple ruins. She was curious about it. She loved any piece of lore that had grand, abandoned buildings and forgotten history.

"Do you want to wait for Anders?" Mirra asked.

"We'll shoot him a party invite when he logs on," Gracie decided. "The Killing Fields aren't packed with mobs. They tend to patrol in ones and twos, so we can just pull as many as we can handle on our own, and— Oh, hey, speak of the devil." Anders had finally logged on, and she pinged him with a party invite.

"Hey, guys." His voice came over the chat, sounding annoyed. "Sorry, got caught in a meeting."

"In a…what time zone are you in?"

There was an awkward pause. "I have coworkers over in Asia," Anders said finally, "so sometimes I have late-night conference calls. I just bring my laptop home. Yeah."

"Uh, okay. Listen, we were going to head over to the Killing Fields. Meet you there?"

"Sure. I'll repair my gear and head over."

The party ran smoothly now. They'd learned a few tricks, as well as the timing of each other's special abilities.

It was just habit now for Gracie and Anders to step out of the way as the amarok lunged forward to rake enemies with its claws, and Fys was careful to move it from enemy to enemy so it didn't build up too much threat and drag enemies away from Gracie. Mirra, meanwhile, was becoming comfortable enough with regular heals that she was able to switch to damage-dealing for parts of most fights.

It wasn't long before they had the components needed for her stage of the quest, and they all trooped along to the tavern for her to turn them in. Anders had ordered a beer and was holding it up, staring intently at the way the liquid moved and the bubbles rose inside.

"Can you not figure out how to drink it?" Gracie asked.

"No, look at the foam." He held it up. "See how it clips the edge of the mug asset?" He shook his head.

"Come on, man." Grace pushed out an elbow to nudge him before remembering that he wasn't really there. She had nearly overbalanced a few minutes before when she tried to lean on the bar.

This game, in addition to being a surprising workout, could help one acquire a surprising number of bruises. She had also acquired a healthy respect for the virtue of cleanliness after she managed to step in a container of lo mein she'd left by the coffee table the night before.

Anders looked at her.

"The game works so well," Gracie said. "You aren't going to nitpick the whole thing, are you?"

He paused, then smiled. "No, you're right, I should appreciate it. I, uh, have a friend who works in QA for video games, and he tells me a lot of details. I just see that stuff now, you know?"

"Seems like they QAd this one pretty heavily."

"Yeah. But it's big, and who *knows* what's out there, right?" He grinned. "All sorts of mysteries. Players cause chaos, as they say. Design your game to do X, Y, and Z perfectly, and the players will come waltzing in and all want to do Q."

"Ah, Q," Gracie said. "The most fun one can have in a game. Sec. God, this fucking thing."

"What's up?" He tilted his head curiously.

"Got a new bra, and the strap keeps falling off my shoulder. It's fucking annoying." Gracie looked around at both of the others, who had stopped moving entirely. "…What?"

"You're actually a chick?" Mirra asked.

"Of course I'm a chick. I have—" Gracie gestured at the female body. "I mean, I'm—why did you think I was a dude?"

"Most female characters in MMOs *are* dudes," Anders said.

"You're kidding me. Really?"

"You didn't know?" Mirra was laughing now. "You're this model-looking character with a big-ass sword, so I kinda figured, well, you know. Who wants to be in proximity to huge tits and have a giant sword, after all?"

"Man, what kind of dicks do you know that are *serrated*?" Gracie was laughing. "You should see a doctor, seriously."

Anders sounded like he couldn't breathe, he was laughing so hard.

"All right, what'd I miss?" Fys was standing nearby with crossed arms, and the fact that she was knee-high made that hilarious. The other three descended into a new storm of laughter. "No, seriously, what the fuck is going on?"

"Let me guess," Gracie gasped out. "You're a dude, too? Big, hulking, six feet tall?"

"Accurate enough," Mirra said. "He keeps in *shape*."

"I wanted to know what it was like to be short," Fys said, with great dignity. "I'm Kevin, by the way."

"And I'm Alan," Mirra said.

"Jay," Anders chimed in.

"Gracie." She waved.

"Whoa, wait, whoa." Kevin waved his hands. "*You're* not a dude?"

"*No.*" Gracie threw up her hands. "The sword is just a sword."

"That's good. It's got a greenish tint. Not so healthy."

"See, *he* gets it," Gracie told the other two as she gestured to the tiny Piskie.

She couldn't help but feel a stab of worry, however. She had thought this group was a place she could just hang out without worrying about everything she said, trying to make sure she wasn't going to come off as if she were flirting—or get told off for being cold. It had been a breath of fresh air to log in and play with guys *and* girls.

It was all guys, though, and what if they treated her differently now that they knew she was a girl? She'd had whole D&D groups arguing about her tanking strategy before, even when she had a flawless record. So many times, people had picked apart her decisions and play style even though they never did with the male players, no matter how many bad decisions *they* had made.

"Gracie?" Jay asked.

"Huh?" She realized she'd missed something.

"I said, you need to repair your gear or anything? We thought we could finish up the quest. Fys wanted your take on the final boss." They had all shared blog posts and official game pages the night before, telling the lore of this dungeon and sharing the game mechanics of the minor enemies along the way, and the final big boss at the end.

"Oh, right. Sorry, I was thinking..." Gracie shook her head to clear it. "So, the ghosts have ice power, right? And we were thinking of using an ifrit instead of the amarok? But then I thought, what if we have Anders and Mirra—sorry, Jay and Alan—use some fire powers there and *keep* the amarok, just have it use its non-ice powers. That way, it's still doing damage, and it's not vulnerable to the boss."

"Sounds good to me," Jay said.

"Me, too. Doesn't really change what I do." Alan had his character shrug. "Well, actually, it's probably easier to heal."

"I like it," Kevin said. "Otherwise, I'm trying to keep it moving so it doesn't get in any ice patches. I'm surprised none of the guides suggested that."

"The game is pretty new," Gracie pointed out. "And it's only a starter dungeon."

"Gracie's some sort of weird tactical mastermind," Jay told the other two. "Run a fight with her a couple of times, and she'll start to use these weird combos. They always work, too. It's maddening. Work on a game for years and —" He broke off in a sudden coughing fit.

"You okay, man?" Gracie asked.

"Yeah, I'm good. Should we go?"

The walk to the tomb was quick, interrupted by quick jaunts to grab herbs or ores nearby and punctuated by jokes about everyone's shitty bosses. Kevin seemed to like his boss but had plenty of stories about people up the chain at his company, and Alan, who worked in IT for a university, promised to tell them about the crazy demands his bosses made.

"Seriously," he was saying as they approached the stairs. "One day to build an entire email system. They didn't want to pay a few hundred thousand for a software license."

"What did you tell them?" Jay asked incredulously.

"Oh, I told them they were in luck," Alan said wickedly, "because I could do it for *half* that."

Jay was howling with laughter and had managed to stop moving, his character bent over as he clutched at his sides. "Oh, my God. What if they'd said yes?"

"For over a hundred grand, I'd pour coffee in my eyeballs and give it a go." Alan spread his hands as if it were self-explanatory. With the voice filters and the tiny female avatar, it was hard to think of him as a man, but to Gracie, that only made the whole comedic routine funnier.

Jay stopped laughing and wiped his eyes.

"Quick," Kevin said to Gracie in an undertone. "Pull some mobs before they tell any more stories. We might not get another chance. He's got a *lot* of those."

"His bosses are really crazy, huh?" Gracie smiled at him and padded off, loping up the hill to catch one of the patrolling ghosts. While most ghosts she'd seen tended to look quite old, with wispy hair and trailing robes. This one looked quite muscular, and very angry.

She supposed she would be angry too if she'd died in the nude at a temple.

She stepped out into the pathway when it reached a safe distance from its friends and did a little dance, then high-tailed it back to the group. It gave a ghostly shriek and followed her.

"I've been thinking," Jay said as the others watched her lay a few kicks and punches on the ghost. "We should get a flame-sender."

"If you mean a fire mage, man—" Gracie walloped the ghost in the face "—just *say* fire mage."

Laughter was her answer. "All right," Jay agreed, "we need a fire mage. And that looks like a good level of threat. Let's do this!" He leapt into action with the amarok.

Alan's spells proved valuable for pulling enemies, so they proceeded up the path, clearing as they went. Gracie was panting by the end of it.

"You know, you can just use the combo wheel," Jay suggested.

"I kind of like the workout, you know? I just *stand* all day, and..." She broke off, bracing her hands on her legs. "Oof. Maybe tomorrow. I just have a lot of stress to work out."

Like the fact that Kyle had texted back, and apparently wanted to take her out for a nice dinner instead of coffee. She'd managed to find a dress in the back of her closet, the one she'd worn to her graduation, but putting on makeup and tottering around in heels wasn't her idea of a good time.

It was just nerves, she told herself. She could just picture how happy her mother and father would be. They'd feel like she had made good choices after all, so they didn't need to be on her case, and—

She shook her head and straightened up, looking around her. "I need to punch more things. Point me in the direction of your boss, good sirs." She looked at the other three, who were staring at her. "I grew up watching my mother do that thing—you know the one: 'I would like to speak to your manager.' It actually kind of works here." As an afterthought, she added, "I think I'd have approved more if she killed them with a flaming sword when she talked to them."

They crept into the main boss's chamber, stifling their laughter. Usually, in game, your in-party chat didn't alert mobs to your presence, but there was something about this place that inspired awe.

It really looked like the ruins of a temple, Gracie thought. The sun was setting outside, and the shattered columns threw jagged shadows over the floor. The rustle of wind in the trees outside was so realistic that she almost felt like she smelled it on her skin. She could imagine the scent of greenery and stone...

The summer day faded, and ice began to creep across the floor.

"So you return," the boss whispered. Its voice was not loud, yet it came from all around them. "*Defiler. Despoiler.* I have been waiting for you."

He wasn't a ghost, which was what Gracie had been expecting. Instead, as he came around the corner, the ground shuddered. He was some sort of nightmare construct, not stitched together like Frankenstein's monster, but instead made with magic. The proportions were all wrong, and there was faint motion under the skin like hands pressing against it or faces turning and twisting. One too-long arm dragged a large mace over the ground.

"Holy *crap*," Gracie muttered.

"Guys?" Kevin sounded uncertain. "I don't think this is the normal boss."

Gracie glanced at him. "Like, we should get out of here or—" The doors slammed shut, and magical barriers sprang up in front of the windows. "Of course," Gracie muttered. "All right, guys, huddle up; we can do this. And if we can't, that's what graveyard respawn and armor repair was made for, right?"

"Right," Alan agreed.

Fys hung back for a moment but then nodded. "Right. It's just weird, okay? Like we triggered something we shouldn't have."

There was silence, and the rest of them looked at Jay.

"Any thoughts?" Gracie asked.

"No," he said slowly. "I'm as lost as you are." He sounded deeply disturbed. "Must be a glitch." He readied his weapon. "Let's do this."

"Come on, guys." Gracie looked around. "This is funny, right? And there's only so wrong it can go. Remember, we're not actually stuck in a room with an— Oh *crap*, it's coming for me. Apparently we're doing this! AAAAAAAAAAAH!" She drew her sword, all gleaming greenish and serrated edges, and charged the boss. "Everybody scatter!"

From the silence and the pounding of feet, she guessed they were too busy taking her advice to say anything else.

The boss, running heavily now, swung its mace up and

backhanded Gracie's character across the room. The sky wheeled across her vision and she smashed against the far wall, sliding down it. The dazed debuff made the room look blurry, and her character couldn't stand up.

She could see that it was coming for her, though, and primal terror gripped her.

"Come on, get up," she pleaded with her character, watching the timer count down. "Come on, come on, *come on.*"

Her view cleared, and she managed to throw herself sideways just in time as the mace slammed down. Pivoting, Gracie saw her opportunity and slashed the back of the thing's legs before stomping hard for a shock blast.

The monster bellowed, but there was a new scream in the mix, too, and as she watched, a slimy monster with no eyes pulled itself out of the wound and flopped, dripping, onto the floor.

Gracie shrieked. Jay shrieked. Kevin was making gagging sounds. Alan sounded like he was having a panic attack.

"Oh, Jesus *fuck,*" Gracie managed. She was backing away, holding the sword in front of her like a talisman. "Oh, I hate this thing. This thing is the worst." She pointed her sword at it. "Is it *filled* with those?"

"Gracie!" Jay called. "It's holding its leg, and it's not attacking. Kill the thing while you have the chance!"

Gracie dove forward, slashing at the monster. It ducked away, surprisingly fast for being blind, and hissed at her, but she kept her momentum going and whipped her sword around in a circle to cut it down from the same side it had ducked to. It screamed as it collapsed into crystals of ice.

She wasn't a moment too soon since the boss bellowed and turned. Its hit points, which hadn't gone down at all with her slash, now showed a loss.

"*That's* how we kill it!" Gracie called. "Take out each monster. Jay, you and I will try our luck getting in shots to pry each little monster out, okay?"

"Okay," Jay called back.

They bounced it back and forth between them, Gracie often drawing its fury and then fleeing while Jay slashed at it. Each time, it howled in pain and stopped moving while its smaller counterpart climbed from the wound and attacked.

"This is not getting any easier to watch," Alan yelled.

"*Don't* watch," Kevin called back.

"I can't…*not* watch. It's like a train wreck. A gooey one," he clarified.

"*Ew*," the whole group chorused.

Then the boss turned to them, laughing, and began to shrink. Where there had been a monster, now there was a cleric in long, flowing robes. He was bald but had a long beard, and he stared directly at Gracie.

"You think that was all there was?" he asked contemptuously.

He snapped his fingers, and the twenty monsters on the floor came to life once again.

"Now," he said with a terrible smile on his face, "you will die."

CHAPTER NINE

There was a pause. The skeletons stared at them, and they stared at the skeletons.

"Shitsticks," Kevin said succinctly.

"Agreed," Gracie said. "Alan—"

"On it." Their healer laid down an AOE for their team, a glowing circle that would provide healing for every team member standing inside it.

"All right, here's the deal," she told them. "I'm going to pinball around, pick them all up, and Mirra—Alan, sorry— is going to keep me alive while the amarok and Jay pick off anyone they can. Got that?"

"Got it," everyone chorused.

"Okay, but why aren't they moving?" Gracie asked. Two of the bodies morphed into one another with a wet *shlorp* sound. "Oh, you have got to be *kidding* me. Everyone, kill these eyeless bastards!"

With a yell, Jay charged into action, and Gracie did the same. The amarok shrieked and snapped its teeth as they cut their way through the group, slashing down each of the monsters before they could merge once more into the shambling mess they had first seen.

But with each death, there was a *ding* and the cleric seemed to pulse brighter, until, as the last monster fell, he was shining as brightly as a sun. In the light, Gracie could dimly see his head thrown back and his arms spread wide.

"Karenar!" His voice was as desperate as it was fervent. "Guide my power! Strike down our enemy!"

The light rushed into him and exploded outwards, so visceral that Gracie threw her arms up and braced, sure she was going to be knocked from her feet. Her field of vision shook as if the entire place had rocked in some unseen explosion.

When the light cleared, the temple was whole. Its walls gleamed with frescoes picked out in fresh paint. Curls of smoke rose lazily from braziers, and the statues stood whole at the corners of the room. The vaulted ceiling was held up by tall carved columns.

And in the center of the room was a warrior. He seemed more than human, slightly out of scale with the rest of them, and although the tip of his sword lay on the ground and his head was bowed wearily, there was no mistaking his power. It seemed to ripple under his skin like fire. When he raised his eyes, there was triumph in them.

"I am made whole," he said, "as I once was. And you will return to nothing, as you once were."

Gracie didn't have time to think when he rushed at her. She raised her weapon and fought for her life. No one could have told her at that moment that it wasn't real. The haptics shook and her muscles were on fire, already tired from fighting her way in and defeating every monster in this place, some of them twice. The breath was harsh in her lungs, and she almost thought she could taste blood as she thrust and parried desperately.

She was trying to survive, nothing more. This man hated her, and his hatred seemed personal. Why, she did not know, but she didn't question it. It didn't occur to her, as it would have in a normal video game, that this was something happening in the world of the game. No, she was *here*. It was happening to her.

When her opponent broke away, only to shudder and have his health bar dip sharply, she realized that Jay and the amarok had taken up for her—and had to stop herself from screaming that this man was *hers* to finish. She was dangerously low on health, despite Mirra's best efforts. She needed to stay away for a moment.

Burning muscles notwithstanding, she was back in the fight the moment her health bar was full again. This time she pulled no punches as she fought. She was beginning to learn the boss's rhythms—his attack chains and his preferences—and she fought him with the same hatred he felt for her.

Or...maybe she did. Without understanding why he wanted vengeance, it was hard to say for sure. With a flash of humor, she wondered if he was simply a ghost who had forgotten who he was really angry at.

There had better be a good cutscene at the end of this.

Once more, she was forced to break away, and once more, she danced anxiously on the balls of her feet, waiting to go back into the fight.

The third time was the charm. He was growing weaker, and the game developers had thought to put desperation into his movements. There were cuts on his fiery skin now, and he was crying out to his goddess to help him.

At last, he fell to his knees, swaying.

"*You* locked yourself in here with me," Gracie told him as she advanced. "For revenge. You wanted me to be nothing. Why?"

"Karenar curse you," he spat, and dissolved. The cleric's body thudded to the ground, small, wizened, and clearly dead.

Around them, the temple walls dissolved again until only the ruins remained. In the distance, a bird trilled.

Silence.

Gracie looked around. "Did we... What the hell just happened?"

"I just got an achievement for Stage 1 of something called 'First Among her Followers,'" Kevin reported. "Does anyone know what that is? And the other quest is marked as complete, even though I swear that's not the one we did."

There was a scuffling noise from Jay's mic, and a moment later, he said curtly, "I gotta go, guys." His character blinked out of existence without another word.

"That was weird," Kevin said. "But *damn*, Gracie...that was some *fighting*. You keep cranking out DPS like that, we won't need a whole party, huh?"

Gracie grinned. She was panting and could feel herself coated in sweat, but she couldn't stop smiling. This was lore, heroism, and mystery, all wrapped up in an experience that felt more real than her real life. Going through the motions every day at her job, dealing hands, smiling at the people as they came and went...this was better. None of them saw her, and none of them cared.

But here there was a whole world to explore, a world like the one she had always wanted.

She was grinning as she swiped a hand over her brow. "Okay, I need a rest after that. Don't know about you guys."

"I need a drink," Alan said succinctly. "I haven't been that stressed since I presented my Master's thesis."

Gracie chortled and teleported back to the tavern to log out. She pulled her VR headset off her head and barely made it to the couch before her legs gave out. She felt amazing...and totally drained.

Her phone buzzed nearby, and it took two tries to pick it up.

CONGRATULATIONS! read the subject line; the sender was identified as Metamorphosis Online.

Inside, a banner of confetti hung over the excited proclamation that Gracie's account now sat at $150 for the month.

"Son of a bitch, they charged me for... They're sending me congratulations for—" She broke off, confused, and read the email again. She had *made* money. She had made more than her first month's membership fee, by a *lot*. "Why?" she asked her phone. "*How?*"

Her phone, fully occupied with making the confetti banner work, had no answer for that.

Gracie sat back in her seat, frowning, but a smile was tugging at her lips. As much as she wanted to be, she could hardly be too upset about this. This put her over the amount she needed for the month for rent and gave her a bit extra to buy donuts at her favorite place this weekend.

"Hot damn," she muttered.

She was still smiling when she caught a whiff of herself. After the fighting, she did *not* smell pretty. She hustled off to take a shower, aching and muttering complaints about getting older.

But she couldn't stop smiling.

Jay was sweating as Sam walked him down the hall to Chris's office. All of a sudden, his choice to bunk off and play games during work hours seemed completely indefensible. He could see all of his petty justifications about how he was *supposed* to be play-testing and hearing from the players vanishing into thin air.

He was going to get fired.

Chris looked worried when Jay was shown into his office. He was probably trying to figure out how to fire someone. After all, what with being in the midst of launch, they weren't exactly rolling in workers. They had a lot to fix and run, and even with a well-staffed company, there weren't enough employees to do everything.

He braced himself, and felt his jaw drop when Chris said, "How many people know about that bug?"

Jay scrambled for an answer.

"There were three others in your group," Sam prompted finally. His voice was soft. "Does anyone else know?"

"Not that I...I mean, it was weird, but—"

"It's *expensive* is what it is." Chris swiveled his monitor around. "That *glitch* gave an achievement of $150 per player."

"What the *hell?*" Jay leaned over the monitor and tabbed through the data. "That wasn't the quest we—" He broke off, clearing his throat. He wasn't supposed to be on quests.

Chris hadn't noticed. "I'll need a full report," he told Sam as if Jay wasn't in the room. "All of the mod powers your team has, and have all of them run that quest. Some in chosen groups, some in PUGs, some solo if it can be run solo. Match as many of the variables as you can from Jay's run and then iterate. See if any of the rest of them can get that glitch to go. We need to get ahead of this thing before the C-suite hears about it."

"It's not a super-big deal," Jay said, holding out his hands placatingly. He heard Sam hiss a quiet warning but didn't pay attention. What was the problem, after all? "Some endgame content got triggered, but like the monthly dungeons, it must have adapted to our level. We'll figure out the connection, and no one will ever know. I say we just leave the money in those players' accounts. $150 is chump change for—"

"You don't *get* it," Chris interrupted. He grabbed his monitor back, stabbed a few keys, and then turned it so roughly that it tipped over. "It's put *this* player in the top ten globally."

Callista. Jay stared at the avatar and fought the urge to grin. She was going to find this *so* funny. Some statistical glitch, some—

A thought, not quite formed, made the smile fade.

He still wasn't quite sure why he was worried when Chris said, "Do you know how this game got funded, Jay?"

"I...no." Fuck, he should have a better answer to that.

"By our sponsors," Chris said in a much-too-pleasant voice. "Lox Graphics. Gr8p Drink. Brightstar. Every one of them is sponsoring players and guilds, and every one of them wants their logos splashed all over the top ten. Now we have a player who's *glitching* their way into the list. Placement on this list is expensive, Jay. If they don't get placement, they don't fund us. They don't fund us, we *shut down.* So go write that report and figure out what's going wrong so we can fix this before they start pulling their ads. *Now.*"

Jay backed out of the room, nodding silently.

Sam didn't join him, and Jay could hear his immediate boss trying to persuade Chris. The words were indistinct, but the tone was similar to someone trying to calm a horse. Sam was putting his job on the line to defend Jay because Jay had opened his fat mouth.

For the first time, he felt slimy as he sat down at his desk, and the slimy feeling wasn't from the sweat that was coating him after that impromptu fight.

He'd loved the idea of the global rankings. He hadn't even blinked at the idea of sponsorships. After all, tons of companies sponsored *StarCraft* players.

But those companies weren't demanding that *StarCraft*'s developers change the game so their sponsored player would win. This...this was different.

Jay sat at his desk while his shift bled away and the rest of his team left. He was still working when Sam walked by on his way out. Sam lingered for a few moments, but Jay was so immersed that he didn't look up and say hello.

When he finished the report, Sam was gone

That was good, because he had a hunch he wanted to test now that his team was gone and the next shift was coming in. After all, none of *them* knew who he was. No one would ask what he was working on. Jay shut the door of his office and began digging through the game files. He found Callista easily and began to trace her very first steps in-game.

She'd started out, gone to the pool, killed the wolf...

His eyes narrowed. They were feeling grainy now, and a little dry. He was swaying in his seat, but he kept digging.

It was three hours into the next shift before he spoke, and he said only four words.

"Son of a *bitch*."

CHAPTER TEN

J ay bounced his feet nervously as Chris tapped his fingers on the desk. Chris was pissed, he could tell, and he didn't like that. Chris was one of those people who *liked* being angry. They almost enjoyed it when their employees disappointed them because they just loved to give dramatic speeches and exercise their power.

Normally, that bugged the hell out of Jay, and it was one of the reasons he did everything in his power to steer clear of Chris. He didn't want to say something he would regret. Something that would cost him his dream job.

There were bad eggs everywhere, right?

Right now, he was too tired to be annoyed, though. He'd gone home and tried to sleep, which had been a wasted effort. By the time he'd eaten the fast food he'd gotten on the way home and showered—he reeked, frankly —he was so tired that he couldn't sleep. He tossed and turned while gray light filtered around the edges of the shades, then finally got up and went back to the office.

Sam was running late, and Chris was getting more

annoyed by the second. Finally, they heard Sam's voice in the corridor, and he rushed into the room, laptop bag bouncing against his side.

"Sorry, sorry, the drive-thru was *super* slow, and my daughter didn't want to go to daycare this morning..." His voice trailed off as he took in the mood in the room. "Everything okay?" he asked finally.

He was braver than Jay would have been. With Chris, that was practically poking the bear.

"I don't know yet," Chris said in a tone that conveyed the considerable patience it took to deal with someone as disappointing as Sam. "*Jay* didn't want to start until *you* arrived, and you just got here."

Oh, good, this was going to be an equal-opportunity beat-down. Jay gave Sam a strained smile that said, "Let's just get through this."

Sam gave a tiny nod and settled into the other guest chair. "So I'm guessing you figured out what was going on, then?" He didn't look at Chris.

"Yeah." Jay cleared his throat. It was scratchy, as were his eyes. "So, here's the deal. There was an Easter egg quest that this player found. It grants a pretty big ranking boost for completion, which is shared with anyone in the party, and it kind of...goes off randomly."

"What," Chris said, "does *that* mean?" He was really warming to his angry mood and bit off each word crisply.

Jay sighed and rubbed his scalp. It was itchy. All of him was itchy. He was *not* young enough to pull all-nighters anymore, apparently.

Wasn't twenty-six too young to be feeling the first sting of aging?

"So, when she went to defeat the ghosts at the Blood-choir Temple, for instance, the boss who *actually* appeared was totally different than the one who should have, given the quest they were on. I think it's all going to happen like that."

"You...*think?*" Chris looked like he was going to flip the table.

Jay was beginning to feel the same way. He'd been up all night tracking this quest through the code, and even though he'd barely managed to find any of it, he'd done a much better job than Chris would have.

"The quest isn't documented," he explained as patiently as he could. "In a *normal* quest, I'd be able to look at the fights and conversations and see what gets triggered by each successive completion." He shrugged. "Well, in a normal quest, I wouldn't have to. We'd have documentation about what the quest did, what stages it had, and where to find the bits of it. If I wanted to, it would be easy to find the code. In this case, none of it seems to be...indicated correctly. I know how she started the quest, and I was there during the boss fight, so I had some information to work with, but even with that, I couldn't tell you where any of the code is to say what's coming next."

Chris stared at him for a long moment, and Sam cleared his throat.

"In something the size of this game," he said delicately, "we have to have very strict naming conventions for dialogue, quest chains, et cetera, or it quickly becomes impossible to find anything. If the dialogue and achievements specific to a quest aren't tagged with the quest name —which is I *think* what Jay is saying, right, Jay? Right—so if they aren't tagged, they'd be almost impossible to track down." His brow wrinkled.

Jay knew what that wrinkle meant. "I was able to find some of the conversations by searching the database for certain strings from the boss fight. Unfortunately, the things I found followed no naming conventions I could see and were in sections I couldn't navigate to, so I couldn't find the rest of the quest. And," he sighed, "it's done with conditions, not with scripts."

Chris's face settled into a stony mask, and at last, Jay felt a wave of anger. Chris didn't like being reminded of his lack of skill in coding, which would be annoying enough on its own. He worked at a game company, for Christ's sake! But more than that, he'd had numerous opportunities to get more competent with the code. He just hadn't ever taken them.

"What Jay *means*," Sam said, breaking in with a worried look at Jay, "is that the code doesn't say where things go next. Instead, whatever happens next, happens because certain other conditions are met. So if a quest has part A and part B, instead of part A finishing with instructions to go on to part B, part B is set to happen when part A finishes."

Chris looked at Sam, then at Jay, then back to Sam again. "So?" he asked finally.

"So there's no way to know what's coming," Sam replied. "It could be anything."

"Not. Good. Enough," Chris said.

Jay snapped. "Look, from what I've seen, it was written by Harry Kouper. It looks like his stuff. And..." He cleared his throat.

"Yes?" Chris said much too nicely.

Jay decided not to mince words. Nothing here was secret, not exactly. "This was the sort of thing Harry did," he said with a shrug. It was part of why Harry had gotten bought out after a long and increasingly vicious power struggle with the other two founders of Dragon Soul. "A prank like this?" Jay said. "Well, it's hard to know if he would do it just because he thought it was funny or to screw things up for us down the line, but it really does sound like him."

Even Chris knew enough to know that much. He sat back in his chair, uncharacteristically quiet for a moment.

"Well, at least you found out what we are dealing with," he said after a moment. The words didn't have his usual sarcastic bite to them. He was genuinely grateful. "When I tell the Ds—"

He broke off as Jay and Sam exchanged a quick look. "The Ds" meant the other two founders of Dragon Soul productions, Dhruv and Dan. Harry and Dhruv had been freshman-year roommates at MIT, and Dan had transferred in their junior year from RPI. They'd begun working on *Metamorphosis Online* from the dorms, and the game was littered with references to Boston and their various colleges and classmates.

Chris still wasn't talking, and Sam motioned for Jay to stay silent as he took the plunge. "Dhruv and Dan are best placed to fix this," he told Chris. He could see that Chris was worried about bringing up a problem and not a solution. "They might recognize an internal joke—or whatever —sooner than an outsider would. They are more familiar with his code. They'd want us to bring this to them immediately."

He'd messed up in suggesting what to do. Chris gave him an unfriendly look. "Yes, and in the meantime? We just punt it their way and tell them to deal with that *and* the mess in the rankings? Which Jay did *not* fix, by the way."

Jay swallowed. He'd completely forgotten about that. Following the trail had turned into an obsession as the night wore on, and between what he knew for certain and his hunches—hunches he hadn't shared and wasn't intending to—he'd forgotten to undo the ranking.

He cleared his throat. "The only way to fix the rankings would be to make a manual adjustment, which wouldn't be..."

Chris raised his eyebrows when Jay paused.

"Well, it wouldn't be fair," Jay said. The words sounded lame even to him. "If she's noticed her ranking, and she logs in and sees that we've adjusted it? Well, I mean, she *did* complete the quest. She earned those points."

"Then, *if* she submits a ticket, we tell her that the original boost was a mistake," Chris told him as if explaining something to a particularly stupid child. "We'll deal with it. Better to play it as a glitch than to let people know there are a bunch of hidden ways to manipulate the rankings when we don't even know what they *are.*" He gave Sam and Jay scathing looks. "I'll handle this."

"Wait." The word came out automatically.

Sam and Chris looked at Jay, which was awkward. He didn't actually have a follow-up. There was no plan at all.

So he made one up on the fly. "Let me look at the rankings and come up with a good PR-sensitive way to address it, *and* an idea of the adjustments we'd need to make. We can tag her account so that any big ranking boosts get sent to one of us for approval, maybe." He was still scrambling, but ideas were coming to him now. "If Harry did this, there might be more. There might be more even if it wasn't him. We know programmers like to hide little bits of code. My team might have to handle this again in the future, so we should come up with a plan. Just tell Dan and Dhruv about the report—I'll send it to you—and that we're working on the rest of it."

"Are you sure?" Sam asked him. "You need to go home and get some sleep."

"No." Jay wasn't sure why he was so adamant about this, but he was. "I'll have the report to you tomorrow night," he told Chris. "I'm going to go get some caffeine and start working."

He left without being dismissed. He needed to get out before he snapped.

At his desk, he slumped into his chair and groaned. He wasn't even sure what was upsetting him about this. He just knew that the phrase "I'll handle this" had put his hackles up.

It didn't matter, he decided finally. *He'd* find the solution. *He'd* figure it out.

Because if his hunches were correct…

He wasn't going to think about that yet. His hands were shaking as he put on the VR suit. This was crazy. He was doing something crazy, and the Ds might figure out what was going on and stop it all in its tracks. He wasn't sure if he hoped they did.

The world calmed him, though, as it always did. He

stared out at the gently waving grasses and the spread of stars across the night sky and felt his tension melt away. When he was here, the rest of the world didn't seem real.

There was a ding in his headset, and a second later, he got a voice chat request. His heart started to thud.

"Hey," he managed.

"Hey, yourself." The Aosi voice, all echoey and epic, made the informal language sound hilariously out of place. "Can't stay, actually. Glad I caught you."

"Oh? Why?"

"To…tell you I can't stay?" Gracie sounded a bit confused. "I just didn't want you all to be waiting for me. I'm sorry."

"Oh. Right." Jay fought a smile. She'd actually logged in to tell them she wouldn't be here. She cared. "Well, have a good night."

"Eh." She didn't sound too enthused. The flicker of boredom actually worked pretty well with the Eternal Perfect Being voice. "We'll see. But you all have some fun."

Jay was still trying to figure out how to tell her that he probably wouldn't when she logged off.

He sighed. At least this gave him time to figure out what the hell to do about this mess.

───────

In the living room, Gracie stripped off the VR headset and nearly had a heart attack when she saw Alex lurking in the corner of the room.

"Jesus fuck, you scared me. How long have you been

standing there?" It couldn't have been long. She'd only just put on the headset.

"I just got home." Alex blinked at her attire. "Is this, uh... You know what? I'm too tired to be witty. What's with the fucking dress?"

"Oh. Right." Gracie looked down. "Uh, date."

Kyle had suggested an upscale restaurant for dinner and hadn't been willing to take no for an answer. Fortunately, Gracie had found some clothes lurking in the back of her closet, bought for her by her mother, who was eternally optimistic that if she could just get Gracie to look the part of the preppy corporate climber, the personality would follow.

Alex made a fart noise and gave her a thumbs-down.

"I know," Gracie said, throwing her hands up. "And..." She checked her texts. "He was supposed to be here to pick me up like twenty minutes ago, and nothing."

"Because he's a douche," Alex said.

"Hashtag not all Kyles," Gracie said, with a wicked grin. Her phone blooped, however, and she groaned when she saw it. "Or maybe all Kyles. He got stuck in a meeting and can't meet up tonight. He'll call me if he's free later."

"He'll string you along," Alex predicted. "This is all to put you off-balance. Which is working, I might add. You're wearing makeup."

"I know. It feels itchy."

Alex was still laughing as Gracie kicked off her heels. "Ugh. Enough of that, then. Let's order a ton of food—I'm fucking starving—and then log in. Wait, are you actually home tonight, or do you have to go back to the office?"

"Actually home." Alex spread his arms beatifically.

"No shit! You managed to get that dude off the hook?"

"Not really. He seems to have decided to leave the country. Management is putting up the pretense of a fight before giving the IRS the raw data, but since he's not paying his accounting bill…"

"Oof. Well, let's get you some giant wolves to beat with a stick, huh?" Gracie grinned. "You order food, I'm going to go wash this stuff off my face."

CHAPTER ELEVEN

G racie wasn't entirely sure how she was feeling. There was no way to know if Kyle was being a jerk; that was the thing. Totally reasonable people *could* get stuck in meetings, after all.

But what if he *was* being a jerk and she was handing him chances to keep doing that? Or what if he'd met some high-flying executive with perfect hair and he was going with the better option? Between a blackjack dealer who couldn't make her rent and someone with a career, it wasn't too hard to pick, right?

She craned and stretched her arms to get the zipper down, then tossed it across the room with her foot and grabbed last night's PJs off the floor. With her hair in a ponytail and an old tank top on, she finally recognized herself in the mirror, at least.

Food had arrived by the time she went back out, and she wolfed down eggrolls without saying anything.

"Hey." Alex's voice was quiet.

"Huh?" Gracie looked at him. She felt her cheeks color.

She was suddenly aware that she'd let a date derail her entire night.

"I actually dated a bit after I got here," Alex said. He cleared his throat awkwardly.

Gracie frowned. She wasn't quite sure where this was going.

"I just mean, I get it, okay? You get ready for a date, you don't even *like* the person that much, and then something goes wrong, and it still feels shitty. You tell yourself it's stupid and…it doesn't help." Alex shrugged. "I talk about how marriage sucks and all of that crap, but the truth is, I felt like an idiot the whole damned time."

Gracie managed a laugh, and she nodded. "Yeah. Yeah, like I wasn't even sure I wanted to go. I was dreading it, and now I feel like shit." She put her fork down with more force than was strictly necessary. "God, being human sucks."

"Well put." Alex raised his plastic fork in a mock toast. "You know what *doesn't* suck?"

Gracie looked at him suspiciously. "Are you going to say video games?"

"I absolutely fucking am. And, since you know the ropes in *Metamorphosis*, you're going to help me out, right?"

"Depends. How many bears are going to attack me?" She began gathering up the takeout containers.

"I'll get those." Alex piled them into the plastic bag. "You get things set up. You want a seltzer?"

"No. I'll one hundred percent spill it on the VR suit. But thanks. I'll get us logged in." Gracie padded out into the main room and brought up both logins. "Your password is the usual, right?"

"Nah, made a new one," Alex called back. "OMGWTFB-BQ84 exclamation point. All caps."

Gracie was snickering as she logged in. "All right, it's loading. Getting all suited up. Or...do I have to pee? This game is hell on bathroom breaks." As soon as she dropped into the game, however, she felt nothing but contentment. "God, I love everything about this place. Are you at the tavern? I'll come get you."

Alex met her at the city gates, lurking to one side as a stream of people passed him. The game was getting more crowded by the day, Gracie had noticed.

"What's the 9 over your head?" He asked her.

"I don't know?" Gracie craned her head up. "Crap, I can't see it. What does it look like?"

"A nine."

She crossed her arms and gave him a look.

Alex threw up his hands. "What do you want me to say? It's a big glowy gold 9 above your name."

"Okay, well, I don't know what that's about, I'm Level 15." Gracie shrugged, then heard a ding. "Oh, I know someone who will know, though. Inviting them to the party. Yo, Kevin."

"What's up?" Kevin's voice came through high and squeaky in the Piskie filter.

"All right, it's just weird hearing a Piskie female voice and calling the person 'Kevin,'" Alex commented.

Gracie laughed. "Kevin, this is Alex. Alex, Kevin. Alex is my roommate, and Kevin has been part of the group I'm in. We're helping each other level up. Would you mind helping Alex get up to our level tonight, Kev?"

"No problem," Kevin said easily. "After last night's excitement, I could use a night of frolicking in the flowers."

"We had this weird boss thing," Gracie explained to Alex. "Ah, yep, there's Alan. And oh, hey, Jay's still online. Whole group. What's up, guys?"

"Not much." Jay's voice was scratchy, and they heard him cough and clear his throat. "Sorry about that. I, uh, might just have to leave suddenly tonight."

"Ooooh," Gracie teased. "Hot date?"

"Er. No."

"She's just salty," Alex chimed in. "She, in the grand tradition of dating, got stood up by a douche."

"Been there," Alan said glumly.

"Twice this week," Kevin agreed.

"After the first time they stood you up, you let them try again?" Gracie said skeptically.

"Nah, someone else. Same night, too."

"You…"

"He has the devil's own luck," Alan said. "And—this is the big one—guys are just easier to date than girls."

"Let me tell you, man, that is *not* true." Kevin was emphatic, which sounded hilarious in the Piskie voice. Everyone burst out laughing. "I'm serious! Stop laughing. Goddammit, guys!"

Jay recovered first. "All right, go on. Tell us about it while we all get to—where are we meeting, city gates?" There was a chorus of yeses. "Come on," Jay cajoled Kevin. "We promise we won't laugh at the voice."

Kevin harrumphed. "There's no 'about it' to tell," he said finally, still sounding a bit prickly. "It's just, dudes are every bit as crazy as girls. You think there's less drama when it's two guys dating? You're *wrong*, pal."

"I have to agree," Gracie chimed in. "Well, all I know is, my cousin has a bunch of stories from dating guys *and* girls, and from what she says, it's always a clusterfuck."

"I'd be willing to believe that," Alex said contemplatively. "People get dumb when they date, right? Although, having enough dates to get stood up twice in one week…"

"I should have known we were coming back around to that," Kevin grumbled. He appeared at the end of the street, his Piskie running along, her hair easily half again her height. "Listen, I date that often *because* people are crazy. You gotta play the odds if you want to find a good one, right? And there are seven billion people. That's a lot to go through. I mean, even three and a half billion is— *Whoa*. Whoa. Gracie. Whoa."

"I'd ask if I had spinach in my teeth, but I don't think they programmed the game that thoroughly," Gracie joked. "Oh, and since you're here, you'll know this—what's with the glowing 9 thing Alex says I have above my head? Assuming he's not pranking me."

"Oh, no," Jay said.

"What's up?"

"Nothing. Nothing. Nothing. I just…spilled something." He cleared his throat. "So, where are we questing tonight?"

"That 9," Kevin said, ignoring Jay, "means you've hit the *global rankings*, Gracie. You're in the top ten."

"The top ten? Whoa, wait, the top ten *players*?"

"Yeah. So, you hiding some Level 50 alt somewhere or something?"

"I…no?" Gracie looked at Alex, baffled. There was no

emote for baffled, but after a moment, his character gave an elaborate shrug. "It has to be a glitch, right?"

"Right," Jay said, his voice sounding stronger. There was a pause, then he sighed. "No."

"No what?"

"I mean, it's not a glitch."

"How do you know?" Gracie waved as Alan joined them and pointed toward Jay, who was walking their direction from the surrounding countryside. Everyone set off together.

"I just mean, if you've got that ranking, there's a reason, right?"

"I don't think there really is." Gracie shook her head. "We're all Level 15, right? We should have the same ranking. We haven't done anything different, have we? I mean, Alex and I had that weird bear thing we fought off, but that *can't* have that big an effect."

"You did that quest with the jewel, right?" Alex interjected.

"I suppose. And there was that thing last night—"

"Let's get leveling," Jay broke in. "Before I have to go, right? Oh, we have a low-level."

"This is Alex," Gracie explained. "He's my roommate. He got me into the game, but he's had to work late the past few nights. Figured we could help him level up."

Alex bowed. "Gary Swiftbolt, at your service."

"Gary Swiftbolt?" Gracie snorted. "You are *such* a dork."

"We're all dorks here," Kevin said philosophically. His Piskie made a grand, sweeping gesture. "Let's get Swiftbolt here leveled up before we lose you, Miss Number 9, to one of the big guilds."

"Oh, good point." Alex shrugged. "I need to kill some wolves by a magical spring, by the way?"

"Ah, we'll show you the way." Gracie set off. "What's a good point? And what about guilds?"

"He means," Jay said, "that you'll be getting headhunted if you stay in the top ten. Even close, really." He didn't sound entirely pleased.

"Or she'll get a sponsorship," Alex chimed in. "All right, Teef, take it away. Go get me a wolf." He sent his panther racing off into the sunshine. The days passed quickly here in the game world, and the sun climbed noticeably if you took even a moment to look at it.

"She *might* get a sponsorship," Jay said.

"Uh, guys? Little help here?"

"Right." Jay nodded to Gracie, and the two of them took off for the fight as Alan began healing. Kevin's demon oozed along beside them as they ran, and all three of them slammed into the wolf at once. It went flying, one-shotted easily by three Level 15s.

Gracie pointed in two directions and she and Jay took off, one-shotting another wolf apiece.

"Excellent," Gracie said. "Well, there's that quest sorted out."

"I'll go get the next one," Alex called.

"Cool. Alan, you want to go with him, keep him out of trouble, and heal him if anything comes out of the woodwork?"

"Sounds good," Alan said.

"You know," Jay said, as the other two started off, "you should think about looking for sponsorship."

"It's a glitch, man." Gracie looked at him, grinning, and

then remembered to make her character emote. "I've only played this game for a few days. Wait. Son of a bitch." She sighed. "I just realized that the email I got about making back my monthly fee—that's probably the same glitch. Argh."

"Or it's *not* a glitch," Jay argued. "Gracie, what if—" He broke off.

"What if?" Gracie prompted.

"It's nothing. Not important. Just remember it's not a glitch, okay?" His voice was oddly intense. "All this money you're making every day? That's yours."

"I make money every *day?*"

"If you're in the top ten, yeah," Kevin chimed in.

"Yeah." Jay wasn't looking at her. "And your roommate's right. You should try to get a sponsorship."

"What do sponsorships even do? How do they work?" Gracie looked around. This all seemed ridiculous, but no one else seemed to be noticing that. *It's a glitch,* her brain insisted.

"Well, they pay some living expenses, make sure you have good internet, stuff like that. And you rep their brand."

"I don't know. If I'm already making money every day, why do I need more?" Gracie shrugged. "Hell, if I get higher in the top ten—"

"Which you can do more easily with a sponsorship," Alex chimed in. "Imagine not having to work so many hours, Gracie."

"Oh, that *would* be nice." Gracie let herself dream for a moment. "Ugh, I don't know." She shook her head. None of this was real. No matter what Jay said, it wasn't real, and she was going to have to give that money back. "Let's just go play for a bit, okay? Good old-fashioned slicing things open with giant swords."

"Thrusting," Alan corrected. Since they'd found out Gracie was a girl, the Gracie's-sword-is-a-penis jokes had become *more* common, not less.

She snickered.

They managed to boost Alex's level considerably over the course of the night, trading jokes and lobbing creative insults at each other and their various opponents. By the time Gracie logged off for the night, she was feeling quite content.

That was, until she got into her room and saw the dress lying on the floor. A few beads winked at her in the dim light and Gracie caught sight of herself in the mirror, dressed in old clothes and her hair straggling out of its ponytail. The mirror also caught, in stark detail, the bare walls of the room, the cluttered nightstand, and the mattress on the floor.

She checked her phone. She'd given Kyle a brief, polite acknowledgment, but he hadn't responded after that. He hadn't contacted her after work, either.

She sat down on the bed with a thump. She hadn't wanted to go back, to have the life her parents wanted for her, but more and more, she was beginning to wonder if she'd just left because she couldn't hack it.

If she was just running away from the truth.

After all, what evidence did she have that she could be a success?

CHAPTER TWELVE

"It's the only solution that makes any sense." Jay fought the rising urge to slam his hands on the table.

Or better, Chris's head.

No, *worse*. That would be worse. Right.

"He has a point," Sam said cautiously. He wore the expression of someone venturing out onto thin ice. Jay had to hand it to Sam; the guy really was trying to keep him safe. He was just very, very aware that this situation was getting dicey, and that he didn't know the rules of it. He cleared his throat and smoothed his tie. Unlike the rest of them, Sam dressed like he was coming to an office. "I think a sponsorship would resolve this nicely."

Chris looked at them as if trying to determine how much of this they had planned beforehand. "And when our *other* sponsors ask why this teen-level character has so many points?" he asked. "When they ask why she's rising so fast? Because the questions are already starting."

Jay swallowed before he could stop himself.

Chris leaned forward. "Get her into one of the big

guilds," he said, "and the questions go away. Sure, she'll have a rankings boost, but it'll lift all of *their* rankings, too. We can claim she's getting their spillover, they'll be glad to have her on board, and we'll have time to figure this out."

Jay looked down at the table and tried to think of something—*anything*—to say.

Chris was right; a guild *was* a better solution. When Gracie was on her own, her rank was more noteworthy, and more of an insult to the guilds that cooperated and garnered sponsorships. If she were subsumed into one of the bigger guilds, however, they would have a vested interest in her keeping her ranking. Each member's individual ranking, after all, both boosted and was boosted by their guilds.

It was only Jay's selfishness that kept him from accepting the solution. He liked playing with Gracie. He liked the banter and wit their little group shared, and Gracie fit as the leader of their party. In a big guild, she'd be just another newbie, maybe a little bit favored due to her rank, but certainly not a guild officer.

She deserved better than that.

"Jay?" It was Sam, his voice a little worried. "Chris is right. Until we figure this whole thing out, it makes sense to have her boosting a guild and being a little more hidden in the rankings."

"No," Jay exclaimed in a sudden stroke of inspiration.

Chris sighed and looked heavenward.

"Because if we take the ranking away later, we're dropping a huge and well-sponsored guild down," Jay said. He was still grasping at straws, but from Chris's expression, he was on to something. "It doesn't matter if you decide it was a glitch. It was something they had, and we took it away. They'll be *pissed*."

Chris groaned and dropped his face into one hand.

"All right, I'm calling it." For once, Sam cloaked himself in authority. He didn't generally throw his weight around, and the sheer unexpectedness meant that both Jay and Chris looked at him with automatic attention. "We're overlooking one of the easiest solutions: we reroll the character, give it the same gear, wipe its achievements, and manually put it back in the quest chains it's *supposed* to be on. We give it the rankings level it *should* have." He stressed the words faintly. "Harry's quests won't trigger anymore, we'll give this Gracie person the money she made to keep, so she'll stay quiet, and everyone else will calm down. It's a big game, and everyone knows games have glitches."

Jay stood frozen. *No.* They couldn't let Callista get rebooted. She'd started the quest, she'd—

"I'll do it," Chris said. He gave Sam a hard look. "Why didn't you suggest this before?"

"It didn't occur to me until just now." Sam sounded faintly prickly. "And *I'll* handle it. I'm more familiar with the code." He stood up and left before Chris could retaliate.

Jay grabbed his papers off the desk and rushed out behind Sam. "Sam, wait."

"Not now, Jay." Sam looked weary. Whatever brief flirtation he'd had with being a commanding leader, it was gone now.

"Yes, now," Jay hissed back.

Sam swung to face him. He wasn't a tall man, but with his hands in his pockets and the assessing look in his eyes, it was easy to forget that Jay was looking down at him. "All right, help me understand. Why do you care so much? You've been fighting us on this from Day One. You want her to keep this ranking. You don't want her in a guild. I don't even think you want her to have a sponsorship. *Why?*"

Jay stood frozen for a long moment. This was dangerous. He had to tell the truth, just maybe not all of it.

Definitely not all of it.

"You don't know what this world means to me," he said finally. "You don't really play." When Sam raised his eyebrows, Jay hastened to explain. "You're not a jerk about it, you just have people in your life who care who you are, okay? A lot of us don't. We don't have anyone who respects us the second we walk out of these offices."

Sam blinked at him.

"Whenever anyone logs into *Metamorphosis*," Jay said, "the *only* things that matter are their skills, and who they are as a person. It gives everyone a fresh start, and a chance to be judged for the things people *should* be judged for. Gracie…" He caught himself. "Callista. You have to see her to understand, I think. When someone needs her help, she doesn't think twice about giving it. She loves the world, and she's building something; a guild of her own."

"Okay, so—"

"No, hear me out," Jay pleaded. "So Harry was a dick; I get that. He probably *did* write this quest to screw the Ds, honestly. But the reason Callista got the ranking was that she *did* do something. She walked into an unknown amount of danger to save a bunch of *pixels*, Sam. The kobolds hadn't ever done anything for her, and you know how overwhelming the game is at first. It feels real, and the danger feels real, but she did it. Anyone could have, but they just sold the jewel for money. I watched the Hill Warden tell a bunch of players that fragment of lore and none of them did anything with it."

Sam rubbed at his forehead and sighed. "That's as may be, but—"

"I helped build this world so people could get what they deserved!" Jay's voice was rising. "To just change the rules so she doesn't get the boost anymore? It goes against all of it."

Sam gave him a long look. "Okay," he said finally. Jay sagged with relief, but Sam held up a finger. "For now," he said. "I will present all three options to Dan and Dhruv."

"Four," Jay said numbly. "Leaving it be. That's the fourth option."

Sam held back a sigh. "Right. Four options. *They* choose. After all, this world was their idea, right?"

"Right." Jay accepted the reprieve.

"Go home, Jay." Sam put his hand on Jay's shoulder. Right now, he was every inch the father of a stubborn toddler. "I spend too much time trying to convince my three-year-old to go to sleep, to have to have the same argument with a guy pushing thirty. You'll get paid. Just go home and get some rest."

Jay managed a laugh. "Yeah, yeah. And you won't—"

"No, I won't re-roll the character while you're gone, and yes, I *will* manage Chris, and yes, you *will* buy me a nice bottle of something for Christmas this year."

"Roger that," Jay said. His heart was pounding as he headed home.

He didn't mean to fall asleep when he got home, but

after a shower and another hastily-devoured meal of fast food, he was almost tired enough to go to sleep right on the kitchen table.

He barely made it to the bed before he passed out.

He woke blearily a full sixteen hours later and pushed himself up to look around the room. He was ravenous, but he actually felt human for the first time in almost a week. He checked his phone out of habit, felt the familiar, dull disappointment that he could drop off the face of the Earth for sixteen hours and apparently not have anyone care, and called for delivery as he wandered into the main room.

He knew what people would advise him to do at this point: go out into the sunshine, do some errands, and be a productive member of society. Sam, especially, would tell him to do literally anything except log into *Metamorphosis Online*.

He logged in.

By now, the VR set felt familiar on his body, as if he *should* be wearing it and it had just been missing for a while. He was relaxing and smiling to himself when the ding sounded for an incoming message. He gave a laugh of surprise.

"Fancy seeing you here at this hour."

"I might say the same," Gracie said. "I thought you worked during the days."

Of course, Jay realized. He usually played late at night, so she would assume that. "Day off," he said, skirting the issue. "Really needed to take a break after this big project."

"Ah." Was it his imagination, or did she sound a little bit sad?

"What do you do?" Jay asked, genuinely curious.

"I'd, uh... I'd rather not talk about it." Her voice, still echoey with the Aosi filters, nonetheless sounded very small.

With a jolt, Jay remembered his big speech to Sam and felt like an incredible jerk. "Hey, you want to see the sunrise from that temple? You know, the place where shit went sideways? I hung out there a bit ago, and it's fucking gorgeous. We really—" He coughed to hide his misstep. "*They* really built this place to be an experience."

There was a pause. "Sure," Gracie said cautiously. "Meet you there?"

"Yeah."

They arrived at the base of the hill at the same time, and their characters began to climb with the untiring gait only a fake character could maintain. The view around him seemed so realistic that Jay had to remind himself his legs weren't really going to get tired as the path sloped up.

Gracie seemed lost in thought. She didn't stop to pick up any of the ores that appeared along the side of the trail, and she didn't really speak. The 9 was still over her head, and Jay decided not to comment on it. She hadn't seemed very keen on it the last time they'd played.

In the temple, now cleared of ghosts and strange stitched-together monsters, they made their way between toppled columns and saplings that had pushed themselves through the cracks in the floor. The temple wasn't restored, but the game seemed to be suggesting that, at long last, it was a place where there might be life of some sort.

"You think this place is supposed to be from before that big war?" Gracie asked finally. She had stopped to brush her fingers through the leaves of a sapling, and she crouched to look at a column. "Before they scattered the races?" She looked at Jay.

"I hadn't thought about it," Jay said honestly. He looked around. "Yeah, that's probably what it is."

"I like it," Gracie said. "This whole world waiting to be discovered. I wonder how much is hiding around here? Stuff like that kobold tomb." She stood up. "Did the other races keep the peace between the kobolds and the fae? I bet we won't know. It's just one of those things that got lost when the races were scattered. Historians would spend generations trying to get everything back, and they still wouldn't know all of it."

Jay watched her, smiling slightly. Sometimes he got so caught up in what the game was in terms of friendship and camaraderie that he entirely forgot what an achievement it was in the sheer scope of the art and the story.

Gracie walked to the edge of the cliff, eyes focused on the horizon as the sun began to dip. She looked cautiously down the slope. "Do you get totally wrecked if you fall off a cliff here?"

"Yep," Jay said. It wasn't speculation. There had been a contest in the office after the open beta to see who could make the most impressive splat.

After that, management had decided to make the splatter graphics a *bit* less realistic.

Gracie nodded. Her arms were crossed over her chest as she looked out at the horizon, and eventually, she said, "I deal blackjack. That's what I do." She looked at him. "You asked," she reminded him.

"Yeah, I—"

"I was embarrassed about it," she explained. She'd gone back to studying the horizon. "I went to college and majored in math, and then I did nothing with it."

"Bet you know a hell of a lot more about blackjack odds than most people," Jay pointed out.

There was a pause before she smiled; it was strange getting used to the emotes in the game. "That's true. But it's like this game, I think—people think they're playing the *game*, and I think some are, but the people who run it are playing a totally different game. The sponsorships, the guilds..." She sighed. "I keep having to turn down invitations, by the way."

"What?" Jay felt a spike of worry.

"I keep getting invitations," Gracie said. She shrugged, and her shoulders stayed hunched. "People who think my ranking means something. It's a glitch. I need to submit a ticket about it."

Jay wanted to laugh. He wanted to cry. Of course. They'd spent the past three days scrambling to figure out how she was going to take them to the cleaners, and instead, she was trying to do the right thing.

Why hadn't anyone ever expected *that* situation?

"Honestly," Gracie said, "all of them make my teeth ache, anyway. Like, they seem super smarmy, and you get the sense that they'd be totally insane when it came to how often you had to log on, you know? It's just annoying."

Jay swallowed and nodded. "Yeah. I get that."

"Anyway, I like our group." She smiled again. Her shoulders had relaxed. "We need a few more to try to run a month-end dungeon or whatever, right?"

"Yeah. The proper dungeons are all ten-man. Most

guilds have more than that, though." Jay sighed. "Then it's a whole thing about who gets picked to try for the month-first. You know, to see which guild can get through the run before anyone else? The top guilds load in pretty much immediately, and they're just trying any combination they can to figure out the puzzle before other people do."

Gracie shook her head. "Eh, I don't want to be going crazy in my off-time. I just…you know, I think we'd have a good time going through, right?"

"Yeah. We definitely would."

"And there's so much more to the game. I still have to explore it all. On the other hand…" She sounded wistful now. "$500 isn't chump change, you know?"

"I know." Jay watched as she had her character clamber onto the slope of a column. She sat down and patted the space next to her.

"Good view from up here."

He went to join her, and they sat contemplatively as the sun dipped below the horizon and the stars wheeled above them.

"Thanks for bringing me here," Gracie said. "You were right; this place *is* amazing."

"It is," Jay agreed.

CHAPTER THIRTEEN

The sounds of sniffles came from the bar as Gracie watched, half-hiding behind a column.

The woman who came to her table had just had a fight with her boyfriend. Gracie had seen it all unfold. Seen the security personnel swing smoothly into action, suited and outwardly deferential but with looks in their eyes that said what the patron started, they would finish—and probably not in a way the patron wanted.

So the boyfriend had left, and the woman, after brushing off the security guards, had looked around, seen Gracie as one of the only other women nearby, and come to sit at her table.

She was still crying when she arrived, which didn't faze Gracie. You saw a lot of people in Vegas on a false high, and you saw a lot of others who were realizing just how false the high was. It wasn't that she didn't see happy people; she did. The unhappy ones just stuck out more.

"Take your mind off things?" Gracie asked, nodding to the table.

The woman hiccupped and caught her breath, and then her face crumpled again. "He has all my cards and chips. I didn't have any pockets in this dress, so he has my stuff. Oh, *God*." She hid her face in one hand, her voice rising to a squeak as she tried to hold off the sob.

What happened next, Gracie would find herself defending to a long succession of suited individuals. The casino was dead, no cards were dealt, and there were no chips on the table. She gestured to clear her hands for the cameras, then came around the side of the table.

"Hey. Hey, it's not so bad, okay? Let's get you some water at the bar, and then we'll call your hotel and get you into another room for tonight. Get you a new key, okay?"

The woman looked gratefully at Gracie. She didn't seem able to say anything, just gulped and stared in mute appeal.

"Come on," Gracie said. She looked around to see if she could catch Matt's eye, but she didn't see him, so she helped the hiccupping woman over to the bar. Lara was there, a former cocktail waitress who'd lobbied for some hours behind the bar. She saw the woman's tearstained face and gave Gracie a wide-eyed look. "She needs a glass of water," Gracie said, "and to use the phone." She pointed to where the phone behind the desk was. To the patron, she added, "Are you okay?"

"Yeah. I—yeah." The woman gave a hiccupping nod and pulled Gracie into an impulsive hug. "Thanks. It was all so overwhelming for a moment."

Gracie smiled and extricated herself. She was halfway back to her table when she saw Matt—and *his* boss, Vince. She felt her stomach drop, but steeled herself and nodded toward the bar. "I was getting that patron sorted out."

"You aren't supposed to leave your table," Matt said somewhat despairingly. At Vince's cleared throat, he said, "Let patrons handle themselves, Gracie. We've had this discussion before. Call Security if you can't get them to leave."

"She didn't need Security," Gracie said. Her pulse sped up. "She just needed to get to the bar. No one's in tonight, and there are dozens of other tables—"

"*You don't leave your table,*" Vince said.

"There were no cards dealt, there were no chips, and I cleared—"

"You don't leave your table."

"What harm did it do?" Gracie demanded.

"You don't worry about that." Vince leaned toward her. "You don't make judgment calls. You follow the rules." He punctuated the last sentence with gestures for each word. "Are we clear?"

Matt apparently recognized Gracie's expression, because he stepped in between them with a practiced smile. "Perfectly clear, Mr. Wallace. Gracie, come with me."

Gracie managed to bite her tongue until they were in the back corridor, but she couldn't manage a single moment longer than that. "Oh, come *on*, Matt. You know it was the right decision."

"Gracie—"

"What's better for literally *every* patron on the floor? To watch a sobbing woman get hauled out by Security, or to step away for *thirty seconds* to give her a good client experience and—"

"Gracie—"

"Dammit, Matt!" Gracie swung around to face him. "Haven't you ever just had a bad day and needed someone to be nice to you?"

"*Yes*," Matt said emphatically. "And if you'd give me a moment, I'd tell you that. But Gracie, this isn't about 'needing someone to be nice to you' or 'the best client experience.' We've been through this before. Tons of times." His eyes were serious. "You *know* Vince is a hardass about the rules. That's just how things are. You *don't* make judgment calls. Even if I keep sticking my neck out for you, I may not have the power to help you keep your job."

I don't even want the fucking job, Gracie thought resentfully. She'd dodged two more entreaties to become a cocktail waitress, and Vince was beginning to hint that she might get reassigned whether or not she wanted to be.

Between that and this, she was busting her ass to keep a job she had never really wanted. She was scrabbling just to...*what?*

She sighed and looked away, her jaw tight.

"Take a bit," Matt suggested. When she looked up warily, he said, "Not like, take some shifts off. I mean, just take a few minutes right now. I'll tell Vince I put you on backroom duty. Take a break, read something. You don't have to clock out."

Gracie swallowed. "Thanks, man." He really was doing all he could for her; she knew that.

"Yeah." Matt nodded. "But, Gracie..." He looked at her and waited for her to say the words.

All of Gracie's resentment came back in a rush, but she

forced herself through the statement. "I don't make judgment calls," she enunciated precisely.

Matt nodded silently—he knew better than to push his luck—and disappeared down the hall, and Gracie headed back to the break room, silently fuming. She hated this. Before, her job had just been something she had to do to make it. She'd been happy enough to have her own place on her own terms that she had mostly been amused by the various annoyances of patrons and management.

Somewhere over the past few months, that had shifted. It had shifted a lot.

In her locker, she rummaged in her bag and pulled out her phone. Her eyebrows shot up when she saw the screen, and to her annoyance, she felt another surge of something that felt like claustrophobia.

Kyle wanted another date.

She stared at the message as she slumped into a chair, then typed back a short message. His had been assumptive bordering on rude—that he'd pick her up for their date on a certain day. She wasn't working then, but he hadn't known that.

She put the phone down without answering. In the mood she was in, she'd tell him to shove his head up his ass, and there would be her first chance at a date in months, down the tubes.

"Come on, Gracie," she muttered to herself. "You *have* to be able to do better than this."

But what *was* "this?" A successful guy, handsome, who made her laugh. And it wasn't like this was a movie plot where it was Kyle against the plucky, poor-but-lovable underdog.

This isn't some stupid rom-com.

No, there was no one else, just like there was no alternative to this crappy job. Gracie had been trying to do things her own way, and it straight-up wasn't working. She picked the phone up and gave a groan as she typed the text her mother would want her to send: "Looking forward to it. See you then."

Then she switched over to a PDF she'd been reading on her tablet and resolved not to think about the depressing state of her life.

After Jay logged out the night before, Gracie had finally opened a ticket to get her ranking resolved, reasoning that she'd at least be free of annoying guild requests when this was all straightened out. The rising balance on her game account had been pretty to look at, but the money wasn't hers, and the sooner she got everything fixed, she told herself, the easier it would be for everyone.

They'd been pretty vague about the whole thing, not giving her any indication of how the process would work, but she told herself that the game had just launched and they were probably overwhelmed with tickets.

In the meantime, Kevin had sent her the link to a blog he followed that broke down a lot of existing boss fights in the game, not just from a battle perspective, but in terms of the lore that was showcased.

Gracie pulled out a pad of paper and scribbled some notes as she read. Her writing had always been a massively untidy scrawl that no one else could read, but she could usually make things out—especially when it was just numbers.

The more she read, the more she struggled between

admiration for the creators of *Metamorphosis Online* and annoyance with them. They reminded her of casino owners, in a way.

Oh, it was always *possible* that they had designed the game mechanics this way for other reasons than she suspected. Possible, but massively unlikely. The game relied more heavily on buffs and debuffs than any Gracie had seen, and some of those varied by proximity or armor or location, while others varied linearly, and still others varied on exponential decay—

In short, the game was complex enough that players would often not be able to understand the exact math behind what was happening.

Just like a casino. Players weren't fighting against the boss, they were fighting against the *game*, just like they were with all of the arcane rules that governed ranking. Gracie didn't envy whoever was trying to figure out *her* correct ranking right now. They must be deep in the weeds.

All the same, she had to admire the game's creators. Obscuring game mechanics was a highly successful technique, and the math *was* technically doable. It wasn't that it didn't work out, it was that most people couldn't make sense of it. There were so many moving pieces that it was difficult for most people to understand why things went wrong when they did.

Gracie, however, wasn't most people. She read through the fights, her left hand moving across the page as she took notes and her lips moving too, both of them lagging the calculations that were falling into place in her head. More than once, she shook her head at some of the conclusions the blog writer had drawn.

Some of the things they put down to obscure and so-far-undiscovered mechanics were, in fact, ably explained by mechanics they had either not understood or forgotten about entirely.

Most of all, Gracie was confused to realize that other people didn't seem to develop the same instinctive sense for the rules that she did. She remembered drawing back out of the way of swipes or AOE attacks, judging the distance by instinct—or, rather, the calculations she didn't bring to the forefront of her mind.

From what she'd seen in other games, players *did* develop a sense for those things. It seemed, however, that this game was complex enough that people weren't accounting for all of the mechanics.

She might disagree with the blog's author about the math of the game, but she fell head-first into the lore descriptions. *Metamorphosis Online* explored the ruins of a long-forgotten history that included all four races, which could only be understood by figuring out what each race had brought to the table.

The catch, of course, was that each race had developed new lore over the years, transforming the events of the past into legends that twisted and blurred the events. Actual historical stories were no more than cautionary tales now, populated by gods instead of mortal beings.

Gracie caught herself, her lips twitching. There was no *actual* history here. The game was so immersive that she kept forgetting that.

Her favorite so far was the tale of King Cedory, a Piskie

monarch who had managed a successful alliance not only with the Ocru, but with the kobolds and the fae as well. One of his palaces, haunted by an enemy of his, had been a month-end dungeon three months ago, and Gracie was enthralled by the description of each little nod to Cedory's history and alliances, including artifacts and murals from the other races he had allied with.

When she looked up, a full hour had gone by, and Gracie grabbed her sandwich and took huge bites of it as she shoved her phone back into her bag and put it all back in her locker. She'd use half of this as her lunch break so Matt wouldn't get in trouble with Vince.

She chewed a piece of gum a few times as she checked her appearance in the mirror over the sink—a necessity, given the strict standards of neatness for all employees— and headed back out to the casino floor. She was trying to mask her disappointment as she went, and not doing an outstanding job of it.

But she plastered a fake smile on her face and walked out onto the floor anyway, even giving Vince a nod without letting her smile slip.

She might hate this job, but she still needed it. She felt her blood pressure ease as she imagined the view from the temple yesterday, and used that to calm herself as she took over for another employee at their table.

She couldn't help wishing *that* was her real life, not this.

CHAPTER FOURTEEN

J ay had just arrived at his desk when Sam sent a message over the internal system:

Meeting in Chris's office, Dan and Dhruv want to hear about your research.

Jay's eyebrows went up. He looked down at his shirt and winced. He was wearing a Dragon Soul Productions t-shirt from one of their holiday events a couple of years ago and a hoodie with the Dragon Soul logo embroidered on it. He probably looked like an ass-kisser.

Nothing he could do about it, though. He took a gulp of his coffee, having forgotten how hot it was, and choked on it before heading down the hall to Chris's office.

Chris wasn't there. Dan had taken his chair, and Dhruv prowled restlessly behind the other founder. Tall and lanky, Dhruv had always struck Jay as someone who was too hyperactive to be a legitimate coder. How did he sit *still* long enough?

Apparently, he managed. The man was legendary.

Dan, meanwhile, had the strained smile of someone who didn't particularly enjoy being in the spotlight. He had taken over being the front man for the company since Harry had left, and he didn't seem to like it much. Whatever else Harry was, he had been indisputably good at schmoozing. Dan wasn't.

Still, he'd learned certain protocols. He stood up and extended his hand. "Jay? Good to meet you. Thanks for bringing this to our attention."

Jay, obscurely comforted by the other man's unease, nodded and sat when Dan gestured for him to do so.

There was a pause while Dan looked over his shoulder at Dhruv, and the silence stretched so long that Jay cleared his throat and said, "Uh, so, *was* the quest coded by Harry?"

Sam made a tiny movement at the edge of Jay's vision as if trying to get him to stop talking. The Ds, meanwhile, winced in unison. Dhruv gave an annoyed, elaborate shrug, and Dan curved his lips in a strained, humorless smile.

"We don't know, and we haven't been able to get an answer from him."

Harry, Jay remembered, could be incredibly vindictive. During his last few months at Dragon Soul, he hadn't even had a secretary, because so many of his had quit. Jay could just imagine how he'd responded to questions about the quest.

He ducked his head. "Sorry I asked."

"Not a problem." Dan didn't look like he meant that, but he also didn't look like he was holding it against Jay. "Here's the thing: we're hoping you can help us with this. You did some good digging. You got a lot farther than we would have been able to, and we want to put you on this full-time. Not only that, we're hoping you can search the database for anything else that seems like it might be another Easter egg quest."

"Sure," Jay agreed cautiously.

"We do have more data for you," Dhruv said, still prowling. "Whatever he set up, it doesn't trigger for anyone else now—we tried a few people—and it isn't solved by a reset."

Jay, who had been looking at some papers Dan had passed him, looked up. "Reset?"

"We rerolled the character," Dhruv said with a little shrug. He didn't think this was worth looking over for.

"You—" Jay looked at Sam.

"Wasn't my call," Sam said. There was a warning in his voice, the pity almost wholly lost in it. "Be smart, Jay," his eyes said.

"Sam was right," Dan said. "It *was* a good idea. What can't be solved by turning it off and on, huh?" The tired joke was still funny to anyone who had ever done tech support. "Not as satisfying as figuring out what the problem was, but quick—and quick is good right now."

Dhruv gave a snort that might have indicated either derision for Dan or for the sponsors and guilds making a fuss. Or he might have been agreeing; there really was no telling with him.

"We tried just re-rolling the character on the same account," he said, "and deactivating and recreating her user account. Both things *should* have worked. Neither did. The quest is still linked to her account. How, we don't know."

"Change the character name?" Sam asked.

"We tried that with the character reroll," Dan said. He shook his head. "It's a mess, but Jay, I think, can figure it out." His attempt at being the jovial executive was painfully bad, but Jay didn't get a slimy vibe from it. Dan really *did* want his employees to feel valued. He just wasn't a natural when it came to anything social.

So Jay nodded despite himself, despite the anger pounding in his blood. Sam had *promised* him—

It wasn't important. He took the papers and stood, forcing a smile. "I'll get to work on this."

Dan nodded. So did Dhruv, though he didn't look over.

"One more thing," Dhruv said as Jay left. Jay paused to glance back, and Dhruv gave him an angry look. It wasn't until he spoke that Jay realized the look wasn't really directed at *him.* "I don't know what that asshole did, but it's literally impossible to adjust her ranking manually anymore."

"Maybe the answer is to make her stop wanting to play the game," Dan said half-jokingly.

"Not a bad idea," Dhruv said shortly.

"I'll get to work," Jay said again before they could go any farther down this line of inquiry.

He left without looking at Sam.

Jay wasn't there when Gracie logged in. That was a bit unusual, but she supposed he had another big project to work on. She'd have to ask him what he did. If he'd asked so casually, he must have a job he wasn't ashamed of.

She wondered with bitter amusement what that was like.

Not all of the mechanics in the game were spelled out, so her first order of business had been to figure out exactly how each of her own talents worked. Some were helpfully titled *Decreases in force with distance*, but just how *much* did the force decrease?

She intended to find out.

To that end, she spent her time dancing into and out of range of her opponents. She'd chosen the particular type of opponent with care, venturing to a fairly remote corner of the map to find a spell-casting harpy with a particularly long casting phase. This allowed Gracie as much time as she needed to pick her range exactly and then use her abilities.

She was probably also, she thought wryly, developing a place in the lore as a genocidal maniac. Callista Harpy's Bane. Callista the Scourge. Callista Doombringer.

She could really go for that last one.

"You know, this isn't personal," she told one of the harpies. She slashed at it and scooted out of range. "You're just—*hold still*—the *type* of person I need to work on killing right now. Whoa, that sounds bad. I'm a psychopath."

The harpy shrieked in agreement.

"All right, but *this* one isn't my fault," she said to another harpy. "*You* aggroed. You started this. I'm just the finisher." She swung her sword in a shower of particle effects. "A finisher with a real big serrated sword." She slashed again. "Which is just a sword, not a penis."

The harpy, being dead, had nothing to say to that.

After about an hour of smashing harpies, she felt she

had a good handle on how her skills worked on their own. She needed the rest of the group to do proper tests on how their skills amplified hers, and how different mob types might dampen them.

Contemplatively, she stripped off the suit without logging out—having positioned her character in relative safety on a hilltop—and wandered over to rummage through the kitchen cabinets.

Between her getting sucked into the game, and Alex having his work crisis, neither of them had gone grocery shopping in ages. The cabinets held oddly-flavored crackers neither of them had liked, an almost-gone tub of peanut butter, and stale soda crackers that—Gracie squinted at the label—might predate either of them in this apartment.

Maybe Alex never looked in the cabinets. It was possible.

She threw those away and turned her rummaging to the fridge. One exceedingly wilted head of lettuce was in the crisper drawer, which she threw away with a silent thank you that she'd caught it before it turned to slime, and the rest were condiments, bad milk, and various old takeout containers.

She had polished off the peanut butter and was, against her better judgment, eating the dry crackers when Alex arrived home with groceries.

"I could kiss you," Gracie said.

"Sure. Anything, as long as I get to lie down." He punctuated his exhausted words by dropping the bags on the kitchen floor and wandering over to a chair. He waved a hand at the groceries. "I'll put those away sometime."

"You got them, I'll put them away." She kept out a few items for cooking as she stowed the rest in the fridge and the cupboards. "Hope you like rice and beans. Or is it a cereal-for-dinner night?" She didn't have to think very hard. "Yeah, it definitely is. You want some?"

"Yes." Alex had pillowed his face on his arms, and his voice was muffled but emphatic.

"One bowl of cereal, coming right up." Gracie prepared his and plunked it down next to his head, poking him in the shoulder. "Eat. I need you for experiments in-game." She went back to preparing her own bowl.

There was the noisy sound of several large, crunching bites, then Alex asked, "Whasperiments?" He swallowed. "What experiments?" he repeated a bit more clearly.

"I have a handle on how all of my skills work," Gracie said, "but we get a lot of party buffs and mob debuffs, and I need to play around with those." She leaned against the fridge as she ate. "I should really make a spreadsheet," she said thoughtfully.

"Oooh." Alex gave her a fellow mathematician's smile. "I love it when you talk dirty."

"There'll be inter-sheet linkages," Gracie whispered seductively. "Color-coded cells."

He raised an eyebrow. "That's the stuff. You gonna make some formulas?" He wiggled his brows suggestively.

"Oh, yeah, baby, you know it." She lost her deadpan expression and started giggling.

Alex grinned and drank the milk from his cereal bowl. "Well, let's get started on this debauchery. Who says you need to go out drinking to have a good time?"

"We get hot for spreadsheets, it stands to reason that

someone must get hot for overpriced cocktails," Gracie pointed out reasonably. "Hey, my headset's blinking."

Alex craned to look. "I think that's the chat indicator."

"Oh, shit! I left myself logged in." She threw the bowl in the sink and hightailed it into the living room. "Coming coming coming *coming. Fuck,* there's a lot of suit to get on. Hello?"

"Hey, there," Jay said, sounding amused. "You didn't need to rush, you know. Something about you standing motionless in harpy territory told me that you were AFK. What're you doing over there?"

"Experiments," Gracie said succinctly. "If you've got time, you should head over. And one sec. Alex?" She pulled her headset away from one ear.

"Yeah?" Alex came around the corner from the two bedrooms, having changed into non-work clothes.

"That cereal is *not* gonna hold me. Can you order us something? Anything. My wallet's in the usual place."

"Right-o." He disappeared again.

"Back," Gracie told Jay.

"I have to say," Jay told her, "between you and Alex and Kevin and Alan, I'm beginning to regret not having a roommate. I thought all roommates were terrible."

"Not all," Gracie said, "but I've had some annoying ones in my day. In high school—"

"You had a roommate in *high school*? Hopping an airship, by the way. I'll be over there in a few minutes."

"'Kay." Gracie prowled up the mountain for no other reason than that she could. It was clearly not meant to be explored, but she had fun seeing if she could find unexpected paths and vistas. "And, to answer your question, my parents tried shipping me off to boarding school when I was sixteen. It didn't last."

"Did you get expelled?" Jay sounded impressed.

"Nah, it was just a lot of money, and I wasn't any nicer to the teachers *there.* And since they couldn't go flutter their hands and play the concerned parents at the drop of a hat, they brought me back for my senior year. At least they couldn't complain about my grades, right?" Gracie had given the speech before, so it was easy to let her mouth say the words while her mind determinedly didn't think about it.

"Huh," Jay said noncommittally.

"What?" She jumped, missed her target, and went sliding downhill with a muffled curse.

"I don't know; you just wrangle *us* all pretty easily, so— getting off the airship, by the way—so I figured you'd probably been some high-school all-star. The high achiever, you know?"

"I suppose I was," Gracie said cautiously. "Eh. I mean, some of my teachers liked me. Sometimes. I did good stuff. I just never quite measured up to my sister."

"Oh. Say no more. My cousin's family is like that. Two brilliant kids, super cool, and my aunt and uncle pit them against each other like it's some kind of deathmatch. Now, *I,*" Jay's voice was wryly amused, "managed to be a disappointment without even having any siblings they could measure me against."

Gracie gave a peal of laughter and felt something in her chest ease. The vibrations in the floor nearby had told her that Alex had come back, and he logged in.

"What's all this merriment?" he asked severely.

145

"We're discussing being disappointments," Gracie explained.

"Oh, I can so win at this game!" Alex warmed to the theme. "Already divorced, childless, living with a room-mate, not dating anyone—and let's not even *start* on how I won't move back to Charleston. It's deeply embarrassing for my parents to have to keep explaining to their church group that I'm living in the City of Sin, don't ya know."

"Vegas?" Jay guessed. "No shit. Well, I suppose with Gracie's job... Nah, that could be anywhere. Casinos all over, right?"

"And tax-dodging douches," Alex agreed cheerfully, "which is where I come in. Unfortunately, I'm helping the douches, but...well, we all need a paycheck."

Gracie could see Jay running into range now, his barbarian cutting a path through the harpies. "Coming to you, Jay. Just going to watch for a while if you don't mind to get a sense of your ranges. Could you use Power Surge and Recoil Punch a few times? I don't have those."

"Sure thing," Jay said, sounding bemused.

"So, what is it you do?" Gracie asked as she clambered down the mountain.

"Oh." He seemed surprised. There was a pause. "I work in software development," he said finally.

"Really?" Alex sounded interested. "What company? Between Gracie and me, we have a *ton* of—"

"I freelance," Jay broke in. "Just...finding bugs. Helping people smooth things out."

"Wow," Gracie said. She didn't really know what to say. She wanted to ask about his recent project, but something about his tone told her he really didn't want to talk about this. "So, uh, these harpies... See how they wind up on things? I want you to play with range a bit. Alex, by the way, when you show up, let me know and we'll run over to get you. Some of these things might still mess with you at your level."

CHAPTER FIFTEEN

She wished she was playing *Metamorphosis*.

Gracie wanted to groan. She was staring a menu of food she could *never* have afforded on her own, and a wine list she could barely even afford to *read*, and all she wanted was to be back in her apartment, in her old PJs, eating lo mein out of a paper box and playing *Metamorphosis*.

For one thing, this dress wasn't at all comfortable.

"Grace?" Kyle prompted her.

Gracie looked up at him and then the waiter. "Gracie," she said reflexively. To the waiter, she added, "Um, the bruschetta." At least she knew what that *was*.

"Really?" Kyle raised one eyebrow. "The wild mushroom crostini here are legendary. I thought you knew."

Are you kidding? When am I going to be coming to places like this? But Gracie plastered a smile over her face. "Oh, of course. That, then." She gave the waiter a self-conscious smile.

"And a bottle of the 2012 Chateau Paillauc," Kyle added.

"Of course." The waiter nodded to them both and melted away unobtrusively.

Kyle put his menu down and smiled at Gracie.

"Uh…" She looked at her menu. "What are you having?"

"The veal." Kyle raised his eyebrows. "You haven't decided yet?"

I'm still holding my menu, asshole. Okay, tone it down, Gracie. She kept the smile firmly fixed in place. "The agnolotti, I think." It was one of the cheaper things on the menu, and she already felt guilty enough.

Though she wasn't entirely sure what agnolotti was.

"Mmm." Kyle gave her a smile, and something flashed in his eyes—an assessment of her order, probably. "That will go well with the wine."

"Oh, good." If she'd been quicker on her feet, she would have said she'd known that. Then again, he'd probably know she was lying. She looked at the menu as she put it down carefully and tried to reset herself; reset *anything*. When she looked up, she was smiling. "It's good to be out with you." *Fake it 'til it's true.*

Kyle nodded. His eyes traveled over her, taking in the dress and the makeup.

"Honestly, I don't usually get all dressed up," Gracie said, feeling the obscure sense that she'd been found wanting.

"I understand," Kyle said easily. His smile was reflexive enough that Gracie relaxed a bit. "But, as they say, dress for the life you want to have, hmm?"

Not sure if that was a reprimand, Gracie sat in silence while the waiter brought the wine and Kyle sampled it. She watched the way he swirled the liquid in the glass, sniffed it, and sipped it. She knew each of those steps had to have meaning, but right now it looked mostly like Kyle was putting on a show.

Maybe he was nervous, too. She told herself to go easy on him and toyed with her fork while the waiter poured her a glass, nodding a thank you to him before he left again. Then she held out her glass to clink.

Kyle gave a faint smile as if this was impossibly quaint, but clinked glasses before taking a sip. "So, tell me about your job search."

Gracie paused, her glass coming down from her mouth. The wine was good, she thought; she was sure she couldn't say *that*. She should say something smart about it.

Why couldn't they have gone someplace that had beer and normal, recognizable food?

"I'm sorry?" she said finally, setting her glass down. "My job search?"

"Well, yes." Kyle looked faintly amused now. "You told me where you got your degree. I assumed your...*stint* as a blackjack player—"

"Dealer."

"Dealer." He shrugged slightly. "Was an aberration," he finished.

"Well, yeah," Gracie hastened to say. "I mean, obviously, in the long run—" She broke off. "I'll definitely want to job-search." She leaned back as the waiter brought the wild mushroom crostini and set it on the table.

"So, where are you looking?" Kyle took one of the crostini, but he didn't eat it.

"I haven't started looking." Gracie wanted to crawl into a hole and hide. She could just see this same conversation playing out at her sister's engagement party: *And where are you working, Gracie, dear? Oh? How strange. And where are you looking for a new job? You haven't started looking? Why not?*

"Why not?" Kyle said right on cue.

Gracie took one of the crostini and put it on her plate. "I don't know." It was hard to keep from sounding like a surly teenager. "Just waiting for everything to settle, I guess. After college." The excuse sounded weak.

"You can't ever wait for things to settle," Kyle said with certainty. "Never settle. Always keep pushing."

"Tell me about *your* job," Gracie said a bit desperately. She folded her sweaty palms in her lap. "What's it like being on...well, the other side of the floor?"

"*Better*," Kyle said meaningfully. He held her gaze as he took a sip of wine. "Gracie, you're a smart girl."

Girl?

"You should be up in administration at your casino by now," Kyle said. "Or at least looking at management on the floor." His tone said he didn't think much of trying to progress through her current trajectory. "I mean, there are stories of CEOs who started out at ground level, right?" He seemed to be reassuring himself, and doing a good job of it.

That was good, since apparently *she* couldn't effectively reassure him.

"I don't think I want to be a CEO," Gracie told him.

"Were you intending to stay home after having children?" Kyle inquired now. His brow furrowed. "I suppose I can see that, while they're young. But daycare is really—"

"No, I just mean... Well, I don't know. Maybe? I hadn't thought about it." *About any of that.* She could feel the claustrophobia of her parents' ideal life plan choking off her air.

It was blindingly clear to her all at once why she hadn't gone searching for a better job. That job was one plank, a husband was another, and then a big mansion and kids, and before she knew it, she would have built herself a coffin, and she'd die trapped.

She took a gulp of wine, aware of him watching her.

"I really just wanted to work in academia," she said finally with a shrug. "Or maybe not academia, but do research, you know? Write papers."

Kyle stared at her blankly. "Have you been working on papers?"

"I...no." Things had gotten away from her, she supposed. When she came home from work, she was exhausted. She needed to unwind. She thought, with a squirming feeling of guilt, of the math textbooks stacked up next to her dresser.

She *had* meant to be doing something with her life. Something. *Anything.*

"Well, do you intend to work as a blackjack dealer all your life?" Kyle inquired finally. "Because if you don't, you'll have to look for something else. I'm just being honest."

Of course he was. Weariness settled over her, and with it came the years of ingrained responses.

"I know," Gracie managed. She took a bite of crostini and tried not to cry. She knew she was inadequate, after all. Why did everyone need to remind her about it when she felt bad enough to start with? Why couldn't they let her be quietly miserable on her own?

Of course, when she was in *Metamorphosis*—when she was with the group—she *didn't* feel miserable, and she *didn't* feel inadequate—but she knew better than to bring up any of that to Kyle. He'd tell her she was ruining her life. He'd tell her that video games weren't real.

Still… Some strange recklessness took over her. "Have you heard of *Metamorphosis Online?*"

Kyle, who'd taken a bite of his crostini as well, raised his eyebrows as he chewed and swallowed. "The video game, right? They were discussing it on *Money Matters* the other day."

"Oh?" Gracie was on more familiar ground here. She'd seen her parents watching similar shows each morning. "What's their take?"

Kyle warmed to the topic. "That it's about time the game companies got in on the sponsorships." His brow furrowed. "Apparently, players have been being sponsored for years."

"In competitive play, yes. Things like *Starcraft.*"

Kyle shrugged. "In any case, paying the players is risky."

"Not really." Gracie sat forward now, her food and wine forgotten. "You see, it creates a tournament pay schedule."

Kyle's brow furrowed at her.

"Like in golf," Gracie said. "Or any sport, really. The person who comes in first makes an incredible amount of money, right? And then it decreases exponentially from there. Now, see, the *dream,*" she gave him a smile, "is that *you'll* be one of the people at the top. It's not out of the question, after all, right? It's a game of skill. You learn the rules, and you could be the Cinderella story."

Kyle blinked. He was giving her a curious smile.

Gracie continued, "Like casinos. Of course," she inclined her head meaningfully, "that's just the dream.

People get confused and think they're coming to play a card game. This is more straightforward, allegedly."

"Allegedly?" Kyle gave a little laugh and took a bite of crostini. "They didn't go into this on *Money Matters*, I'll tell you."

"My roommate plays." Gracie fought a squirming sense of guilt. She knew she should just say she played, but she also knew that Kyle wasn't going to think much of it. "Anyway, I was intrigued, so I went digging. This one really *is* like a casino. People think they're playing against the mobs and against each other, but they're really playing against the game company, and like a casino, they're losing. This isn't a golf tournament."

"They have to know," Kyle said.

"They do on some level." Gracie shrugged. "But there are so many *ways* to win, you see. You get a bonus if you get certain achievements, you get a bonus for your ranking; all these things. So people feel like they can do it, but they lose sight of how little they'll really make. And because only certain ranks get payouts, the game companies have limited the risk to themselves while allowing the number of players who pay full price to swell as large as... well, as it can."

Kyle sat back in his chair, clearly thinking. "Well, there's your paper," he said finally.

"*Oh.*" Gracie had been lifting her wine glass to her mouth. Now she put it down, smiling curiously. "I suppose it is. Maybe. I don't know how interested math people would be in a financial case study. Maybe if I presented it as a risk analysis? Well, that would just be re-creating theirs. Still..." She was staring off into space.

See? This wasn't so bad. She had just needed to give him a chance, right? And she could already feel the warmth of her parents' regard if she came home in July with Kyle on her arm. They'd have to admit that they were wrong, that maybe Gracie wasn't the disappointment they thought—

"You have to think bigger." Kyle gave her an encouraging look. "This kind of assessment, Gracie... You can think on your feet like this, can't you?"

"I mean..." She'd been thinking about the paper. She focused on him hastily. "Yeah. I guess."

"And if you were to dress up a bit. You know, try to look better," he gestured at her clothing, "you realize you could *be* on *Money Matters*, right? Or have your own show."

Anger hit her so hard and so fast that Gracie went entirely still. Her fingers clenched on the edge of the table.

Don't say it, Gracie. Don't. "Excuse me?" Her voice shook slightly.

"Oh, come on." Kyle rolled his eyes and gave a sigh. "Don't give me that crap."

"I beg your pardon?" Ironically, she was channeling her mother right now. This was what it was going to be like, she realized. Always. They'd have these moments of humor or quick thinking...

And then there'd be this.

Kyle sat forward, giving her a disgusted look. He made sarcastic little finger quotes as he spoke. "'It shouldn't matter what I look like,'" he said in a mocking, high-pitched voice. "'It's what's inside that counts.' Live in the *real* world. Here? People judge by appearances. I don't make the rules. I'm just saying, if you want to win—"

As quickly as it had come, the anger was gone. Gracie felt a smile break over her face as she looked down at her lap.

"What?" Kyle asked.

"I *don't* want to win," Gracie said. She found herself smiling as she looked back up. "Not the game you're playing, because you don't win that game, Kyle. No one wins that game except money."

Kyle was frowning at her, stunned into silence.

"*You're* not going to win it," Gracie said now. She could hear the venom in her voice and some part of her brain was yelling at her to stop, to keep from pissing him off. "There's a thousand more where you came from, Kyle, all buying the nice suits, all making sure they know just how to swirl a glass of wine, all making sure they know," she leaned forward, "just the set of steps to take to set a girl off-balance, to make her owe them something. That's how you do everything, isn't it? In favors and secrets, like you can rig the whole world. They could say on *Money Matters* that little favors have outsize payoffs, and the next day, every one of you would come in with an extra coffee for the boss."

He was frozen, staring at her.

"People judge based on appearances," Gracie said. "I get that. Believe me, I'm well aware. So let me guess what you saw. You saw a chick in cheap clothes who'd be grateful for a night on the town. You started breaking me down the second I walked in here. I was never going to measure up, was I? Because no one ever measures up. Everything's a quest for just the right appearance, and you never finish it, do you? We'd spend the whole rest of our lives with you telling me my hair wasn't the right shade of blonde, or my job wasn't quite prestigious enough for you to brag about at the office party."

She stood up, reached into her bag, and pulled out her wallet. Driven by some urge she hadn't understood, she had gone to an ATM earlier and taken out a bigger chunk of cash than she could really afford.

Now she knew why. She didn't want to owe Kyle a damned thing. She dropped the fifties on the table, shaking slightly.

"So, go on. Tell yourself you don't make the rules, and that's an excuse to treat people like crap. Tell yourself you're just 'playing the game' and doing cool 'life hacks.' I'm going to play a different game." She leaned forward slightly and lowered her voice. "And *I'm* going to win."

She turned on her heel and left, giving a faint, embarrassed nod to the waiter as she passed him. People at a few other tables were staring at her, and Gracie kept her head up and prayed fervently that she wouldn't stumble in these godforsaken heels until she was out of the restaurant.

She was outside before she remembered that Kyle had driven her here, but thankfully there was a taxi waiting not far away. Gracie slid into the seat and gave her address, her voice shaking harder now as the rush of adrenaline left her. More money. More she really couldn't afford to spend.

When she slammed into the apartment, Alex looked over in surprise from his game, pulling up the headset. "Oh, thank God. I thought someone was breaking in—" His voice trailed off at the look on her face.

Gracie pulled on the VR harness and logged in without saying a word.

"Uh, Gracie?" Alex's voice disappeared as she settled the headset. He'd been covering his mouthpiece, but now he spoke in-game. "What's going on?"

"Everyone here?" Gracie hated the way her voice sounded. She saw the whole team online and already in a party with Alex. "Let's run Blackbeard's Gauntlet."

"Whoa, hey." Kevin was laughing. "We are *not* the right level for that."

"I will pay everyone's repair costs," Gracie said through gritted teeth. "Right now I need a fucking win, and I need to not think about anything but this game. So, you all coming?"

There was a pause.

"Yeah," Jay said finally. "I'm in. Everyone?"

"Yeah," Alan agreed.

"I'm there," Kevin added.

"Of course," Alex said quietly. In the real world, his hand brushed her arm blindly, and she reached over to squeeze it for a moment.

"Good," Gracie managed. "Well, let's find some more party members and head in."

CHAPTER SIXTEEN

Harsh breathing echoed in Gracie's ears. Her own, certainly, but the coughs and the varying pitches of the mutters let her know she was not alone in being exhausted.

The entrance to Blackbeard's Gauntlet was an unassuming path into the jungle, winding from a black-sand beach toward a live volcano at the center of an island. Dropped onto the island by one of the game's portals, their small group had basked in the sound of birdsong and watched the light slanting down through the trees.

Gracie appreciated the attention to detail. *Metamorphosis Online* had a free pass to be a bit buggy or cut corners. It was the first MMO of its kind, and the game was massive. People would have forgiven them for making the environments tightly controlled and linear. However, the game's developers clearly embraced its role as a virtual reality. There were often pauses like this to help the players sink into the world.

Then again, she reflected as there was the twang of

bowstrings and a battle cry and Kevin gave a shout of alarm, maybe all of this was just to lull them into a false sense of security.

Sneaky bastards.

Gracie swung into action against foes with painted faces, camouflaged in the jungle and coming in waves that propelled the group forward, ever forward. They ran along the path with shouts to one another, Alan and Gracie alternately shouting orders for who needed to get healed or take point on a fight until they came to the warren of caves below the volcano.

The true genius of the game designers, Gracie thought, was that they could convey so much without certain key elements. In the jungle, with the rustle and lap of the water, she could almost have said she smelled the greenery.

Here in the caves, creaks and groans let them know how fragile the walls that stood between them and the lava were, and the shimmers in the air and sweat beading on their faces almost made Gracie feel the stifling heat.

Then again, after that run through the jungle, she really *was* dripping with sweat.

"Not much farther," she told the group as they edged along the passageways.

There was a chorus of agreement. The tunnels seemed to be getting smaller, until the hulking pair of Ocru they'd picked up—confusingly named Freon and Chowder—complained that they were having to crouch to get through. Gracie could see that she was going to have the same problem soon, which meant Jay would, too.

At least Kevin would be able to get through, she thought with amusement.

"Is it possible we came the wrong way?" asked the human woman who rounded out their group, a warrior named Lakhesis.

"I don't think so," said Chowder. "I didn't see any turnoffs. I think they're just trying to put us off-guard, you know?"

"Yeah, fuck that," Gracie muttered. On another night she might find it funny, but tonight, she was uncomfortably reminded of that date.

It had *all* been a set-up; she could see that now. Kyle hadn't really thought she would know about the wild-mushroom crostini. He'd taken her somewhere he could throw his wealth in her face to make her feel small.

In fact, she was pretty sure that if she looked online, she'd find a play-by-play spelled out on some blog somewhere.

She really wished she had something to punch right about now.

Maybe Kyle's face. Maybe you could pay an extra fee each month and get to punch whoever you wanted to. *Bad Gracie, creating a cyberpunk dystopia.* Her lips quirked as she peeked around a corner...

And gasped. She whipped back around and motioned the others to be still, holding one finger to her lips. When she motioned them forward again, all of them crept very slowly and very carefully.

"Hoooooly..." Jay muttered. "Goddamn, I forget how incredible this all is sometimes."

Gracie gave him a curious look, but he said nothing more. The two Ocru were taking screenshots of each other emoting in front of the view, and Kevin had edged over to the abyss to look down.

If there was a perfect marriage of pirate ship with evil villain lava lair, this would be it. Lava ran around the edges of the room in shining streams spanned by rough stone bridges, while dozens of flags hung from the ceiling. At first, Gracie thought they must be denoting the ships in Blackbeard's fleet, but then she recognized the flag of the Aosi and realized with a chill that these must be trophies.

It shouldn't feel real, but it was so immersive that for a moment she thought she could smell the salt spray and gunpowder and hear the screams and the splintering of wood as the cannons roared and belched flame.

She cleared her throat hastily.

"What are you thinking?" Jay asked. He'd come to stand next to her, the hulking barbarian's frame covered in soot and sweat.

"Two things," Gracie said. "First, they made this game *really* realistic, and I kind of want to see if I can draw pictures on your chest, it's so dirty. Second, if they could figure out how to package whatever heat-shielding technology they're using to keep those bridges from melting, they could be rich."

Jay gave a choking laugh. He craned his head to look down at his body as he dragged his fingers over his stomach.

"Nope."

"Well, it took a while, but we've finally found the limits of the game's immersion."

"So you mean I *can't* sneak up behind you and cut your hair?" Kevin joked.

"If you can reach it, Piskie, you can cut it." Gracie gave the summoner a feral grin. "All right, let's plan." She went to crouch at the edge of the ledge that overlooked the cavern. "We've got some patrols, some guards... Wait."

She squinted toward the end of the cavern. It was even set up like a ship, with the contents in a long rectangle down the center, benches even set out at the edges as if for rowing...what, the whole island? Gracie grinned.

But it was something about the guards flanking the throne that had caught her attention. The throne looked rough and was backed with a ship's wheel that framed Blackbeard's head like a spiky halo. *A for effect, there, buddy*, Gracie thought. He was lounging, one booted leg swinging over an arm of the chair, and the guards around him...

Were skeletons. Gracie jerked back when she realized. Her eyes darted to the patrols and the drudges—all skeletons, she now saw. Given the way their clothing hung from their bodies, she had thought they were prisoners, emaciated and starved into submission while Blackbeard's crews were away.

Now she saw that they were pirates pressed into eternal servitude. Even death had not freed them. They wore the marks of their deaths on their tattered clothing, and their bones gleamed even through the soot down here.

There was a loud rumble, and the roof shifted.

Run, Gracie wanted to order. *It's not worth it. We don't need to die here just because some maniac built a pirate-inspired pillow fort in a volcano.*

But this was the beauty of *Metamorphosis Online*; you got to do things you'd never do otherwise. Gracie looked over her shoulder at the team and saw all of them looking up at the ceiling instinctively.

"I think it's safe to say the game devs put a clock on this one," she said simply. "All right, here's the deal. Freon, I want you and Mirra standing together while we attack. If I yell, 'Scatter!' head in different directions, but try to meet up again after, all right?" Both of them nodded. "Same for Fys and Gary Swiftbolt. Freon's also on backup healing," Gracie said. "Cool? Cool. If shit hits the fan, I want one of you two to tell us to self-heal. That means all of us use potions, and summoners, keep track of your pets."

Everyone nodded.

"Okay. That leaves me, Anders, Chowder, and Lakhesis on the front lines, along with Teef and—Fys, does your demon have a name? No? Okay, the demon, too. I want all of you on the opposite side of the boss from me *unless* there's a breakaway. Anders, you'll take point on that." She'd fought with Jay enough to trust that he'd be aware of what was going on and keep the squishies from getting...well, *squished*. "Gary Swiftbolt, you're Anders' backup on that."

"I love how you use my full name each time," Alex said, grinning.

"You called yourself 'Gary Swiftbolt,'" Gracie said. "I think it's pretty necessary. Okay, all, ready for some trash pulls? We'll try to creep up the near side and pull Blackbeard away. Gary Swiftbolt, your service is needed for the pulls."

"You have my bow," Alex intoned softly. "You know, maybe I could get a new nameplate for my desk at work. I think I'd really like to have clients call me—"

Without warning, the rough stone path down to the cavern floor collapsed, sweeping the group down toward the center of the room...and all of the mobs.

"Oh, shiiiiiit." Chowder sounded more anticipatory than worried. "It's gonna get *real*."

"Fuck!" Alan, with a healer's eye, saw only the fall damage waiting for all of them at the bottom. "Potions ready!"

"Wheeeeeeee!" Kevin, making full use of the Piskie voice filter, was clearly trying to get Fys to surf. Her demon was oozing along behind all of them as if manifestly untroubled by the avalanche in which they found themselves.

"*KILL THE INTRUDERS!*" Blackbeard yelled. There was a hiss of assent from the skeletons, and bones rattled and clanked.

The party slammed to the ground with a thud of haptics, and the world spun crazily as Gracie's character rolled and came to her feet. She didn't even think, unsheathing the sword as she rolled to her feet and gave a battle cry.

The skeletons had rushed her as soon as she got to the ground, and she heard the team calling to one another as they scrambled into position and she waded into the fray. The other three melee fighters would let her build up threat before coming into the fray, something Jay seemed to judge expertly.

Gracie heard his command and charged forward, all of the mobs swinging around to face her...and leaving their backs to the rest of the group. She hacked and slashed, every once in a while slamming her sword point-first into the ground for a shock blast.

"This would be—a terrible way—to treat a really nice weapon," she panted as she fought.

"Yeah, don't do that with your dick," Alan advised sagely from the side of the room as he sent a major heal Gracie's way. "I do *NOT* have a spell to un-bruise that."

Groans and laughter filled the air as the next wave arrived. The group had developed a rhythm, Jay fighting with Alex's panther and Kevin's demon, Lakhesis and Chowder backing each other up, and Freon sending bolts of ice to slow various mobs who were trying to retreat and pull new enemies into the group.

"Mirra, how you doing over there?" Gracie called out.

"I should be good. I'm getting a fantastic boost from Freon, and my mana is refreshing at a good— *Oh shit!*"

"What?" Gracie spun, ducking under a wooden stave brandished by a hulking skeleton. "Mirra?"

Then she heard it. The battle cry echoed off the roof of the cavern and kept echoing. It came from everywhere and nowhere, and the group making it could be twenty or a hundred—or a thousand. The pirates had returned, and everything from the thud of their feet to the heft of their weapons proclaimed that they were going to be much tougher adversaries than the skeletons.

"They're flanking you!" Kevin yelled. "Gracie, pick a side!"

Gracie looked left. She looked right. She looked at Blackbeard.

And a plan formed.

"Anders! Come with me!" The rest of you, round up

these pirates and *hold* them—looking at you, Freon! Gary, Fys, keep your pets on anyone who tries to break away." Before the two waves of pirates could close in from the sides, Gracie took off straight for Blackbeard. Behind her, she heard Jay give a whoop.

"Foolish girl," Blackbeard boomed. His guards rattled to attention, helms wobbling on their bare skulls. "But the Aosi always *did* believe the myths. You know what you are, Aosi? You're Ocru. Ocru warped by magic, telling themselves lies about their origins. You're nothing special."

Gracie didn't waste breath replying. She slammed into the group at full speed, ramming her sword into the platform that held Blackbeard's throne. The shock wave funneled the guards to her, and Jay, understanding her plan without her spelling it out, circled around to the back of the platform.

Gracie swung, dislodging a skeleton's skull from its shoulders and disassembling its ribcage with the next stroke. She was breathing hard, just angling her sword to slash at the next one when her chest haptics went nuts. She saw the ceiling of the cavern and realized she'd been flung off the platform. She just had time to snatch at thin air before she came down on solid rock and her whole chest shuddered.

"Ohhhh, that had to hurt." She got to her feet, her character moving more slowly than it should as she tried to run back to the platform before Blackbeard could get his hands on Jay. A shower of glowing particles around her let her know that Alan had sent her a huge heal.

"*Watch* that guy, Gracie!" Alex called. "Christ, he swiped you off that platform like you were nothing."

"Yeah, if you could *not* have that happen again, your friendly neighborhood healer would appreciate it!" Alan added.

"Sorry, Mirra. You're a champ. Totally sprung this whole thing on you. You're doing great."

"Yeah, yeah, yeah. Does this guild have year-end bonuses?"

Gracie laughed as she reached the platform. Blackbeard had indeed turned his attention on Jay, who was dodging and weaving desperately to stay away from him. Gracie considered, then went up the stairs in a rush and leveled a major strike at Blackbeard's back.

"What's up, bastard?" She raised her weapon and brought it down as hard as she could. "What'd that do for your— Oh, *shit*, he's a glass cannon!"

"On it!" Jay launched a flurry of his heavy cooldown strikes and Gracie did the same, dodging as Blackbeard yelled his fury and wound up for another punch to send her flying—

He fell unceremoniously, and the battle from behind them ceased almost at once. Gracie, panting, looked around to see that the room was still. The pirates were gone as if they'd vanished into thin air, only a few gold coins remaining to say they'd ever been there.

On the platform, a chest carved of bone was cracked open, with light shining from inside. Gracie instinctively looked at Alan, who readied a healing spell and nodded at her. If it was a trap, they were ready.

But it was armor; piece after piece of it, far too much to fit into that little chest.

"Baby's first loot chest," Alex said, coming over to sling

YOU NEED A BIGGER SWORD

a digital arm over Gracie's shoulders. "Fys, I'm going to go out on the limb and say that toddler-sized number is yours."

"You be careful, or I'll stab you in the shins," Kevin warned. "Gracie, that's some incredible mail armor."

"Isn't it?" Gracie was running her hands over the mail, reveling in its shimmer. "It really moves. They made it move. And look at the gems." Sapphires winked in the dim light.

The ceiling groaned again.

"Everybody grab the loot and get out!" Gracie yelled, and they scrambled to obey. As the portal opened to take them back to Kithara, their last moments saw the cavern ceiling break open, with lava pouring into the space where they had just been.

"Ohshitohshitohshitohshit—" Alex was still saying as they materialized in the main square of Kithara. He broke off. "Ohhhh, that's going to haunt my nightmares."

Gracie was laughing. "Wimp. All right, everyone put on the good stuff; let's see what we got. Nice, Lakhesis. Oh, Freon, that really accentuates your, uh…"

"Magnificent ugliness," Freon said contentedly.

"Yeah, that," Gracie agreed. "Jay?"

"Gotta go." Jay's voice was suddenly tight. "By the way, did everyone else get a new quest stage to complete?"

"Oh, yeah," Alex said. "First Among Her Followers."

"That's the achievement we got when that one boss battle went sideways," Kevin weighed in.

"We weren't there for that," Chowder pointed out, "and we all got it too."

"Mmm." Jay sounded very pleased. "Well, I'll see you all

tomorrow for that. Night, all. Hope you feel better, Gracie."
He was gone before she could formulate a response.

Then she noticed she had a new quest stage too, for Long May She Reign.

"Huh," she muttered.

Jay took his headset off and nodded to Sam. "What's up?"

Sam gave a meaningful look at the screen. "Playing during work hours?"

"The dialogue is how I found the last piece of the quest." The lie came easily to Jay's lips. "This time, everything seems to have gone as it normally would." He didn't mention the new quest, and he didn't mention that he was intending to hold the next information he found hostage.

And it was just as well he didn't, because Sam swallowed and looked down for a moment.

"Look, I... Well, I wanted you to hear this from me first. And I want you to know I argued against it, okay?"

"Argued against what?" Jay asked carefully. His voice was impressively even. Probably too even, truth be told.

Sam swallowed. "They're banning that woman from the game," he said finally. "For ranking manipulation."

CHAPTER SEVENTEEN

"Jay, *think* about this," Sam pleaded as Jay strode down the hallway. "They left ten minutes ago. You're probably not going to catch them anyway, and it's *better* that way."

"Oh, yeah?" Jay spared him a glance. "That's why you didn't tell me, huh?" His voice was bitter.

"No," Sam said. He cleared his throat. "I may not *play* the game much, Jay, but I know better than to interrupt someone in the middle of a boss fight."

Jay gave a grunt. Sam had made a good point, but he hated to admit that right about now.

Dan was still in the lobby talking to one of the higher-ups Jay didn't know so well, and Sam made a last futile grab at Jay's arm. "Please, man, just go home. Sleep on it, and if you're still angry tomorrow—"

"Tomorrow, after she's logged in and her character's already gone?"

"Jay—"

"No. This is wrong." Jay ran his hands through his hair.

"I can't believe I have to explain this to people! She didn't engage in rank manipulation. *You know that. They* know that! So why are they throwing her under the bus?"

"We're not," said a new voice. Jay stiffened, and Sam's eyes closed briefly. Dan came to stand next to them. He looked at Jay somewhat owlishly.

"You're banning her," Jay said. "A permanent ban."

"Yes." Dan said nothing else.

"Forgive me, but how is that not throwing her under the bus? You're going to make a statement about it, right? She won't be able to play anymore, right? And she didn't do anything wrong."

"Do you know that for a fact?" Dan asked.

"Yes!"

"Really? How?" One might have mistaken his interest for something genuine—except, of course, that he knew Jay couldn't prove it. When Jay said nothing, Dan said, "You've spent *some* time in-game with her. That does not prove she isn't working with Harry."

"Oh, for fuck's sake, she's *not* working with Harry!"

"You cannot *possibly* know that," Dan said simply. "We have a character we cannot delete, hooked into a quest we cannot find or control, wreaking havoc on our ratings and throwing our sponsorships and game mechanics into doubt. Do you know what happens if people stop trusting that, Jay? It's very simple: we lose the sponsorships. We become another failed, corrupt company."

Jay said nothing. The blood was pounding in his ears and he wanted to say something, but he was finding it difficult to do so in the face of Dan's earnest, quiet demeanor.

"The whole thing reeks of Harry," Dan said. "You know that as well as I do. It's why you suggested to us that he might be responsible for it in the first place. Frankly, I think it's a tossup whether she's his accomplice or just an unwitting pawn, but either way, we have someone taking advantage of an opportunity others don't have."

"That's not true," Jay pointed out at once. "Any player could have turned in that quest. She was just the first one to do so. I told that riddle to a *lot* of players."

"Yes, and we're never going to figure out who edited the Hill Warden script to put *that* in." Dan dropped his head into his hands and scratched his scalp despairing. "God, this is a mess."

"A mess with someone involved who didn't do anything wrong—"

Quick footsteps sounded nearby. Sam grabbed Jay's arm to cut him off, and a moment later, Dhruv appeared. He looked surly.

"I can't delete the account," he said. "There's no way to ban it. It is *hooked into the game.*"

Jay tried to hide a snort and didn't manage to do so. Dan and Dhruv both rounded on him, furious, as Sam gave a despairing groan.

"Oh, come on," Jay said, annoyed now. "What do you want me to say? You were going to take the quick, dirty way out. Turns out you can't. It's hard to act like this is some great tragedy and you've been wronged by the universe."

Dhruv's face went cold.

"Uh, Jay?" Sam cleared his throat.

"What?" Jay looked at him. "You want me to act like I'm

sad about them not being able to delete this account and ban her for something they know she didn't do?" He held up a hand before Dan could start. "I know, I know, I can't prove she didn't do it. But you can't prove she did, and I think you *know* she didn't."

Dan said nothing.

"You'll help us," Dhruv said abruptly.

"*Excuse* me?" He couldn't have heard that right.

"You found pieces of the quest before," Dhruv said. "We couldn't have duplicated that research. You can figure out what's wrong with her character. Fix it, or if you can't, make it go away."

There was a pause. Everyone stared at Jay expectantly, and he stared back with the realization that they actually expected him to say yes. This was unbelievable.

"No."

Dan rubbed his forehead and sighed.

"Jay." Sam gave him one last chance. "*Why* don't you want to do this?"

It was an offering, and Jay took it—but not the way Sam clearly hoped. "Because I don't think this is a glitch," he said far too honestly. "I think this is a world with myths and legends where doing the right thing is rewarded, *the way it should be*. And now there's a quest that does that. I'm watching someone bring people together, forge a community, and help this world—and I like that. Not only am I not willing to punish her for something Harry did, but I also don't even think I dislike the quest."

If he had hoped for a receptive audience, he'd hoped in vain.

"Then you're fired," Dhruv said unceremoniously. "Give me your badge."

"Whoa, now," Sam started. He cut off when Jay put a hand on his arm.

Jay unclipped his employee badge and held it out. "Oh, and one more thing." Dan and Dhruv looked at him warily, and it was hard for Jay not to smile. "You ban her, and I'll spill all of this."

"Your employment contract specifically forbids—"

"Yeah, so you'll sue me," Jay said. He couldn't stop the grin now. "But you won't be able to get that genie back in the bottle, gentlemen, so think carefully."

He strode away without another word to Sam, but a few blocks away, he stopped to send a text:

Sorry to dump that on you and leave without a goodbye. You deserve better than to get tarred and feathered for my mistake. Just throw me under the bus, okay? You did tell me not to do it.

Sam clearly started typing and then stopped again more than once. Finally, the message came back simply:

Tell me if you need anything, Jay.

I will. Jay put his hands in his pockets and kept walking, trying not to let doubt creep in.

It wasn't long into her shift before Vince showed up. Gracie scanned the area for potential players before looking at him.

"What can I do for you, Mr. Wallace?" She kept her tone irreproachable, but she knew there was a bite to it.

"We received a complaint about you," Vince said. His face didn't flicker when Grace's jaw dropped.

"Not possible," Gracie said at once. "The only people who leave my table angry are the really belligerent drunks, and everyone has those—and I have fewer than other people!"

"It wasn't a customer," Vince said. "Precisely. It was someone from the Bellagio, who passed along as a favor to us the fact that you were advertising your association with the Torrino *and* behaving inappropriately in public."

For a moment, the sheer inanity of that choked Gracie silent. The cocktail waitresses at the Torino wore skirts that qualified more as belts. There were burlesque shows in some of the halls. This was *Vegas,* for crying out loud. Complaining about it being inappropriate was patently absurd.

Then it hit her.

She knew exactly who had filed this complaint. "You mean Kyle Johnson, don't you?"

Vince gave a nod. "Apparently, you were very rude to Mr. Johnson the other night. Now, he's prepared to let this go with an apology. In fact, made it very clear that he was not asking us to fire you."

"Of course he wasn't," Gracie said. "Which neither of you believes, but which allows him to plausibly play the part of the reasonable, gracious man when we all know a gracious man would have asked for an apology in public—"

"Ms. King—"

"I'm not finished," Gracie said. "A gracious man would only have asked for an apology where one was warranted, not stood me up. Not insulted me multiple times. If you want someone who is behaving inappropriately, look at Mr. Johnson. All I did was refuse to put up with him."

Vince looked at her; just looked. Gracie lifted her chin and looked back. If he thought he was going to wait her out until she cracked and said she was wrong, he was badly mistaken.

She won...after a fashion. Vince sighed. It was delicate, far too delicate for a man of his size. Clearly a fake sigh.

"I hoped I would not have to explain this to you, Ms. King. An adult should know there are certain rules in the world. One of those rules is that social status confers certain benefits. Mr. Johnson is a well-respected member of—"

"Oh, please." Gracie shook her head. "Spare me the, 'I don't make the rules' speech, *Mr. Wallace.* I got that the other night from Mr. Johnson while he was defending the fact that he was insulting me. You don't actually have to take the easy way out and do the wrong thing. You know that, right? You're choosing to." She cleared her hands for the camera and unclipped her badge from her waist. "So let me demonstrate for you. Kyle has put together a lovely catch-22 where I'd have to either lie and humiliate myself or get fired. I'm choosing not to lie and humiliate myself. Walk me out."

She hoped she saw a flicker of something in his eyes, but she knew that was just wishful thinking. Vince wasn't going to feel bad about this. He probably wasn't even going to remember it.

As Gracie walked out into the sunshine, divested of her badge and her brocade vest, she squinted at the fountains she so loved to watch, then set off determinedly in the other direction.

Somewhere along the way, the glitz and glamor had worn off. This city wasn't anything but—

But the real world. The real world looked like this everywhere. Gracie realized, to her horror, that her eyes were prickling with tears. She *hated* crying.

It wasn't that Las Vegas had stopped being the city she genuinely loved. It was just that it had decided to spit her out.

Well, fuck life. She would beat life inside a virtual one or die (probably lots of times) trying.

CHAPTER EIGHTEEN

"Gracie?" Alex looked worried as he came out into the lobby. "What's going on? What's up?"

"I..." Gracie felt the tears starting to break through. When she'd left the Strip, she'd been full of purpose, but as her anger bled away on the drive toward home, she'd wanted anything other than to go back to an empty apartment.

An apartment she probably couldn't afford anymore, truth be told.

She wished she hadn't come to see *Alex*, of all people, but she hadn't managed to make any other real friends since working here.

"Gracie?"

"I thought you might want to go to lunch." She wasn't going to fall apart here.

"Yeah, I saw your text right before Jen told me you were here." Alex nodded at the receptionist, a perfectly-coifed woman with equally perfect makeup. Gracie had no doubt that she was intended to warm up the Vegas higher-ups who did their taxes here, but when Gracie arrived, Jen had seemed to understand that Gracie was about five seconds from bursting into tears and had given her a smile that was jarringly genuine.

Now she smiled at Alex. "She's a lunch meeting," she said meaningfully and pointed at her computer.

"You're a dream, Jen." Alex gave her a nod. "I'll bring you something back." He held the door open for Gracie to go out into the sunshine, and led her along the sidewalk for a bit in silence.

"I got fired," Gracie said finally. At her side, she saw Alex stop, and when she looked up at him, she saw that he looked worried. "All right," she admitted, "I quit."

To her surprise, Alex's face split into a grin. "That's my girl." He clapped her on the shoulder. "That calls for a proper celebration, then. Let's go get a beer."

"A celebration?" Gracie scrambled after him. "Alex, I was already not going to make rent this month, and that was even before I gave that douche $100—"

"I got a bonus the size of Chuck Norris' balls for my work on that one project," Alex said, unconcerned. "Plus, last I saw, you were making a tidy amount per day by having that rank." He opened the door to a dimly lit restaurant, and they followed the host to a table. As they sat, however, Alex raised an eyebrow. "But what's this about $100?"

"*Ugh.*" Gracie gave a brief recap of the date, only to have Alex laughing by the end of it. "It's not funny!"

"Okay, it's not funny, but can you imagine how he felt?" Alex grinned at her and took out his ID. "Come on, pick a beer."

Gracie scanned the list. "Ever heard of Surly Brewery?"

"Nope."

"Well, I like the sound of Todd the Axe Man right about now, so I'm gonna try that." Gracie fished out her own ID as Alex flagged down their waitress, and they both ordered. "And about Kyle—"

Alex guffawed. "Bet it stopped him in his tracks. He's used to throwing his money around and having that work for him. And it usually does, but *man*! What does a guy like that do when it stops working?"

Gracie tried to smile, but she couldn't quite bring it to the front. "Use his contacts to file a complaint with her work, demanding she either apologize or get fired?"

Alex's face went still. "Gracie, he *didn't*."

"He did." Gracie wished she had that beer. "And Vince pulled the exact same, 'I don't make the rules' shit, so here we are."

The waitress put down their beers. "You need another minute?"

"Oh." Gracie looked at the menu. "I'm so sorry. I, uh…"

"Want me to?" Alex asked, correctly interpreting the look on her face as I Can't Do One More Fucking Thing Today. At her nod, he looked up at the waitress and rattled off their order: "Two Cowboy Burgers, medium rare, and an order of mozzarella sticks." To Gracie, he added, "That sort of fuckery necessitates melted cheese."

The waitress snorted quietly with laughter and gave him a grin as she left.

"She *liiiiikes* you," Gracie said in a sing-song voice.

"Does she?" Alex looked over in interest. "Now, *there's*

something. Huh." He shook himself after a moment. "What were we talking about?"

Gracie snickered as she took a sip of her beer. "Oh, this is good. Why the hell couldn't Kyle take me someplace like this? *Beer.* Burgers."

"You know the rules, Gracie," Alex said mock-seriously. "If you allow yourself to like *lower class* things, you'll start a downward slide that crushes all your hopes and dreams of owning a tiger and being cryogenically frozen when you die."

Gracie paused to raise an eyebrow. "Real expenses you've seen on tax returns?" she guessed.

"I can neither confirm nor deny that." He took a sip of his beer. "Oh, that's *good.*" He turned to her. "Look, Gracie, you gave it a shot. I'll bet you really did. But I'm glad you didn't apologize." He held up his beer for her to clink. "To better dates with non-douches."

Gracie clinked with a grin, then smiled at the waitress as she brought the mozzarella sticks over. "Thanks."

The woman nodded and left with a shy smile at Alex.

"She *so* likes you," Gracie said. She jerked her head at the woman. "Leave her your number."

Alex grimaced. "Ughhhh, too much effort."

"Lazy." Gracie rolled her eyes.

"I'm talking about divorces." Alex raised an eyebrow as he downed the beer.

"Uh-huh, and I should never date again because the world's full of douches, right?" Gracie saw him open his mouth to protest and grinned. "See how crazy you sound? Checkmate."

"I hate it when you make good points. Eat your fried cheese." Alex took another sip of his beer.

"So…" Gracie took a bite of her mozzarella stick. "Oh, you were right. The cheese does make it better somehow. Anyway, guess I'll go home and job search."

"Nope." Alex shook his head.

"Listen, Alex—" she started before he held up a hand.

"I'm not saying don't get a job." He laughed. "But my last roommate stank up the place with weed, and the one before that stole the fridge. You're actually nice to be around. I don't want to go looking for another roommate. And frankly, Gracie, you're going to get a job. I know you. So just…take the *day*, okay? Take a day, and maybe play some *Metamorphosis*."

Gracie toyed with a mozzarella stick. "You want to hear something weird? I think that game is kind of to blame for me quitting."

Now he gave her a curious look.

"It's just… Who was I before that, right?" Gracie hunched her shoulders. "Some random trash bag with a terrible job. But I log in there, and suddenly people *listen* to me. I'm actually someone who matters. I make a bad call, I get pretty instant karma for it. I make a good call, things work out and people respect me." She took another bite and chewed contemplatively. "It made going to work so much harder, you know? I nearly got written up the other day for helping this sobbing woman over to the bar. Literally for being nice and doing a nice thing. What kind of bullshit is that?"

Alex nodded reflectively. "I guess I hadn't thought of that. I'll want to be careful, then. People don't treat us quite as badly as your bosses treated you, but I don't want to find myself running my mouth and getting fired. At least, not until *you* get a job."

Gracie laughed and held up her glass in a mock toast. "To gainful employment."

He waved his glass at her. "Hey, just putting it out there *again*: you get a sponsorship and that ranking money together, and you'll be out-earning a dealer job." Alex leaned back as the waitress put down their burgers. Gracie noticed he avoided looking at the woman, although he was clearly very aware of her.

She mentally rolled her eyes. She understood why Alex was gun-shy. From the very little he'd told her about it, his divorce had been deeply unpleasant.

But this was ridiculous.

"I still think the ranking's a mistake," she said, taking a bite of her burger. "I— Oh, *fuck*, this is good."

"Right?" Alex asked around a mouthful of his own.

Gracie gave a wide-eyed nod. "A-ey-way...mmf." She swallowed. *"Anyway*, I was saying, I think that ranking's not going to stick. I'll have to give that money back."

"I don't know. That quest you mentioned last night? Long May She Reign? It's not in any of the stuff they've put out, and I don't see it in the forums," Alex said. "I think it may be an Easter egg, and you've gotten a ranking boost from the temple thing. I bet they come back and tell you it's all real."

Gracie shrugged. Privately, she didn't think he was correct, but the burger was too good for her to want to talk.

They chatted as they ate, and pretty soon Alex looked at

his watch. "All right, I think I've hit the limits of a business lunch." He pulled some cash out of his wallet. "Will you take care of getting this to her?"

"Yeah." Gracie smiled at him. "Thanks for talking. I feel better. And for lunch. And for helping me with rent this month."

"Gracie, it's fine." He grabbed his napkin and wiped the burger off his hands. "Damn, I need to go wash up. But seriously, Gracie, it's fine."

"It's not. I'll pay you back."

"I know. That's why it's fine." He gave her a grin and a shoulder clasp as he headed out.

Gracie waited, tapping her fingers, and then, in a stroke of inspiration, fished a pen out of her bag and scribbled on one of the napkins. When the waitress came back, Gracie was waiting—and because she was watching, she saw the woman's face fall when she noticed Alex wasn't there anymore.

"Aha!" Gracie said.

"What?" the woman asked.

"Uh, one sec. First, this is for lunch." Gracie held out the cash. "That covers it, right? One sec, let me get more for the tip. There you go."

"Thank you."

"No problem. And *now*..." Gracie held out the paper napkin. "This is my roommate's number. Saw you checking him out, and he's a good dude. And he's *definitely* interested. Just a bit gun-shy."

"I know the feeling." The waitress flexed her hand to look at where a wedding band would have sat.

"Ah, you *do* know the feeling." Gracie nodded at the slip

of paper. "Give him a call."

"I... Yeah, I think I will." The waitress looked at the piece of paper, then back up. "I mean, if you're *sure—*"

"Very sure," Gracie assured her. She headed out with a wave, very much cheered up by her lunch.

The apartment didn't seem quite as grim as she'd anticipated. After hearing Alex's perspective, she was able to let herself relax as she flopped on the couch. She *would* get a job. There was no shortage of jobs, after all. She'd wait tables if she had to.

In the meantime, she would enjoy taking the rest of the day off without having to dread her next shift at work.

Gracie took a long shower, humming to herself, and fixed a snack before heading back to the couch. For some people, a giant burger with cheese and bacon, not to mention a heaping side of fries, an order of mozzarella sticks, and a beer, would be enough to keep them for more than an hour. Not Gracie. She looked at the assortment of food she'd brought, then headed back to the kitchen and grabbed a bag of potato chips as well.

She'd play some *Metamorphosis*, she decided, *then* go grocery shopping.

When she logged on, though, she was surprised to see Jay online. He was at the temple, but unlike his usual, there was no chat invitation.

Frowning, Gracie headed to the mountain and trudged up the paths. She thought she heard some fae laughing, flickering at the corners of her vision, and she smiled at how lifelike this place was now.

She found Jay sitting on a toppled column, looking out at Kithara.

"Hey." Gracie came to stand beside him. "You okay?"

"Not really." Jay sighed. "I got fired today."

"No shit." Gracie looked at him. "Me, too. Why'd *you* get fired? You don't have to tell me," she added hastily.

"No, it's okay. I just... Well, they wanted me to do something that wasn't right, and I wouldn't do it." He shrugged. His arms were crossed over his chest. "I just threw away my dream job. I know I did the right thing, but it still feels like shit."

"God, I'm sorry." Gracie felt a twist of sympathy. "Well, you did the right thing, yeah? And I'm sure anyone you *want* to work for will understand that on your record."

"Right." He didn't sound convinced, but he did sound pleased for some reason. "Well, what's done is done. The bridge has been thoroughly burned."

"You know," Gracie said, "one of my college roommates used to say that sometimes you need to burn bridges to make sure you don't walk back over them."

Jay was silent as he looked at her. "I like that," he said finally. "I like that a lot."

"Yeah, she was always braver than me." Gracie shrugged. "Anyway, what do you say we totally ignore our problems for today and dick around online?" A ding sounded. "Oh, hey, Chowder's online."

"Let's party up," Jay said. He sounded much happier. "Now that I've had some time to wallow, I could stand to hit a few things."

"I also suggest beer and fried cheese," Gracie said.

"Solid. Now I have dinner plans as well." He was laughing. He stood up and clapped his hands together. "There, I invited you and Chowder. Let's go smash stuff."

CHAPTER NINETEEN

"Hey, guys." Chowder loped over to where Gracie and Jay were standing. "Whoa, this zone is crazy."

"Isn't it?" Gracie gazed at the vista that surrounded them.

They stood at one end of a long, curved plain that cradled them like a spoon and rose into sharp peaks at the far end. Stars hovered close above their heads; a patchwork of orbs, some with planets that could distantly be seen circling.

"It's supposed to be the birthplace of the Aosi," Jay told them. "Look at Gracie, and how she seems to match this place. That's why."

"Oh, sorry," Gracie explained to Chowder. "We've been using our real names. I just used our character names the other day to make it less confusing. I'm Gracie, this is Jay."

"Katie," Chowder said enthusiastically. She laughed when Gracie cracked up. "I suppose that sounds kinda weird in the male Ocru voice, huh?"

"Ridiculous," Gracie agreed. "But I like it. And it'll blow the guys' minds. They were sure *I* was a dude, so I can't wait to see what they say about you."

"Best way to keep from getting creeped on," Katie told them with feeling. "No one harasses a tall, ugly-as-sin dude, I'll tell you. Even in video games."

"Solid point." Gracie shuddered. "I've got messages piling up in my folder that I'm afraid to check."

"Yeah, definitely don't check those." Katie pulled out her weapon, a massive scimitar that was dented and scratched to hell but still wickedly effective. "So, what are those things down there?"

"No one knows," Gracie said.

"What? Is this some sort of uncharted zone?"

"No, I mean, in the lore. The thought is that they're something left over from the creation of the Aosi, or maybe the first try at making them." Gracie squinted at the plain. "Unraveling that mystery is part of what you do in this zone. I read up on it, but I was careful not to read any spoilers, so if either of you *does* spoil me, I'll kill ya."

"She means that," Jay told Katie from long experience. "Our fearless leader has quite a temper."

Katie laughed, the sound coming out as a raspy bellow. "So I saw. I like that."

They descended down into the plain carefully, picking their way around moon-bright rocks and through scrub brush that would have reminded Gracie of the American Southwest if the color palette hadn't been completely different.

"So, who's waiting for the month-end reveal?" Katie asked.

"Eh?" Gracie scrambled up onto a rock to peer ahead. "Okay, we have one patrol coming this way. Ready to find out what these guys are made of?" Up close, the mobs did indeed look like mutated Aosi—tall, but with their bodies bent out of shape. They had no color beyond their eyes, which seemed to reflect a cloudy, star-filled nebula.

Altogether, Gracie was pretty sure they would haunt her nightmares.

"Yep. Want me to pull?" Katie volunteered.

"Go for it." Gracie waited with Jay, and it wasn't long before Katie came running back toward them with two of the monsters following her, shrieking and howling. "All right, bitches, let's see how you like a shock blast." Both of the monsters, caught in the threat-generating AoE, turned on her at once. "Oh, you *do* like that, huh? Yeah, let's see it. Show me those strikes. I wanna see what you're—" She backed up a couple of steps, her voice rising. "Oh *crap,* that's terrifying!"

One of the monsters had unhinged its jaw as it lunged for her, and Gracie slashed up at it out of instinct.

Jay and Katie leapt into the fray, taking down the other monster as Gracie battled hers, and finishing hers off a moment later.

"Okay, so—debuff, big snake-jaw bite-y attack, otherwise they swipe at you for a piddly amount." Gracie was breathing hard. "But they swipe a *lot,* so we may need to keep an eye on that with bigger groups." She looked down at the ground. "Oooh, are those opals?"

"Looks like." Katie picked them up, and they automatically divided themselves into the group's inventory. "I wonder what we do with them."

"Maybe it's like that kobold quest I told you about," Gracie suggested. "Anyway, what's this about month-end?"

"Oh, the month-end announcement." Katie nodded as they set off again. "Each month, around now-ish, Dragon Soul drops the details on the next month's dungeon."

"I still don't get how those work," Gracie muttered.

"It's a little different from raiding in other games," Jay offered. "They wanted it to be a skill game, not a gear game, right? So you could sort of have a Cinderella story; anyone can do the month-first dungeon clear."

"*Really.*" Gracie, recognizing the same phrase she'd used with Kyle, stopped to contemplate the sky. "Okay, tell me more."

"So, the idea is, every group that loads in, each class gets the same gear according to their spec. So, if you're like Chowder here, you'd have whatever they give two-hand fighters. For you, they'd have whipped up a set for tanks, etc. Right?"

"Okay, so people really are starting on an even footing."

"Kind of." Jay sounded like he was grinning. "But they don't release too many details about the fight, first of all, so it's hard to know who to bring...and video of every run is available online until someone finally manages to clear the end boss."

"*Oh,*" Gracie said in sudden understanding. With those being the rules, a top guild that made the run and failed would not only have blown *that* chance to be the first, they would also have given their rivals valuable information. She frowned. "Well, that's interesting, then. So there's this competing pressure to be first, but also to wait until you have more intel."

"Yup," Jay told her. "And they have people running the numbers as soon as the teaser trailer drops, so they have a good idea who to send."

"That's another thing!" Gracie pointed out. "Do you send your top people the first time? I suppose you would, right? You can just restart immediately after if you wipe—"

"*Nope*," Katie said, clearly relishing this. "You're on a timer before you can load in again. Either you clear it, or you have to wait whatever time they assigned before you can head in again. If you get partway in and realize you won't make it to the end, you can try sending another group from your guild, but you can't re-run any of those same people until the time resets."

"That sounds like a nightmare," Gracie commented. "Bet there's a bitch fight every month about who's going first and why."

"Oh, yeah," Jay agreed. "*Oh*, yeah."

"There's a lot of speculation about this month's," Katie chimed in. "The past few months have had some really interesting mechanics. For instance, last time they'd been telegraphing that you'd need a frost-mage-heavy group, so one of the first crews logged in with three frost mages. Well, they get part way through and they're just dropping like flies, so two of the other guilds head in with different groups…"

She was laughing already, so Gracie grinned as she waited for the hammer to drop.

"Well, it turned out the trash mobs were all resistant to frost, but the end boss wasn't," Katie said. "So they threw a lovely fake out in there, and the first group still managed to clear it first."

Jay was laughing. "I remember that one. We were all watching."

"Did you used to be part of a guild?" Gracie asked, interested. Jay had been pretty down on the idea of her joining one of the guilds, but he'd never said why. If he'd been a part of one and had a bad experience, that would explain it.

"Yeah," he said after a pause. "It's a long story."

"And now you're bumming around with the plebes, huh?" Katie flashed him a smile as she ran off to pull another group.

The three of them split off the same way again, with Gracie engaging the monsters' attention and the others picking away at them one by one.

"Although," Katie added, hacking one of the monsters to bits with her cool-down attack, "I tell you, I wouldn't mind that $500, you know?" She sighed. Gracie could hear her panting slightly. "Pie-in-the-sky dream," she added after a moment.

"If we all get the same gear…" Gracie began. "Wait. Jay, is it level-adjusted?"

"Kind of," Jay said. "You'll go in with top-level stats but only the spec you have, so if you haven't unlocked what-ever, you won't have it to work with, while the mobs in the dungeon will have— Heads up!"

There was a roar behind them and a crack opened in the earth. Monsters started pouring out of it and Gracie swiveled her head, trying to take in as much of the scene as she could. Eight monsters. No, ten.

Fuck.

"All right, speed is of the essence!" She charged into the

middle of the group and slammed her sword down. "I'm going to kite these bastards around to keep out of that swiping, and you all use as much AoE as you can. Katie, follow Jay's directions on that. He's got a good head for threat."

"Right-o," Katie called as she ducked a rock the size of her head one of the monsters threw at her.

Gracie wove around the rocks, working her way back uphill and away from the more densely populated areas of the zone. Now that she knew monsters could erupt out of the ground at any moment, she was a little bit worried that she might end up with even more to handle at some point. She told herself she couldn't do anything about that.

Best to focus on what she *could* control, namely, keeping up enough threat to make sure those monsters trailed her and allowed themselves to be picked off.

Not to mention, they had no healer. She'd have to be *really* careful about those swiping attacks.

Gracie scanned her abilities list and popped two of the reinforcing evasion buffs before charging back into the center of the group of monsters and making another shock blast. Several of the monsters unhinged their jaws as they howled.

"Gah, that just never stops being creepy, you guys!" She zoomed away again.

It became a game quickly enough, with them calling out whose buffs were up or down, trading mobs if there was trouble, and popping potions whenever they could. The monsters were fairly harmless on their own, but very difficult to handle as a group.

"Last couple!" Gracie called a few minutes later. She

blew out a quick breath and winced at the feeling of sweat trickling into the small of her back. So much for that shower. This battle was going to necessitate another. It was good to have the day off—

No, best not to think about that.

Her health bar was dipping low, and a quick glance told her that Jay and Katie weren't in any better straits, so Gracie made a quick decision.

"Everyone, to me!"

"What?" Katie asked a bit nervously.

"I've found that you should just follow her suggestions and ask questions later," Jay called back. "Come on!"

The two closed in, and Gracie popped her last evasion cooldown. It wasn't particularly strong, but it was what she had. The two monsters closed in, both disturbingly high-health and high-energy.

Gracie bared her teeth even though the expression didn't translate into the game, and she was just staring down a pile of pixels anyway.

"To my left first. Wear him down. Throw *anything* you have at him. Immediately!"

"*Gracie!*" Katie called.

But it was too late. Between the swipes and one monster's ultimate ability, Gracie's character flew forward and the screen went dark.

"*Fuck,*" she said with deep feeling.

When everything cleared, she was back at the nearest inn—a rather disturbing place bartended by one of the monsters. His name was displayed in green to indicate he was friendly, but Gracie was still anticipating an attack as she edged up to the bar.

"Uh, so how are you guys doing?"

"Well," Jay said, "let me tell you."

He appeared in the center of the bar a moment later, with Katie coming in as well.

"Oh, God, I'm so sorry, guys. I really thought that was the best idea." Gracie sank her head into her hands. "This is not my day for good decision-making, apparently."

"It may have been the best idea, you know," Katie pointed out. "Dead is dead, after all, but letting us all buff each other was a good thought."

"Right." Gracie sighed and forked over some gold for the repair costs on her gear. "Ouch, that one hurt. Oh, and we lost all of our opals. Hope those weren't important."

"We'll just wait for Alan before going back," Jay suggested. "Maybe hang out in some lower-level places for a bit after this, you know?"

"If you two still want anything to do with me, I guess," Gracie said skeptically.

Katie laughed. "What, because we died once, you think we want to leave?"

"She takes the tank thing *really* seriously," Jay said in a stage whisper.

"Do you think she knows that people die all the time in MMOs?" Katie whispered back.

"Guys." Gracie leveled her sword at them. "All I'm going to say is, if you two want to hang around in half-destroyed armor, whispering in each other's ears, I'm gonna need you to get a room."

Jay guffawed. Both he and Katie fixed their gear, the holes mending themselves and the armor becoming brilliant once more.

"Where to next?" Katie asked. "And I gotta say, if you guys ever form a proper guild, I'm *in*."

Gracie and Jay looked at one another.

"Now *there's* an idea…" Gracie murmured.

CHAPTER TWENTY

"Uh, Gracie?" Alex's voice was very calm.

"Yeah?" Gracie didn't look up.

"Is there a reason you're trying to prove that Pepe Silvia does not exist?"

"Huh?" Gracie looked up, totally lost, then glanced around. Her research into past monthly dungeons was arranged neatly around her in piles corresponding to each fight, with—

Hmm. Well, it had started *out* neat. Now, with different fights linked to each of those in satellite piles, and with her constant perusal of said piles, it looked like she'd mugged a college kid and thrown their notes all over the room.

"Who's Pepe Silvia?" she asked finally.

"*Always Sunny in Philadelphia*? Charlie goes on that rant? You know, with the board covered in paper and string—"

"Ohh, right." Gracie scratched at her ear and gave a laugh. "I'll have you know this is much saner than it looks like."

"They all say that," Alex said to no one as he exited the room. "Oh, hey, you got groceries before you went crazy."

She nodded absently. "I know, I'm pretty great, right?"

"That remains to be seen." Alex's voice came from the kitchen, and he appeared a moment later with a jar of peanut butter and a spoon. "What *is* all this?"

"You know," Gracie told him with great dignity, "I'm having trouble with your assessment of crazy, given that you're eating peanut butter directly out of the jar."

"Sure, Nutella is better, but we don't have any Nutella." Alex gave a shrug and dropped onto the couch, staring over Gracie's shoulder. "So, explain. Otherwise, I'm going to be forced to believe that you're trying to summon demons, and I distinctly remember a no-demon clause in our rental agreement."

He wasn't kidding, but… "I thought that was a joke," Gracie said.

"It was a nod to my ex," Alex said, "so it *was* a joke. But only kind of." He looked a little sad at the memories.

"Anyway, peanut butter is a condiment," Gracie said, returning to a less painful topic. She winced when Alex looked her dead in the eyes and ate a huge mouthful. "Your mouth is going to get all stuck together, and then you'll be sorry. Anyway, this is my research to see if I can predict what the new content will be this month. *And…*" She pointed to three piles beside Alex on the couch. "Dossiers on the competition."

"So *that's* why there's a file labeled 'Demon Syndicate.' I was worried." Alex leaned over to read as he scooped out another spoonful of peanut butter. "When you said 'research,' did you mean 'hit list'?" He pointed with the spoon. "Because this looks like a hit list."

Gracie laughed as she changed tabs on her computer and scrolled down to a series of diagrams. "I just copied down the player names for each guild. I still don't know anyone's spec or anything, or even who they've brought into their month-first runs before. I'll make more notes when I have that."

"Do you wanna, I don't know, run that by me again in a way that gives me a clue what you're talking about?" Alex popped the spoonful of peanut butter into his mouth and then said, his voice strangled, "Wait. You're thinking of doing a month-first run, aren't you? That's what you're trying to do, isn't it?"

Gracie tossed a glance over her shoulder with a toothy grin. "Maybe," she admitted cheekily.

He grunted. "Fuck, you don't think small, do you?"

"Of course, I don't," Gracie said, unconcerned. "Nor should I. The gear part is taken care of. There's no reason we *shouldn't* be able to—"

"Except for the fact that these are guilds who play all day long together, have developed their own language, train for this, and have the best specs in the game!" Alex waved his hands. "You won't be leveled far enough in three days to have your spec all set up."

"So we'll roll with what we got," Gracie said, unconcerned. She looked over her shoulder at him again and grinned. "Come on, there's no real downside. Well, I won't have your rent money if we don't make it. On the other hand, you'll be getting that sooner or later anyway."

Alex sighed. "And this *is* happier than I've seen you since your date with the douche."

"That was *not* a date. That was cleverly disguised torture. Slow death by douche. Oh, *that* is a terrifying mental image." Gracie stared at the far wall for a moment. "Forget I said that."

"I'm trying, but it seems to be burned into my brain." Alex put down the peanut butter. "I think I'm done with dinner, then. Okay, lady, riddle me this: how are we going to play tonight if the entire living room is covered in bits of paper?"

"Oh. Oh, dear." Gracie scrambled up. "Give me ten minutes. Fifteen. Half an hour. I'll get all this moved into the bedroom and keep working in there."

"You're so caught up in this that you're not even going to play?" Alex sounded impressed.

"You, my friend, have never seen me in research mode." Gracie looked up with a smile when a ding sounded. "Ah, the coffee is done."

"Lord help us," Alex said with the sigh of a man who had what he thought he wanted and just realized he had screwed himself. "I'm going to wake up tomorrow and find you strung out on Red Bull muttering buff numbers to yourself, aren't I?"

"There's a non-zero chance of that." Gracie picked up a stack of paper and organized it. "I'm going to exercise my right against self-incrimination and not tell you exactly what the number is." She headed off for the bedroom with Alex's chuckles following her.

Alex called, "Wait. Come back."

"Eh?" Gracie stuck her head around the corner.

"Look, if you're going all crazy about this, I'll help." Alex picked up the phone. "First order of business is dinner. I'll order, then we'll divide up tasks and buckle down. Sound good?"

"There's the Harvey Mudd alum I know and love. Come on...when you saw this, you got a little turned on." Gracie wiggled her eyebrows at him.

"*I'm* going to exercise *my* right against self-incrimination now."

Alex hadn't ever seen Gracie's research mode, but it was just as true that she hadn't seen his, and she was impressed. By the time food arrived, he was so deep into his notes that he didn't hear the doorbell ring. He didn't even stop to eat until Gracie waved the box between his face and the page, and even then, he tended to stop chewing whenever he reached an interesting passage. With Pad Thai trailing out of his mouth, Gracie reflected, he looked a bit like a swamp monster.

"So, they're really skewing heavily toward frost and fire," he said finally. "Either way."

"Maybe they've been watching too much *Game of Thrones*," Gracie suggested. She'd commandeered one of the couch pillows and propped her torso on it as she watched a video of a failed attempt. "But, yes, they seem to go hard on that dynamic. Maybe we want to get a fire mage on board as well as Freon?"

"Sounds good. Who is that?" Alex came to sit next to her, moving her coffee cup carefully out of the way.

Gracie nodded her appreciation. "Scions of Shinra," she said. "They were the top dogs a few months in a row at the start, but Demon Syndicate has been dominating lately.

They've had some close calls, but they always come through. They're scrappy. I like it." She grinned. "Of course, they're also sort of the Goliath to our David, so what do I know?"

"Mmm." Alex narrowed his eyes. "What are they— Oh, shit." The party had wiped, and Gracie nodded as she leaned in to hear the voice chat.

She rewound the video for them to watch again. There hadn't been any obvious sign that the boss was gearing up for such a big attack, or so she thought. It took a third watch-through before she realized that some of the decorations around the top of the circular room had been lighting up one by one. When all of them had lit up, closing the circle, the boss attacked.

"When they wipe, do they start from scratch?" Alex asked.

"I don't think so." Gracie frowned. "But I wouldn't be surprised if that made it into the mechanics. They seem to be trying to find a balance between penalizing failure enough to make it sting and incentivizing trying. In a normal game, I'd say they wouldn't think twice about throwing that out there and letting it all blow up. Here?"

"What?" Alex looked at her. Then his brain caught up with him. "The payouts. The *sponsors.* They don't want anyone crying foul."

"Yep." Gracie nodded. "You *know* people would throw a hissy fit about losing out on 'their' share of the pot. Or, you know, having their company logo splashed up there."

Alex gave her a look. "Would I be correct that you're speaking from experience, here?"

"I may have logged out because I was getting spammed

with guild offers." Gracie rolled her eyes. "At first, I tried to explain to everyone that my ranking wasn't real. Then I lost my voice and gave up."

"That explains the several mugs with tea bags."

"We're out of honey," Gracie said mournfully. "Anyway, it was just too much trouble to be logged in. They're so full of themselves. Not just these three guilds, either. *All* of them are." She sighed. "Well, from what I've seen, the main takeaways are to be ready for frost and fire, look in the environment for clues about what's coming, and prioritize killing the boss over the mobs around him."

"Yeah, that's one of your favorites." Alex grinned. "But be careful—as soon as you think you have it down, they're going to switch it up on you. They're sneaky."

Gracie snorted with laughter, then covered her mouth to keep Pad Thai from going everywhere. "Yes, I'm sure Dragon Soul Productions is very interested in what I, personally, think the next dungeon will be." She grinned. "It's a crazy thing to try for, but it's *my* crazy thing. Unless..."

"Hmm?" Alex had leaned back against the couch and was picking the last of the chicken out of a takeout box. He glanced at her and frowned at her expression. "What's up?"

"Matt texted today." Gracie shrugged. "My old boss? Says he's talked to Vince, and he can get me my job back if I want it."

"Gracie!" Alex winced.

"I know. I *know*. But it's a job, right? It's money, right?"

"Money and misery," Alex said succinctly. "Don't go back there. Aim higher." He jabbed his plastic fork at her for emphasis.

"Fine," Gracie grumbled. "But I *hate* job searching. Everywhere is related to the casinos somehow."

"You'll find something," Alex predicted. "For now, I kinda want to see what's going to happen when you try to do this month-first run."

"Aren't you forgetting something?" Gracie asked sweetly.

"What?" He looked at her, perplexed, catching her gaze. "Oh, I don't like that look."

"You're going to *be* there," Gracie reminded him. She grinned at the look on his face. "So get ready to call in sick, because we're running that dungeon on Day One come hell or high water."

"Oh, no." Alex dropped his head. "Oh, God. This is *so* going to be a shitshow."

"It's going to be awesome, and Teef is going to be the famousest purple panther there ever was," Gracie said. "Cheer up! We're about to be rolling in extra cash."

CHAPTER TWENTY-ONE

Darkness closed around the party, close and oppressive. They were underground, although how the environments team had managed to make that clear, Jay didn't know, because it wasn't possible to see the ceiling of the caves. Somehow, though, they had managed to make the place seem both more vast than any mortal had seen before and yet claustrophobic, locked as it was in silence.

They stood on the shore of a massive lake, its waters deep and dark and moving just enough to suggest that there might be something huge and slimy lurking under the surface. Jay shuddered at that thought as his eyes traced the chain of islands that led to the temple at the center of the lake.

The Lake of Souls had been the month-end dungeon four months before, and it was one of the rare ones that didn't feature ice or fire as a main mechanic in the boss fight. As the lore went, the temple at the center wasn't made to worship the gods.

It had been made *by* the gods.

To worship death.

Jay had to admit that the environments team had done a bang-up job on this one. He'd seen the sketches and watched the videos, but it was very different to be inside the instance.

"Everyone ready?" Gracie's Aosi-filtered voice might be designed to make her sound epic, but right now she sounded like a god-level pep squad of one. "Had a glass of water? Stretched?"

Jay rolled his neck reflexively. Normally that was just an idle question, but in *Metamorphosis Online*, it was important for most of the players. You *could* play the game with a click wheel and some other movement controls, but most people chose to play with a VR body suit. Muscle cramps were, therefore, a very real possibility.

At least it tended to make instances shorter, Jay reflected. When you were actually participating in each fight—as the Dragon Soul teams had during the testing and development —you didn't throw in extra trash mobs just for the heck of it.

Their core group had expanded to a full ten now, and he was feeling good about the new additions. Chowder, Freon, and Lakhesis had come back for another bout, and they had rounded the group out with Dathok, an Ocru back-up healer for Alan, and Ushanas, an Aosi fire mage. So far, she and Freon had proved to be an amazingly deadly team, and even though their spells didn't hurt team members, Jay had discovered just how disconcerting it was to have a brawl in the middle of a rain of fire.

Everyone checked in, their names surrounded by a

green aura as they did so, and Gracie gave Jay a last smile before stepping to the edge of the water. She knelt and placed a shimmering gem in a carved depression, and stones rose soundlessly out of the water to break the surface, forming a path to the first island.

Gracie hesitated before stepping onto the first one, and Jay couldn't blame her—whatever moved the waters had sent a wide, shallow wave lapping over the stones. But she squared her shoulders and marched across first, the others following her tentatively.

Jay brought up the rear as she'd asked him to do, giving the gem one last look. It was forged from the opals they'd gone back to get in the Aosi zone yesterday. Gracie, it turned out, was more than a little obsessive when she failed at something. She'd grudgingly agreed to do something else for a while but had eventually suggested going back to the scene of their earlier wipe.

They'd wiped a few more times, but each time they'd gotten farther, and they'd learned to spot the signs of an ambush. By the time Alan signed on to heal, they hardly needed him.

Jay was enjoying watching her learn the boss fights as well. At first, he'd been bored by how many times she ran through each fight, and frustrated by constant failure. Just when they seemed to have an enemy's fighting style down, Gracie would change some aspect of her strategy.

More and more, however, he respected the process. Gracie had developed not only an uncanny intuition for the way the developers' minds worked, but she also knew just how each type of player interacted in terms of skills, and she was learning the preferred play style of her team, as well.

On the platform, the players spread out to surround a pristine altar. Its shining white stone was, if anything, *too* clean. It looked as if sacrifices had been made here and death had swallowed every last drop of blood, leaving nothing behind.

There was a grinding sound, and the ground beneath their feet shook. Waves lapped urgently at the shore. Above the altar, a ball of light appeared and spun wildly before lengthening into a seam that split reality.

"You dare refuse to give the sacrifice?" a voice hissed.

Jay's eyes sought Gracie. She was standing at ease, waiting. Her sword was still on her back.

The hissing voice laughed. *"Then I will choose from among you."*

Now the sword came out with a ring of steel. "Not. Fucking. Likely," Gracie informed the demon.

It dropped through the tear in the world, a lanky figure made of light and dark intertwined. It straightened up slowly.

Or it would have.

Instead, Gracie was already there, leaping onto the altar and beginning with her standard shock blast. Jay had asked her about it while they were fighting smaller groups the other day, and she had explained that, as far as she could tell from her research, it was the most mana-effective way to generate threat, no matter the size of the party. It was only barely possible for some higher-level skills to edge it out, and Gracie was of the opinion that having a combo she could execute by habit was more important than minuscule gains.

They had watched videos of this run, so when the demon gave an unearthly shriek and threw back its head, beginning to pulse, Gracie leapt away at once with the rest of the melee team.

"Get ready!" she called. "Freon first."

The demon was invulnerable as it began to grow, and once it was done growing, it had a quick combo that would devastate anyone it was near. It never got a chance to get close, however. Freon's bolt of ice, loosed just as the pulsing stopped, rooted it in place.

"Magic ho!" Gracie called, and the rest of the ranged attackers let loose with their heavy cool-down spells.

"Who you calling a ho?" Alex shouted across the group.

Laughter rang out, including Gracie's, but she didn't spare the time for a comeback. "All right, melee, let's own this bitch."

With the demon down to a fraction of its health and its quick combo-rotation done, the melee fighters darted back in to take it down. It exploded into a shower of sparks and another gem, which Gracie placed in the carved depression at the far end of the island.

She took a look around before stepping onto the stones this time.

"Anyone else get the feeling this place has seen some serious shit?"

"Oh, yeah," Dathok agreed. He'd made himself short for an Ocru, but his muscly frame added a considerable sense of threat to his healer's robes. His healing, Jay knew, came with a side of corruption magic, and even if Dathok didn't roleplay someone with the power of life and death, he certainly played his role well.

"There's something uncanny about gods worshiping death," Alex agreed as they set off. "And something tells me that when it comes to cruelty in live sacrifices, humans got *nothin'* on deities."

A few people muttered in various grossed-out ways and Jay smiled. One of the things that was true of all the group members was that they really took an interest in the lore of the game. As someone who'd weighed in on that lore and watched it take shape, that made Jay happy.

Of course, it also made him feel guilty and sad, but he tried to ignore that part. Sam had left him a voicemail yesterday that Jay still hadn't listened to. He was too busy trying *not* to think about his coming job search.

After working at your dream job, *everything* was a step down.

He was on autopilot as they cleared the rest of the islands. Some of the demons dropped lore hints, and others needed to be defeated with certain kinds of magic or brought imps and skeletons into the fight. In the end, it all came to the same thing: the gods had come here with plenty of unwilling sacrifices, and the demons were used to a certain amount of food. They were grumpy about not getting it.

Gracie did not seem impressed by their grumpiness.

By the time they reached the final boss, everyone was panting, and Gracie called a break. They had a luxurious amount of time before the instance would spit them out, so people drifted off to take bathroom breaks or get snacks, leaving their characters in a huddle. The game had anticipated this, so the characters moved around in idle animations rather than being statue-like.

Jay headed over to where Alex and Gracie were in close conversation.

"Planning?"

Gracie flashed him a sharp-toothed Aosi smile. "Yeah, planning second dinner. All this working out is making me hungry." To Alex, she added. "Either hamburger or pepperoni; I don't care."

Alex looked at Jay for a moment, then laughed. "I was going to offer you tie-break since I don't care, either, but then I remembered we aren't *all* camped out in the living room. I'll be right back."

There was the scuffling sound of his headset coming off, and his character went to idle animations as his panther prowled around the edge of the island. In the distance, they could see the last island, devoid of any altars or features.

Jay knew why, and he suspected the rest did, too—the final island was entirely an altar. The gods, being immortal beings, feared and respected death in a way mortals could not understand.

Of course, the same might be said for the mortals they'd sacrificed here over the eons, he supposed.

"How goes research?" he asked Gracie.

"Well." Gracie sounded pleased. "I believe I've gone about as far as I can. Don't think much of some of the analysis blogs since they're missing really obvious mechanics, but whatever. Everyone's acting like they know what the next month-end one will be, but there's no way to be sure. I have statistics, but nothing solid."

Want in on a secret? Jay wanted to say. *Sometimes we cued up two, waited to see what the rumors were, and decided how much we wanted to mess with people before picking one to release.*

He wasn't going to admit that, though.

"I'll tell you what we could *really* use," Gracie continued, amused.

"What's that?" Jay tilted his head to watch the dark surface of the lake and reflected that it was too bad he couldn't skip stones on it.

Then again, maybe not. Maybe that would wake whatever was down there. The game was saving him from himself.

"A source on the inside." The gurgle of laughter in Gracie's voice told him that she was joking. "Statistics can only take you so far. What we *really* need is some espionage."

Jay laughed but felt a deep stab of guilt. They'd have *had* a source on the inside if he hadn't talked back to Dhruv and Dan. If he'd just had the good sense to keep quiet and…

What? He wasn't quite sure. Maybe he could have pretended to be researching while secretly—

No. That wasn't how his brain worked. He'd just have been lying for the sake of lying.

Still, he was quiet as the other members of the group came back one by one. They headed through a final ready check as Gracie explained their strategy.

"All right, most of you know some of what we're dealing with here. Hrakkun is pretty fast on his feet, so we'll need to work on containment, first of all. Freon's on point with that. Dathok, keep him alive no matter what."

Dathok and Freon nodded. As the story went, Hrakkun was a cunning demon who took advantage of the gods' worship and brought his demons here to feast on the sacrifices. The gods had believed they were communing with Death, and the demons had reaped the rewards. Hrakkun could whisper in your ear as if he knew your deepest thoughts, and also make the ground shake as if *he* were a god, but he was nothing more than a tiny demon, barely bigger than an imp.

It made targeting obscenely difficult.

"Let's go," Gracie said. She set the last gem in place and they started, one by one, over the stone bridge. The waves were stronger now, lapping over their feet, and Jay had the absurd feeling that his feet would slip out from under him on the slick surface and he would go tumbling into the dark water.

On the far side, a highlighted line made it clear where to cross to start the boss fight. The group waited until everyone was across, then stepped over the line together. Blue-white flames sprang up behind them, cutting off any hope of escape. The chamber was sealed.

But instead of Hrakkun's taunting monologue, which Jay had heard a thousand times, water broke across the island and a shape reared above them.

The lake monster hissed, revealing a mouth like a lamprey's, and thudded heavily onto the ground. Water rushed toward them and pooled around their feet, and some of the group bit back reflexive yells of alarm.

The beast slithered out of the water, coil upon coil, its

body easily as wide as Jay's character was tall. The thing was massive, and he felt every bit as overwhelmed as the game designers had intended.

Well, whoever *had* designed this.

"Guys?" Dathok sounded a bit wary. "This is, uh… This is not Hrakkun."

Jay laughed. He couldn't help it. It was funny, he thought. Really funny. He hoped someone at HQ was watching Gracie's character and realizing that things were still spiraling out of their control.

"Yeah," he told Dathok. "This sort of thing tends to happen when Gracie's around." He looked around to rally the others. "Ready for a mystery fight, everyone?"

CHAPTER TWENTY-TWO

"Uh, Jay?" Gracie asked worriedly. "Thoughts?" The beast was still moving, its body leaving the water in a rush of deep green scales glistening wetly in the dim light. It encircled the platform, trapping them.

Jay stared up at the beast's head, which was rearing into the darkness above. He could just see the gleam of its eyes.

Unless those were its teeth.

It hissed, and a ripple of apprehension went down his spine. "Uh, you're the mastermind. Right? Please?" He looked up higher, his voice a squeak. "Mother, please don't let the mean ugly monster use my shinbone as a toothpick!"

Gracie snorted. The sound was a little nervous but also exhilarated. "All right, we go for the front there, and hopefully it'll try to get that part away from us, which will keep bringing its head down to the ground. Then we go for the head."

"The Gracie classic."

"Hear me out, I do have new ideas sometimes." She was

chuckling, but it was fleeting; they only had a few seconds before this thing attacked. She jerked her head at Lakhesis. "Lakhesis will head up a second group fighting the tail. I feel like there's something going on where it might compress and keep squeezing us in, you know? Like fish in a barrel."

"Good call," Jay said at once. "Who's with who?"

"You and Teef come with me. Fys' demon and Chowder go with Lakhesis," Gracie decided. "Squishies, spread out. Anyone sees anything going for the squishies, they tell us. Dathok, you're on backup healing until we know what we're dealing with. Ready? Go!"

They charged. Gracie slammed her sword down for a shock blast as she skidded into place, then whirled up to slash at the lake monster's pale, slimy belly as Teef lashed out with his claws. Jay came in a moment later with one of his own attacks, a double-punch that normally looked epic but in this case, looked more than a little futile.

Video game physics being what they were, however, the beast howled in pain. But instead of thudding down, as Gracie had predicted, it reared up, its head disappearing into the mist with a menacing hiss.

The team looked at one another.

"It's going to come crashing down on us at some point, isn't it?" Gracie asked wearily.

Jay flashed her a smile and a bow. "I see you're getting the hang of this. Shall we?"

They attacked again in unison, their battle cries mingling with the rest of the team's. Gracie was glad to hear from the voice chat that Lakhesis was conducting her little group superbly, watching threat and maneuvering well with Chowder and Kevin's demon familiar.

It only took a few hacks and slashes before the lake monster would rear up, exposing a new part of its belly. Gracie's group was on the third segment when they heard a yell behind them. Spinning to look for a moment, Gracie saw that part of the tail had "died." As she watched, it melted into lake water, leaving only the bones and a few straggling weeds, while the next piece of the tail became pointed.

"Definitely going to try to close us in," Gracie said as she turned back to her own task. "My guess? Hem us all in and throw its head at us like chowing down on fish in a barrel."

"I have a sneaking suspicion you're right," Jay agreed, "and I just know it's going to haunt my nightmares. Can you imagine those teeth plunging down toward you?"

"I don't have to; it's going to happen, and I just *know* I'm going to look up." Gracie managed to hold her shudder until after she'd executed a strike. "And I'm going to regret it. That does remind me, though… Everyone, listen up! When anyone thinks that the head is coming down, try to get out the hole Lakhesis' group is making for us!"

Everyone chorused back a yes to that.

"How are people doing?" Gracie asked.

"There're no return hits on this end, so it's pretty easy," Lakhesis called.

"Eerily easy," Alan agreed. "Too damned easy."

A prickle on the back of Gracie's neck told her that her experience with Dragon Soul's game design was telling her to run. "Everybody out!" she yelled. She hadn't seen any signs, but after watching so many fights and seeing so many enemies, she trusted her instincts.

The group fled, and despite the pound of adrenaline in her blood, Gracie smiled to hear Alex calling for Teef. That panther might be all pixels and controlled by different commands, but humans were what they were. Maybe she should get him a dog.

Not the time, Gracie.

Gracie was toward the back of the group, so she just heard the shrieks of her team members as the head began to come down. Luckily she was spared their looks of horror, but a few of them did point.

She tumbled through the fast-closing gap between the end of the severed tail and the rest of the body and her character rolled, haptics shaking, in time for Gracie to see the lake monster's head smash into the place she'd been standing a few moments ago.

The breath went out of her in a whoosh.

"That was close," Jay was saying when Freon's voice echoed through the group chat.

"*Fuck!*"

"Yeah," Gracie said, resignedly. "I saw it. What happened, buddy?"

"Just didn't get moving quickly enough," Freon said, resignedly. "Got caught on the end of the tail, and it dragged me back in. Let me tell you, that head coming down at you is something you definitely don't want to see."

"Ugh." Gracie had seen the teeth glittering in the darkness. Lampreys were terrifying enough when they *weren't* several stories tall. "Mirra, can you— Oh, *shit.*"

The lake monster wasn't just attacking once. Its head

had reared into the darkness once more, and now it plunged down again. Freon gave an undignified shriek.

"Close your eyes!" Jay suggested.

"Oh God, oh God, oh God, oh God, this is fucking terrifying!" Freon was laughing. "I don't even watch horror movies, and now I'm in one!"

Gracie stood with her hand over her mouth as the head tore at Freon's body and emerged dripping with blood each time. When it had plunged down the first time, the group had given a sympathetic gasp, but now they were laughing and cheering each time it attacked. As far as Gracie could tell, they were just sad they didn't have popcorn. Even Freon was laughing now.

Finally, the attack ended. The snake's head reared back and its coils opened, leaving Freon's body limp in the center of the circle.

"Mirra," Gracie said at once.

"Dathok is already on it." Alan sounded pleased to have another healer on deck.

Gracie smiled. She was also happy to find people who were ready to swing into action and help out. "Thanks, Dathok. Everybody else, attack."

"Anytime," Dathok rumbled in his Ocru voice as the others streamed into place with calls to one another. "Although I'd be happier with fewer unexpected bosses."

"Think of it as unexpected *loot*," Gracie said pragmatically, and she smiled when people made more enthusiastic noises. There was a hiss above them, as if the lake monster objected to being referred to as a piece of loot.

Well, don't attack me, then, Gracie thought with an inner

toothy grin. *I've got a giant sword. What did you* think *would happen?*

This time, the fight seemed to progress at double-speed. The head and tail lashed, the body shuddered, and more than once, Gracie heard Lakhesis' shouts for her group to get out of the way. She didn't intervene, not yet; she wanted to let Lakhesis handle things if she could.

Not long after, however, Lakhesis' voice came across the voice chat, panting. "All right, boss, it's been a good experiment, but I think we need more DPS on this one."

"On it," Jay said after a nod from Gracie.

Which left Gracie and Teef staring down the head on their own.

"Gotcha covered, Callista," Freon called. Several ice bolts landed, and the section of body Gracie was fighting slowed to a lazy waver.

"Doing what I can for the cause," Ushanas added, and several fire bolts whizzed by as well, landing with crackles, the fire spreading under the ice like an armor-piercing round. "Eat sparks, slimeball."

"You *know* ice is superior to fire, right?" Freon said good-naturedly.

"Oh, *hell* no, I don't."

Gracie rolled her eyes as the good-natured bickering continued. As long as they kept trying to outdo one another, she was just going to sit back and enjoy the insults —or hack and slash and enjoy the insults, as the case might be. She kept herself in motion, reflecting wryly that getting into a video game had resulted in her being in the best shape of her life.

She could just picture the July vacation now: *You look*

like you've been working out, Gracie. What do you mean, it's from a video game? Is that your job now?

Her lips twitched with humor.

With Jay on board, the melee team was making good progress with the tail. A cheer went up as they killed another section, and Gracie redoubled her efforts on the neck.

"We're almost there!" she called to the others. The lake monster's overall health bar was dropping down lower and lower. "Maybe one more coil up and we'll be home free."

"Then we can get on the forums and figure out what the crap we just fought," Dathok said.

"Bets that it's not going to *be* on the forums?" Kevin asked aloud. His tiny summoner hopped and gave an overblown gesture as she leveled a corruption spell at the lake monster's head. "The last time this happened, there wasn't any record of it." After a moment, he added, "And for now, I'm keeping it quiet. I've started writing it up, Gracie—er, Callista—but I figured I'd wait until we finished the quest line to post anything."

"Good idea," Jay said instantly. "Keep it under your hat for now."

Gracie wondered briefly about that. Jay had had very strong opinions about this quest from the start, but he didn't seem willing to explain. She was just making a mental note to ask him when the lake monster shrieked and began to convulse. Its health bar had gotten low, and its head flopped to the ground as its body contracted into coils and then opened again.

"Everybody out!" Gracie called, but people had already

begun to run away, demonstrating an excellent sense of self-preservation.

They stood back as the beast convulsed in its death throes and at last melted away into lake water. All that was left after it died was a blue jewel.

"No way," Gracie muttered. She exchanged a look with Jay and headed toward it, kneeling to touch the jewel she had left in the kobold tomb. "How did this get to—"

The shield that sprang up around her swirled with colors like the surface of a soap bubble. Gracie looked around, hearing the calls from her teammates, and cursed her stupidity. She shouldn't have gone to touch this alone.

Then her teammates' words caught up with her and she whirled.

She hadn't seen anything in the lore about giants, but that was indisputably what this thing was. It was easily twice her character's height, and hulking across the shoulders. His face was lost in a tangle of kelp that served both as long, tangled hair and an unkempt beard. The skin carried a greenish unhealthy tinge.

"Who are you?"

The question made no sense. The bosses were programmed with dialogue, but they didn't answer questions. Gracie knew that.

He said nothing. He was both dead and not, something claimed by the lake.

"You were a sacrifice," Gracie said on a hunch. This being had been tossed away—or had it run—and found an ally in the lake monster.

His huge head nodded once, and she thought he would drop the shield or tell her his story, But then, with a snarl, he produced a whip made of flame, and she felt the tingle of threat. Her hands clenched. For a moment, she almost believed she could feel the heft of the sword and the sweat in her palms.

"I'm not your enemy," Gracie told him. "But if you fight me, I *will* fight back."

To her surprise, the giant laughed. "Then let us fight, claimant. *Let us fight.*"

CHAPTER TWENTY-THREE

The giant did not leave her so much as a moment to catch her breath. He charged at once, swinging the whip in one hand; a knife made of flame appeared in the other. His heavy footsteps shook the island, and Gracie heard screams from outside the shield.

"Everyone okay?" she called. The giant was on her, and she rolled sideways at the last minute. She knew this was a video game, but physics was physics, right? Big things didn't stop fast.

He obeyed that law at least, stumbling heavily in his original direction as she scrambled to safety. He was laughing as he turned, however.

"They can't hear you, claimant."

"What does that even *mean*?" Gracie demanded furiously. "And what do you mean, they can't hear me?"

In the real world, she felt Alex's groping hands catch one of her arms. She swung toward him, her character careening wildly, and felt his fingers clasp hers. The side of her helmet came up.

"Gracie?"

"I'm okay, I'm okay! Got a duel with this prick, though." Gracie saw Alex nod, and he released her helmet and stepped back.

When she looked at him, the giant was watching her a bit too shrewdly. She felt almost as if he knew she'd been speaking to someone outside the shield.

He had to have known. Otherwise, how would he have known to give her that response when she asked if everyone was okay? Her mind raced. Programming him to anticipate any variant on that sentiment would be far too complex. Either there was some sort of language learning—

No. There was someone *in* this boss; someone fighting her, which meant it was someone who was inside the game's programming.

Which meant someone was fucking with her.

The realization flashed through her, and Gracie's eyes narrowed. But as much as she wanted to run this person through with her serrated sword, she wasn't going to show all of her cards just yet. She circled, settling into a fighting stance and watching the giant.

He wanted to play using lore? Then that's how they would play.

"So," she said evenly. "A claimant? What does that mean? *Answer me.*"

The giant laughed and attacked again. He was quicker on his feet than she would have expected, launching into motion with a feral sort of grace. Gracie's character ran into the shield this time as she tried to get away from him.

Trapped and gasping despite herself at the sight of

something so huge bearing down on her, she brought her sword up on instinct, angled down and slashing up, aimed to catch the vulnerable places below armor. Something must have connected, because the giant bellowed and his overhand strike went wild, hitting the shield while Gracie ran for freedom.

This time she didn't wait for him to attack or taunt her. She whirled to attack at once, and her sword connected again with the outside of his leg. Then, even as he turned, she closed on him. You didn't want to be within striking range of your opponent, of course, but that could just as easily mean staying *inside* his range as *outside* it.

And armed as he was with a whip, his range encompassed everything from the tips of his fingers to the edges of the shield—meaning inside was pretty much her only bet.

He was laughing, a sound like a death rattle that made her want to hack her lungs out.

"Clever," he rasped. "She's so clever, the girl who would be queen."

Well, at least now she knew what she was supposed to be the claimant for—a crown, presumably.

Or maybe an even bigger sword that the team could make *new* dick jokes about.

This time she was the one who didn't waste time with answers. She fought for all she was worth, hacking and slashing, and once or twice slamming her sword down to generate threat simply by habit. She had never fought a duel in this world, instead working with party members she tried to shield from enemy attacks.

"Come on, Gracie." She muttered it aloud. "Get it together. It's not a party, it's just you."

Which, unfortunately, meant it was just her and her piddly DPS. She was made to survive, not take down enemies on her own, and her usual strategy of having more hit points than any solo opponent clearly wasn't going to work here.

Not for the first time, she wished that video games allowed her to make one perfect hit; sever an Achilles tendon, for instance, or open the femoral artery. It just seemed unfair that she was less than waist-high on this opponent and she couldn't take him out at the knees.

It was just a good thing she wasn't a Piskie, or she'd be resorting to chopping off his toes one by one.

"Clever," her opponent said again. The sound echoed, not unlike her own voice. "A queen *should* be clever."

"Yeah, yeah, sure. What's this about being a queen?" His compliments were tinged with mockery, and she was in no mood to listen to them. "'Long May She Reign,' right? What does that mean?" *Answer me. Whoever you are behind those pixels, answer me, goddammit!*

"It means your reign will be unshakeable...*if you can take the throne.*" The giant had drawn back.

"*What* throne?" Gracie went to charge him, then thought better of it. She could just picture that flaming knife cutting through her armor like butter. "*Answer* me, damn you!"

He laughed again, and she was sure that this was no program. There was someone in there, and they were amused beyond measure.

"So angry. *Not* a good trait in a—"

"Oh, *shut* up!" Gracie attacked in a whirl before they could recover. Now that she knew they were human, whoever they were, she was going to exploit that as much as she could. This fight didn't run on trip switches, with the reflexes faster and better honed than any human could match.

No, *this* opponent could be outsmarted.

"If I win," Gracie panted as she drove her opponent back, "you'll tell me who you are."

The laugh was delighted this time. "I might."

"You will," Gracie ground out. "Or I'm going to log out and you can flop around here by yourself, making up mysterious-sounding prophecies for your own amusement."

"No, you won't." The tone was sly, and far too familiar for a hulking giant. "You like to win, claimant. You like to win *far* too much to give up now."

"Have you ever heard the phrase, 'The only winning move is not to play'?" Gracie's arms were on fire, but she couldn't have stopped fighting if her apartment was on fire around her. Whoever was running this, they knew at least that much about her. She *wasn't* about to let this asshole win.

They were fucking with her, and she was going to make them pay for that.

She spared a glance outside the bubble and saw that the rest of the team had pressed close, watching the battle as well as they could.

"I can show you," the giant whispered now, "what chaos you have wrought in the world. I can show you your mistakes. I can let you undo them."

Gracie backed away, her chest heaving. She was so tired, and she didn't know what of this was lore or who this person was or what they wanted with her.

"Don't you want to know?" the giant whispered. He stood, waiting. "This is a place at the crossroads of Death, and it knows how much you've given to the underworld."

Gracie waited. Again, Alex's hands found hers. Again, she squeezed them.

I'm okay for now. She didn't know what to say. She didn't want to admit how creeped out she was by this. That felt like a defeat of sorts.

"Didn't you wonder what would happen when you restarted the war?" the giant asked.

Gracie's shoulders slumped. She was too tired, genuinely too exhausted, to have this fight. "What war?" she asked wearily.

The giant laughed. He waved a hand and disappeared in the shimmer of the vision he showed her. War flashed across the wavering dream images, magic coming in flashes and arrows of brilliant color and rising from the ground like specters and nightmares. Wraiths howled between the combatants, seeking souls and whistling angrily like the very wind, making Gracie question just what force made the windows shudder during storms. Perhaps her child-self had been right, and it *had* been monsters coming to eat her.

But that thought was fleeting because the ones she saw fighting were kobolds, wielding magic of water and earth, and the fae, with their bright colors like sunshine and spring flowers—and their sharp, sharp teeth. This might be a battle between the lesser races, as the Aosi had named them, but it was no less vicious for all that. The two armies were hell-bent on destroying one another.

As unbearable as it was, the image faded too soon. In its place was the silent battlefield.

And silent was worse. Now, the demons who had waited here at the altars could be seen drifting among the dead bodies, blood trailing from their half-formed mouths, long fingers reaching inside armor and flesh to pull out still-warm hearts.

"The war was over," the giant's voice said. It rumbled deep in her bones. "It was done, and there was peace. Then you gave the kobolds a weapon."

Gracie shook. It was a game, she told herself. It was a game; it wasn't real. None of this was real.

But it *felt* terribly real. She remembered the kobolds hanging back outside the door of the tomb, and the fae waiting inside. She had thought she was helping them, and instead, she had given them…what?

This. This *war*.

The vision followed a demon. This one did not stop to eat. It prowled, swinging its head back and forth like a blind, half-aware predator. It made the hair stand up on her arms. Onward it quested, and onward…until it came to the form of a kobold dressed in embroidered robes. Something glittered, held loosely in one limp hand.

The jewel. Gracie bit back a cry. That was how it had come to be here in the temple.

"Now you see," the giant whispered.

"Wait." Gracie grasped at straws. "This is a lie. It's been only days since I returned that jewel."

The vision vanished without a trace and the giant was back, the two of them still hidden inside their shield.

"Time moves strangely in the hills, just as it moves strangely here. If the gods had been wise, they might have used it to keep the races apart for longer. But they failed, and now the mortals will pay for it. Just as the kobolds paid for your failure."

Gracie stared at him wordlessly.

"Go on," the giant urged softly. "Ask. Ask the question."

"Can I undo it?" Gracie fumbled over the words. The death and destruction she'd seen were too much to bear. She knew it was just pixels, but that didn't matter to her right now.

"Yes." The giant was smiling now. "Yes. In this place, anything is possible. In this place, you can turn souls away from the realms of the dead. You can undo what was done."

"Then I want to—"

Gracie stopped. She shook her head, trying to think. She was so tired. Sweat was drying on her skin, making her shiver. Was it her, or was this too easy?

The images kept playing in her mind, blood running over the battlefield, but—

"Has the war actually happened, then?" The question came out slowly. She wasn't sure if this was the right question, but it was close. This was her feeling her way around a darkened room.

The giant said nothing.

"*Has* it?" Gracie pressed.

"You exist out of time now."

"So what you showed me was a possibility, nothing more." She had the answer now, and it beat hot in her blood. Anger was rising. "If I can take back the jewel, I could do something else, too, couldn't I? That future isn't fixed."

"Those are your choices. Only those." The giant looked at her, eyes glittering behind the trailing kelp of his hair.

"I don't believe you," Gracie said. Then, straightening up, she said simply, "And I stand by what I did."

The giant laughed. "A murderer, then. A war-bringer. Enemy of peace."

"If you know so much, you saw how the kobolds were living," Gracie said. "You *saw*. So you know that the absence of war is not peace. You know that an armistice is not freedom. They'd been beaten down to *nothing*. There was no war because they were too broken for it. That's not peace. All I gave them was a possibility."

"And they used it to wreak vengeance," the giant said. "Hundreds of their own, *thousands*, died because they could not see any farther than their need for revenge. A need you fulfilled."

"I won't leave them broken!" Gracie's voice echoed so loud that she winced. "You're giving me false choices."

There was a long pause, and then a laugh. "Good. Very good. You pass the test...*Aosi*."

If they'd meant to calm her, they'd done the worst thing for that. Gracie would have thrown the sword if she'd actually been holding one. As it was, her hands jerked into fists. "And are you done messing with us, then? Whoever you are, hiding behind there?"

"Messing with you?" The voice sounded amused. "What do you think this is?"

"A game!" Gracie spat.

There was another pause, so long that she thought the game might have frozen. That would cap off this night, she thought bitterly.

Then the giant spoke again, and his voice was quiet. "*Nothing* is just a game. No virtue is wasted, and no cruelty is either. *I warned them.*" He turned to leave but glanced back. "And no," he said. "I'm not done with you yet."

He vanished, as did the shield, and Gracie looked around. A triumphant sound and a swirl of golden particles announced her victory, such as it was, and the completion of several new achievements. Everyone was staring at her.

"Gracie?" Jay asked.

"*That* was weird," Gracie said.

"If even *you* think that, it really must have been," Kevin joked. "You'll have to tell me what happened so I can write it up."

Gracie looked toward where the giant had stood. "I don't even *know* what happened. But, guys, it seemed like there was actually someone behind that giant. It was a human talking to me."

"What did he say?" Jay asked urgently.

Before Gracie could answer, Ushanas made a sudden exclamation.

"Callista—Gracie?"

"Yeah?" Gracie didn't think she could take another surprise just now.

"Your rank just climbed," Ushanas said. "You're number seven now."

CHAPTER TWENTY-FOUR

"Thanks." Jay gave a smile and a nod to the deliveryman and headed back into his apartment, balancing the pizza as he grabbed a roll of paper towels. It was 10PM—hardly a reasonable time to be eating.

He smiled bitterly. It wasn't like he needed to keep a normal schedule for anything.

He sighed. With that reminder, the pizza didn't look quite as appetizing. He rubbed his forehead before picking up a piece and mechanically taking a bite. He hadn't eaten all day, and he knew he needed to.

On the other side of the room, his headset was blinking. He put down the pizza and went over to put the heads up back on.

"Hey again."

"Are you already done?" Gracie asked in surprise.

"Well, no." Jay looked in the direction of the pizza box, but all he could see was a vista of gently waving tall grass. "I'll, uh, I'll eat later."

"Come on," Gracie said sternly. "You have to eat."

"Are you normally this much of a slave-driver?" Jay joked.

"Of course. Haven't you seen me in raids? I'm always ordering people around." Gracie's character made finger quotes as she mockingly imitated herself. "'Don't stand in the fire.' 'Make sure you stay close enough to Mirra to get healed.' 'Don't draw all the threat, you're squishy.' I'm the worst."

Despite himself, Jay laughed.

"Ha! Made you laugh! Damn, I'm good." Gracie was laughing too. "Seriously, though, why don't we just to do a normal video chat like Knect? That way you can eat—"

"You mean, you can make sure I eat," Jay muttered. His stomach growled disloyally. "But fine. I have Knect. My handle is jaythomas; super-original. I'll log on and then go get my pizza."

"Cool!" Gracie seemed very pleased with herself. "I'll give you a call in a minute. I just have to log in."

Jay grumbled as he logged out of *Metamorphosis* and took off his VR rig, but the grumbling was halfhearted. In reality, he was pleased that his friends cared enough to check up on him. He might not have a job, he thought, or any prospect of a job coming down the pipeline, but at least he had friends.

He still felt a little bit like shit, but he reminded himself that things like this were exactly why *Metamorphosis* was so important.

He grabbed the pizza, headed back to the couch, and paused for a moment before he accepted the video call. His finger hovered above the button. A moment ago, he had been focused on nothing more than pizza and beating himself up about his lack of a job, but in a flash, he realized that he was about to *see* Gracie for the first time.

He stared at the ringing call for far too long, unable to make himself press the button. He told himself sternly just to do it. What was he afraid of? His mind resolutely refused to let him answer that question.

In the end, it was annoyance at himself that prompted him to stab his finger down. He held his breath as the call connected—

Only to see an empty couch and a blank wall. The mixture of relief and amusement at his own stupidity made him guffaw.

"Sorry!" a female voice called from offscreen, barely picked up by the speakers. "I decided to get myself a snack while you were getting your food." All Jay could think was that the voice sounded surprisingly normal. After knowing Gracie only through her Aosi character, he had gotten used to the strange, echoey voice. But a human voice worked far better with the way she talked.

See? Jay asked himself. *Nothing to be afraid of.* He took a big bite of pizza as he heard Gracie say, "Sorry, sorry, sorry, sorry!"

Then she appeared on the screen, and he choked on his pizza.

In his head, he always pictured her as her character. He knew it was ridiculous. Obviously she didn't have blue skin, and she wasn't seven feet tall. From the beginning, he had told himself sternly that she didn't look like that. Hell, in the beginning, he had thought she was a dude. When he had thought about what she might actually look like, his mind had to run the gamut of height, hair color, face shape, and race. He had told himself that he was ready for her to look like anything.

Except for being a dead ringer for her character.

Gracie settled herself on the couch, carefully balancing a plate with two sandwiches and a veritable mountain of potato chips. She was tall and slim, with the sort of body Jay had always assumed didn't really exist. She swept long golden brown hair back over her shoulder with her free hand and looked up at the screen with a smile.

"Hey! Wow, it's nice to actually meet you." She waved. As Jay continued to say nothing, she frowned. "I think the video froze. One sec." She laughed. "You're stuck mid-chew. Ugh, this always happens. I swear, it's a miracle we're able to play *Metamorphosis* without all dying by lag. Come on, Wi-Fi, I believe in you!"

"Um." Jay managed to close his mouth.

"Oh, there you are. Hi!" Gracie waved.

"Uh, hi." Did his voice always sound like this? All squeaky? He couldn't feel his hands.

Gracie frowned as she chewed a bite of her sandwich. She swallowed with a gulp. "You okay? Jay?"

"Uh…" Jay reflected that he normally knew so many words. Why could he not think of a single one of them?

"Hellooooooo." Gracie was grinning. "You look like you saw a ghost, man."

That, at least, gave Jay a lie he couldn't work with. He embraced it gratefully. "You look *a lot* like your character. Only, you know, not blue. It's just a little weird."

"Oh. Sure." She looked confused.

Abruptly, it was just too much. Jay could see it all unfolding in his mind's eye. He looked forward to their meetings in-game and relished the jokes and the conversation, and he had been reasonably sure that she felt the same, but now that she knew what he looked like, everything was going to be different.

There was no way that a chick who looked like Gracie would want to hang out with someone who was painfully average—and that description was being generous.

"You know, I just realized I have to go." Jay forced a smile. "I'll talk to you later." When she said nothing, his smile took on a bitter edge. "See you."

"Jay." Her voice was devoid of emotion, but he could tell there was a storm coming. "You want to tell me what's going on?"

"It's not important," he said flatly.

"Given that you went from being in a fairly good mood to looking like you got hit by a truck and you hate me, I'm going to believe that it *is* important." Gracie sounded angry.

"What do you want me to say?" Jay knew his voice was rising, but he wasn't able to stop it. He didn't want to. He'd been through this so many times over the years, and for once, he wanted the girl to know how it felt. "You look like some crazy—I don't know, *supermodel*—and I'm me."

"What the fuck, man?" Gracie shook her head. "What are you even talking about?"

"I'm *talking* about the fact that you're out of my league." Jay put down the piece of pizza. He didn't want it anymore.

She stared at him for a long moment.

"What?" Jay challenged her. "Nothing to say to that fact?"

She looked away for a moment, and when she looked

back, he was surprised to see that she was absolutely furious.

"What would you like me to say?" She bit the words off. "That games like *Metamorphosis* are important because people judge you on your abilities, not on what you look like? Not on all the superficial shit that doesn't matter?"

"Yeah," Jay shot back. "So people don't just write you off."

"Uh-huh." She gave him a smile just as bitter as his own and threw down the gauntlet: "And what the fuck did *you* just do?"

Jay stopped and blinked. "Look, that's not the same." He shook his head. "I mean, when people won't associate with you anymore because you're not what they want."

"Says the guy who was about to sign off!" Gracie's jaw was set, and to his surprise, tears were glittering in her eyes.

"Gracie—"

"No." She cut him off with a swipe of her hands and wiped her eyes. "God, I *hate* crying. Fuck this. Look, you can go If you want, but you're being a huge hypocrite. You want to know something? Yeah, being reasonably good-looking makes things easier in general. I'm not going to pretend that isn't true. But it also means I've had more than my share of trouble trying to find a group I could just do geeky stuff with. I was so damned happy to find *Metamorphosis*. To find people who cared about each other, people who judged me based on how I made them laugh and how I tanked, not on how they assumed I would behave or how they thought I owed it to them to behave just because they found me attractive."

Jay stared blankly at her.

"I was scared to suggest video chatting," Gracie said angrily, "but I told myself not to be stupid. I told myself that we knew each other well enough now. That we'd been through enough together that you wouldn't just write me off." She paused, and then said, her voice very small, "And then you did, like the rest of the time we had spent together didn't even matter."

Jay swallowed.

There was silence, then Gracie challenged him: "Well?"

She sounded like she was going to cry, and part of him was angry, but he kept hearing in his head, "*And then you did.*" Those words had clearly cost her to say. She had wanted to say something angry, but instead, she had told him the truth.

So he told her the truth in return. "Look, *Metamorphosis* was important to me because people have written me off for not being attractive enough. They can dress it up however they want, but that's why. It's just that… Well, you look like your character, and I don't look like mine. The second I saw you, I thought, 'Well, that's it. She's just going to write you off.'"

She swallowed. "Jay? Those people who wrote you off… were they friends like we are?"

"No," Jay admitted. "But you don't get it. You *can't* get it—"

"No, *you* don't get it." She shook her head. "Listen to me for a second. I'm in Las Vegas. Everything here is beautiful. The buildings are beautiful, the fountains are beautiful, everywhere is full of beautiful people. It's part of the show, and there's nowhere like here, and yeah, I kind of love it.

But it's not a perfect place. Underneath all the sparkly dresses and the makeup and the plush rugs and the money, people are just the same. Las Vegas is about putting on a show, and that's what appearances are—they're a show. They're a mask." When he frowned, she shook her head in frustration. "Everything you said was *true*," she said, waving her hands. "About what's real and what's not. What's *real* is the sort of friendship we built online. In the game. And I know it's scary for you to trust that I will stick around, but please, try to understand how scary it is for me to trust that *you'll* stick around. And for the fucking record?" She gave him a look with a capital L. "You've got a serious complex about your looks. You look perfectly fucking fine."

Before he had time to think, Jay was laughing. He wanted to be cynical, but this was Gracie. The way she spoke, the way she gestured—all of it was so familiar. She didn't have any time for bullshit, and despite everything, he was beginning to believe she was telling the truth.

He gave her a nod, then groaned and dropped his face into his hand. "Ugh, I'm sorry."

"Nah." She sounded sad. "It sounds like you came by your pathology honestly. I'm sorry people suck, but, Jay, I'm not going anywhere. You've helped me through some hard stuff, and right now you're going through some hard stuff too. I want you to be happier. I care about you. I'm here for screwing around in the game, and I'm here just to talk if that would help. Or not, if it wouldn't help."

Jay felt something unusually warm and relaxing spreading through his chest, and had a moment of panic where he wondered if he was having a stroke or possibly a heart attack. Did those feel warm? He gave a small, self-conscious laugh "I, uh—"

"Proposal," Gracie interrupted.

"Er, yes?"

"What if we were just done with this and never discussed it again?"

Jay finally chuckled. "I like your style. Yeah, let's do that."

"*Good.*" She sounded relieved. "So, ready for the new content drop?"

"Yeah." Jay took a bite of pizza and tried to decide whether to tell her where he used to work. "I just feel like —" He heard a door in the background of the call. "Is someone there?"

"Just Alex," Gracie said. "Or a home invader, I guess. Oh, no, it's Alex. That's a relief."

"What's this about home invaders?" Alex asked from offscreen. "And are you *not* playing *Metamorphosis*? Have you been replaced by a pod person?"

"I'm talking to Jay," Gracie said with great dignity. She pointed at the screen. "Say hi."

"Hi?" Jay said as Alex stuck his head around the screen.

"Oh, hey." Alex waved, and Jay had the disgusted thought that it was apparently a whole apartment full of ridiculously good looking people. Luckily Jay didn't have to come up with anything to say because Alex said to both of them, "So, have you heard?"

"Uh…" Gracie shook her head. "Heard what?"

"Oh, my God." Alex looked at Gracie and Jay. "Seriously? How am I the first one to know about this? You both have the day off!"

"Yes, thank you for reminding us that we're both jobless," Gracie said with mock-bitterness. "You're too kind. Really."

"Whoops," Alex said. "Okay, wrong note to hit; I see that now. Well, maybe this will distract you... They dropped the new content patch early."

"*What*?" Gracie and Jay said in unison. Jay scrambled to open his browser and load the *Metamorphosis* homepage, and from the frantic typing on the other end, he guessed that Gracie was doing the same thing.

"Whoa!" He heard her murmur. "This is freaking beautiful."

"It is." Jay just couldn't shake the thought that something was wrong.

A moment later, his suspicions were justified.

"Oh, *shit*," Gracie said.

Oh, no. Jay forced himself to be calm. "What is it?"

"They changed the rules," Gracie said. "Now you can go in with your own gear. If we were even close to being on the same footing as the other guilds before, we're not anymore."

CHAPTER TWENTY-FIVE

"*F uck.*" Gracie slumped back on the couch. "Fuck!"

All it had taken was this one tiny nudge for the whole house of cards she had built to come tumbling down. Who had she been kidding? She had known from the start that the ranking and the money that came with it weren't really hers to keep. She had known it was unlikely that they could ever manage to clear a dungeon before any of the big guilds.

Yet, somehow she had talked herself into believing they could do it, and that maybe she could do this for a living instead of getting another crappy job.

She had thought she was so much smarter than all of the patrons in her old job because she saw the true game behind the façade. When she started playing *Metamorphosis Online*, she had thought the same thing.

Instead, all her experience had done was make her arrogant. She had thought she was so much smarter than everyone else, but she had fallen into exactly the same trap as them.

What an idiot.

Alex saw the look on her face, and he glanced at her computer screen and looked at Jay for a moment as well. "Guys? Can I say something?"

"What." It wasn't really a question. Gracie wasn't in the mood to hear inspirational shit. She could hear the resignation in her own voice.

"Look, it was always going to be a long shot," Alex said. He looked between the two of them again and gave them an encouraging smile. "Isn't that kind of the fun thing about something like this? You take a long shot; shoot for something you have no hope in hell of winning."

"No hope in hell?" Gracie demanded. "Thanks a lot, man."

"Oh, come on." Alex threw up his hands. "Isn't that the fun of it? Isn't that part of why everyone in our guild is so cool? Everyone told me I had to settle down with my girlfriend and get married. After the divorce, everyone told me I had to start dating again and get married so I could have kids. I didn't listen. I came out here, and I'm enjoying the hell out of my life. Gracie, your parents wanted you to be a stockbroker for a CEO or something and marry a douche like Kyle. You didn't listen, and you're much happier because you didn't listen. Jay... Look, I don't know you all that well yet, man, but you didn't put up with the bullshit of your boss telling you that you had to do something wrong. That's what I like about you guys; you aren't afraid to head off in your own direction. Life can be grim enough even when we get all of the fun we can out of it. Don't make it even grimmer by avoiding that."

Gracie chewed on a fingernail. Despite her bad mood, she had to admit that Alex was making a good point.

"And just so I'm clear," Alex's voice held the faintly mischievous tone Gracie knew so well, "why exactly did we decide to give up on this without even trying?"

Gracie shot him a glare. As far as she was concerned, he had absolutely no right to be making such good points, especially not if he was going to look so goddamned smug about it. Indeed, Alex was practically radiating smugness as he got up and drifted out of the room.

"Damn that man," Gracie muttered. "I hate when he has a point."

"Yeah." Jay was clearly trying to sound annoyed, but Gracie could hear a laugh bubbling up in his voice. "He's a real asshole, your roommate."

"You just wait," Gracie said darkly. "Next he'll offer to get everyone online so we can do a run."

"Already on it!" Alex called from the next room.

Gracie gestured in his direction as if to say, "I told you so." To her surprise, Jay wasn't laughing anymore. He was looking into the distance with the grimmest expression she had ever seen.

"What's up?" Gracie asked him.

"So..." Jay sighed. "There's something I haven't told you."

Gracie stared at him blankly. She could not for the life of her think of what he might need to tell her. After all, it wasn't as if the members of their group knew each other in real life, right?

She had a crazy worry that he was going to do something like to tell her he was a long-lost sibling, but before she had too much time to think, he heaved a breath and said, "I worked for Dragon Soul Productions. The thing I told you about, where I got fired because I wouldn't do something that was the wrong thing to do? They wanted me to undo all of the ranking points you got from the kobold quest. And then, when they couldn't do anything, they tried to ban your account."

Gracie stared at him. Whatever she had expected, it wasn't this. It was so out of left field that she literally couldn't think of anything to say.

"Wait…" she said finally. "Wait." Then, still confused, "Wait, *what*?" Out of the corner of her vision, she could see that Alex had drifted back into the room. He was staring at the computer with an oddly intent expression, as if he didn't believe what he had just heard.

Gracie was with him on that one.

Jay had sunk his head into his hands. He spoke now without looking up, his voice muffled. "You triggered an Easter egg quest. Forgot who got ousted from the company —Harry. We think it was his work. The thing is, your character isn't under their control now—"

"Back up," Gracie said. She held up a hand. "Wait. Go back. So, when we first met after the kobold quest—"

"Oh, I didn't know about any of that stuff then," Jay told her. "Honestly, I was just intrigued by the conversation we'd had—" He broke off and ran his hands through his hair. "Right. Back even farther. In order to fine-tune the AI, we had live people behind some of the NPCs. I don't know if you remember speaking to the hill warden?"

Inspiration hit Gracie like a bolt of lightning. "That was *you*?"

"Yeah." Jay looked halfway between proud and terrified. "Look, it was just so that we could get an idea about what sort of questions players would have. It wasn't supposed to be creepy or anything—"

"I didn't think it was creepy," Gracie interrupted. "I mean, it makes sense. Wow." She frowned. "Wait, what was it about our conversation that interested you?"

"You cared about the world," Jay said simply. "You enjoyed it the way I had hoped people would enjoy it. I poured my heart and soul into making that game. I had also stood on that hill and talked to a lot of players, and none of them really cared the way you did. I guess I just wanted to watch you discover all of it, and after we talked when I was Anders, I really liked hanging out with you."

Gracie felt her cheeks go hot. The truth was, she had come to look forward to speaking to Jay every day. When she saw that he had signed onto the game, she always smiled.

When she had been on her date with Kyle, she had wished that she was sitting there talking to Jay instead, because they would've been laughing and having a great time instead of her getting insulted for what she wanted to do with her life.

"Gracie?"

She realized he had kept talking while she'd been thinking about—

Her cheeks flamed. "Sorry." She cleared her throat hastily. She couldn't tell him what she'd been thinking about. "I really liked hanging out with you, too. I'm glad that you—" She broke off, mentally berating herself for being glad. "You lost your job because of me," she said quietly. "That's not okay."

"It's not," Jay said after a moment. "But it wasn't because of you. It was because they didn't want to lose corporate sponsorships, so they were willing to just throw your account under the bus to make a quick fix for a problem they didn't understand."

"Maybe it made sense to—" Gracie started, but Jay interrupted her.

"It's sloppy," he said. "It's sloppy in a way that hurts random bystanders, and they knew that, and they still did it. That would already have been bad, but it was worse because I could see you going above and beyond for people who weren't even real. You would do more for pixels than they would for actual people, and the whole reason I had worked for them was to help build a place for *people*. I couldn't stay, Gracie."

That, she understood. She nodded at him. It was a commonality in their group, she realized now. On the day she had met Alex and she had not been sure whether to move in, she had noticed how he'd picked up the paper on the front steps and brought it to his neighbor, an older man who would have had trouble navigating the stairs. Those little instinctive acts were something she had seen from every member of the group.

And those acts meant a lot to her. This was what she had never been able to articulate to people like Vince and Kyle: that how you treated someone should not depend on the superficial qualities that had been assigned to you by the world. That you should be kind when it was possible, not to get ahead because the person you were being kind to was important, but because being kind was important.

Jay shook his head. "And this...the gear? They're doing it specifically to screw us over. Your ranking is an embarrassment to them. If you were to get a month-first, you'd climb even higher in the rankings. They changed the rules to make sure the other guilds would have the advantage." He gave a snort of laughter. "You know, just in case I thought I had made the wrong decision and they were actually reasonable, moral people, they have confirmed they aren't."

Gracie laughed as well, but she sobered quickly. "God, I feel so stupid. I told myself that ranking wasn't real, but part of me still saw that number on the bank statement and thought maybe I could make a living at this. Maybe I could get out of my shitty job and not have to get another one just like it."

Jay sat back, his eyes narrowed in thought. "I don't think it was stupid," he said. "In fact, I think it might still work."

"They're never going to let me..." Gracie protested, but he shook his head.

"They can't stop you," he said flatly. "They tried to ban your account, Gracie. They tried to *delete* your account, but it didn't work. The game decided you're meant to be there, and you know what? Even if it weren't for all the things you've done—the things that made us all want to be in your group—the fact would still be that you're a fucking good player. You *get* the combat in a way I've never seen before."

Gracie flushed with pleasure. "I love it," she admitted. "I

love learning all the mechanics and just flowing on instinct."

"It's not instinct with you," Jay said. "It's calculations. I can hear you mutter while you're learning the dynamics of different enemies. You're calculating the odds."

"*Never* tell me the odds," Gracie quipped.

Jay laughed. "You know what, then? Let's do it. *Fuck the odds.*"

Gracie started to smile. "Fuck the odds," she mused. "Now there's a battle cry. I like it."

"Guys?" Alex stuck his head around the door. "Everyone is logging in."

"Cool," Gracie said. "Let me just order some food and—"

Alex interrupted her. "No time." He shook his head.

Gracie realized what had happened at the same time that Jay did. He swore, and she uttered one word: "Who?"

"Demon Syndicate," Alex said. "Someone must have given them a heads-up because they're wearing a very weird assortment of gear and they have a strange group, and they went in about five minutes after the content dropped."

Gracie launched into motion. "Jay—"

"On it," he said at once. "See you in-game."

He signed off, and Gracie began putting on her VR outfit. She looked up to see Alex watching her.

"So you've decided to give it a shot." He looked pleased.

"Fuck the odds," Gracie told him. "These people want to screw me over? They want to change the rules? That just means they're going to look even more stupid when we win anyway."

CHAPTER TWENTY-SIX

T had bounced on the balls of his feet and gave a last experimental full-body shrug to see how the VR suit was situated. Everything seemed good, and he grinned.

Outside his VR world, he and the rest of the team stood in a series of taped-off squares in a little gymnasium. As a sponsored team, they had a training space rented for them, with high-speed internet, snacks, and exercise equipment, as well as top-of-the-line VR suits. In addition, each of them was sporting the black pants and top that served as their uniform, emblazoned with the Brightstar logo.

When this was over, and they'd gotten the month-first badge, Brightstar would put images of their fight up on the Demon Syndicate website. The gymnasium was lit along the edges by blue neon lights, the tape and the Brightstar logo glowing under blacklights, all structured to look appealing to a generation on the cutting edge of VR, raised with the memory of TRON.

They had people beating down the door to get into Demon Syndicate these days.

Not Callista, of course. For a moment, Thad's smile slipped into a frown. Brightstar had been insistent that he try to recruit her, wanting to have as many players in the top ten as possible. Gr8p Drink was edging them out these days.

Thad hadn't wanted to do that, but he *did* want the sponsorship—and he wanted the rankings their sponsorship helped him achieve. It was all over the forums that the sponsors had persuaded Dragon Soul to allow people to bring their own gear into the dungeon run this month, and Thad wasn't surprised. Brightstar gave a lot of money to Dragon Soul. They could pull some serious strings if they wanted to, and he'd rather have them doing that for him than someone else.

So if they wanted this Callista person, he'd recruit her.

Or, that was how it was supposed to work. In reality, he'd made the offer to Callista, and she'd turned him down flat. He didn't get the sense that she was any happier about it than he was.

Now Brightstar was pissed, and Thad had something to prove: namely, that he could beat Callista's little group into the dust when it came to this month's dungeon run. That shouldn't be hard, after all. It wasn't like she would even try. She had nothing in terms of a team, just some newbies she'd picked up somewhere.

And even if she *did* try, how far would she get in a dungeon that had been built for top-level gear?

He heard whoops from his team as the opening cinematic began, and his mood dissolved. Thad had always had the ability to dial in when he needed to, and he wasn't going to let some weird recruitment issue get to him now.

He barely paid attention as the cinematic played. His mind was already running ahead to the money hitting his bank account and the flood of congratulations that were going to come in online. People on the forums had been saying for months now that the Scions of Shinra were the real top dogs and Demon Syndicate's rise was just a fluke, nothing more.

Thad was going to prove them wrong.

The cinematic cleared, and his second-in-command Envi, the guild's top healer, sidled up to him. In reality, Envi was a thirty-five-year-old man named Jamie, tall and lanky, with dirty-blond hair. In-game, however, he was an Aosi woman, pale hair and skin carrying just a hint of blue. Only his eyes were dark, so deep a blue that they looked black until the light hit them.

"You're sure about this?" Jamie asked Thad. He looked around nervously at the party they'd brought with them, composed almost entirely of fire mages. "This is a *lot* of squishies to be healing if everything goes south."

"I'm sure," Thad said.

Envi stared at him, expressionless. Even though Jamie knew Thad wasn't really the person standing in front of him, even though he knew that he was looking at an avatar whose face didn't show emotion unless Thad told it to, Jamie was looking for clues.

Thad sighed and took the time to open a private channel. "The information is good, okay?"

Jamie sighed too, the sound coming out less frustrated and more like the epic dying gasp of a Tolkien elf. "What if they're setting us up to look bad?"

"They're not," Thad promised. When Jamie sighed

again, Thad moved a little closer. It was a private channel so no one could hear them talking, but he still had the urge to whisper. "It came directly from Dragon Soul to Brightstar."

Jamie sucked in his breath. There was a pause, and Thad was just about to say that time was ticking away and they needed to go, when Jamie said quietly, "I'm not sure I like that."

Thad stared at him. His character, an Ocru male named Goolax, did his idle animation, straightening up and loosening up his shoulders. "What?" he said finally.

"Look, when we were scraping to try to find out information Dragon Soul didn't want us to know, it felt different. If they help us, it won't feel like we're actually *winning*," Jamie said. "It feels like pay to play."

"It's not different at all." Thad fought a wave of annoyance. He was a hundred percent over people who wanted to get moralistic about tiny situations. "We're not getting people killed or something here, Jamie, chill. We're just winning at a game." When Jamie said nothing, Thad almost snapped, "Who doesn't take an advantage when it's handed to them? That's just good tactics."

"I guess," Jamie said doubtfully.

"And we worked for the armor we've got," Thad pointed out. "Every other victory we've had has been because we worked hard to get good at the game. So what if we have an assist in this one, right?" He grinned. "Plus, I know you've had your eye on that new keyboard, which you can get with the cash from this run."

He'd won, and he knew it. Jamie nodded. "Yeah," the

other man said. His character's pale hair rippled in the moonlight. "Let's go smash this shit up."

"Hey, all." Gracie shrugged her shoulders and bounced on the balls of her feet, trying to burn off nervous energy. Her character was hanging in a void that looked something like a nebula, blues and purples rippling around her.

"Hey." "What up." "Yo." The team sounded engaged and excited.

"So we're really doing this, huh?" Ushanas asked.

"We're really doing this," Gracie confirmed. "Why not, right?"

There was a slight pause, then she heard Alex's voice in her ear over a private channel. "Maybe a bit more inspiring on the speech front, chief."

"Right. Whoops." Gracie's cheeks flushed. She took a moment to think while she switched back to the global channel. "The way I see it, we've pulled off some crazy things in this game, and you know why? Because *Metamorphosis Online* is set up to reward skill, and it's set up to reward people who love playing together. We have both of those things in spades."

Now there was a murmur of agreement.

"I've watched every one of you fine-tune your play style," Gracie said honestly. "You listen to feedback, and you work with your teammates so that each of you does the most you can for the group. You've learned to communicate with one another when things are going crazy—and things *do* go crazy around us, don't they?"

The team laughed.

"We've gotten to see some weird-ass parts of this game," Gracie said, talking through the laugh that was bubbling up in her chest. Her teammates started appearing in the void with her. Alex gave a wry salute, Kevin hopped and twirled as his tiny Piskie character, and Alan had Mirra whirl, admiring the way the light glinted on her robes.

"To be honest," Gracie told them, "I have no idea if what we're about to do is even the same dungeon everyone else will get."

"Oh, shit." Kevin was laughing. "She's right, isn't she? Strap in, guys! It's gonna be a surprise clusterfuck."

"And we'll have a damned lot of fun doing it," Gracie said. "Because guess what? We're going to be streaming live. People are going to be able to see how freaking cool every one of you is. People are going to be making bets on us versus Demon Syndicate, and you know what they're gonna see? That we're *better*."

The team cheered. They were nearly all here now, Freon dropping in with a wave, Lakhesis stabbing her sword into the air, and Ushanas standing quietly, clearly preparing mentally.

"All right, team huddle." Gracie beckoned them all in. "Aaaaand, everyone kneel, or Kevin's going to be staring at our junk." There was a burst of laughter as everyone sat on the floor of nothingness—a dizzying feeling—and put their hands in. Gracie felt a swell of pride in her chest. "We're good at what we do, guys. We're *really* good at it. We have fun with it too, and that's because we're here every night for *each other*. Some of you I've known for ages, some of you I've only known for a few days, but every one of you has proved yourselves. I hope you feel confident with me at the helm."

"Damn straight I do," said Jay. He gave her a nod. "To our very own Callista, who's not afraid to stand in front and get hit with maces, *definitely* not afraid to give orders, and a great friend for getting you out of your funk when you've gotten into one." He gave her a grin and, below her headset, Gracie couldn't help but grin back.

"Hear, hear." Alex clapped Gracie on the shoulder in the real world—a maneuver that involved hitting her more than once—and gave a thumbs up in-game. "Now, we're already behind, so I advise we go now," he continued. "Demon Syndicate logged in as soon as the content dropped, and they logged in with a weird party configuration. I don't know about the rest of you, but *I'm* guessing they had some inside information, huh?"

"What gave it away?" Gracie asked drily. "That, or the fact that Dragon Soul just now conveniently decided to allow players to take their gear into the dungeon runs?"

There were laughs and groans.

"She's not wrong," Jay said quietly, and although few others knew what he meant, he met Gracie's eyes and gave a quiet nod.

"So, I say we teach them a lesson," Gracie said. "You all with me?"

The group pounded their fists on the ground, high-fived one another, and gave shouts of agreement.

"Good." Gracie brought up the ready check. "Time to go catch up with the competition, then. Let's wipe the floor with them."

In the Dragon Soul offices, Sam crossed his arms over his chest and let out a deep breath. His team—Jay's former coworkers—clustered around the monitors that showed the two raids in progress.

Demon Syndicate had just loaded into the beginning of the run. A moonscape, dead rock pitted with impact craters, flickered to show the team appearing. In the distance, across a chasm of space dotted with treacherous paths and patrols of elemental creatures, stood the ruins of a massive palace.

No one was paying attention to them, though. Everyone's eyes were fixed on the second screen, where the tiny doomed team was loading in.

There was a sound behind them, and one of the employees glanced over his shoulder to do a double-take. She nudged Sam in the ribs with her elbow, and he looked back to see Dan and Dhruv watching, their faces expressionless.

Sam met Dan's eyes and then looked back at the screen. He didn't know what to say, and, to his own surprise, he felt a little bit pleased that they were so clearly annoyed. He could say honestly that he hadn't told the team to watch this run, nor had he told them that Jay was involved. Jay hadn't mentioned it, either. Everyone knew, though, and Jay had been a good supervisor.

People were pulling for him to win.

"Demon Syndicate logged in as soon as the content dropped," one of the players on Jay's team said. His name tag identified him as Gary Swiftbolt. "And they logged in with a weird party configuration. Now, I don't know about the rest of you, but *I'm* guessing they had some inside information, huh?"

Everyone watching went still, and a couple of people sucked in their breath hastily. No one was willing to look at Dan and Dhruv.

Sam was smiling now. They'd done exactly what Jay had accused them of doing—throwing all of the rankings integrity out to pander to their funders, and it was coming back to bite them in the ass. Anyone watching the stream had heard what the player said, and within an hour, it was going to be all over the forums.

"Come on," Sam said under his breath. His eyes fixed on Jay's character, then slid to the Aosi woman who was running the show. Callista, her nametag read. She had a sword that was almost as tall as she was. "Come *on*. Bring it home."

CHAPTER TWENTY-SEVEN

The void twisted and swirled around Gracie, and then, with a jolt of haptics to her feet and a crunch of frost, resolved itself into a shattered moonscape. Stars glittered overhead, thousands upon thousands of them lighting the night sky in a ripple that was somehow totally alien compared to the Milky Way.

"Whoa," she breathed, and the game made a puff of crystallized breath so realistic that she shivered and gave a little laugh. She took a few steps forward, looking around in wonder. Her footsteps crackled in the frozen dust. "Every time." Her voice was a murmur.

"Hmm?" a voice behind her asked, and she spun, clapping a hand to her chest. She had totally forgotten anyone else was there, and Jay had surprised her. He grinned and held up his hands. "Sorry, sorry. What does 'every time' mean?"

Gracie shook her head, momentarily unable to find the words. "Every time I load into a new zone," she told him finally. "Every time I even log *in*? It's just so damned beautiful that it takes my breath away. I used to read about places like this and imagine them when I was playing D&D. Now I feel like I'm really here, you know?"

"Yeah," he said after a moment, and she could hear the depth of emotion in his voice, even through the game's filters. "Yeah, I really do." He reached out to take her hand.

She reached out as well, and there was a moment of confusion as their hands passed through each other. Gracie felt her brow furrow, and then she laughed. "Ah, crap. See? This is the sort of thing that happens. It looks so real that I forgot we aren't actually here."

There was a cleared throat from behind them, and Gracie turned quickly, her cheeks heating. She was very glad for a moment that no one could see her blush in-game. She had a sense that it was Alex who'd done the throat-clearing, though, and she just *knew* there was going to be some teasing later.

Oh, God. She fought the urge to drop her head into her hands.

Luckily, she had plenty of other things to focus on—like getting through this run quickly. They were already behind, and there was no time to be sitting around and bemoaning that fact.

She looked around and did a quick check that everyone had loaded in without issues.

"All right, here's the deal," she told them. "I need you to be on-point. That means you let the tanks build threat, and you watch yours. It means you're *very* careful not to pull anything when you spread out. It means *all* DPS takes responsibility for helping the healers. If you see something weird or there's a patrol coming in, say something. We can go gambol around and wipe this thing as many times as we want in the future—just not this time."

There was a burst of laughter, and people nodded.

"You heard the woman," Alex told them. "Same time tomorrow night, we do the run with no gear."

A few suggestive whistles pierced the air and he posed, fake-flexing as if for a swimsuit competition. Gracie was more than a little tempted to take her headset off and take pictures, and she mentally cursed him for having done this at a moment when she had no time to do so.

She was pleased to see that as she took her first few steps into the dungeon, people noticed and followed at once. Alex's panther, Teef, padded along beside her. The various non-melee team members were staying in the middle of the group, with Lakhesis bringing up the rear.

No one was taking any chances.

The first elementals appeared in the distance quickly. They were patrolling in a small pack, small shimmers like tiny nebulas kicking up dust devils on this weird and alien moonscape.

The story of this dungeon was an unusual one. Not star-crossed lovers or an evil genius, but instead, a shamed general who had died with his army, and whose soul could not find rest. He had fled to this prison of his own making in the afterlife and had been driven mad by the thought of truce between the races, for it had been their wars that had destroyed so many lives.

Now he was seeking an army and was determined to take revenge on the entire world of the living.

And they were *here*, so convincingly that Gracie could almost feel the cold wind on her skin. They were here to stand against an evil that would destroy the world. She knew what her mother would say; what Kyle would say. That it wasn't real.

But it was. *No virtue is wasted,* the strange boss had told her when they fought, and Gracie believed it. Her team was here, and even if the evil they fought didn't exist in the "real" world, choosing to stand for what was right wasn't wasted.

She believed that wholeheartedly.

As the elementals drew closer, she turned to make a last, silent ready-check of the team. Everyone nodded to her, and Gracie took a deep breath, drew her weapon, and charged. At the last moment, she went into a spin and down into a crouch, lashing out so the sword bit through the group of elementals like a scythe, its magical blade cutting into them and draining them of their power.

"What up?" Gracie greeted them. "Hear you're trying to destroy the world. Can't let you do that."

"Gracie's monologues to trash mobs are one of my favorite things about this game," Freon commented as he loosed an ice bolt that took one elemental in the chest. "She really wants them to *get* why she's killing them."

"Well, sure." Gracie threw her sword up in the air, slammed her fist down in a shock blast, and caught the sword as it came back down. "Otherwise, it's just rude, you know?" The elementals shrieked and converged on her, surrounding her with a dizzying array of colors as they tore at her. "Like, for instance, right *now* I'm going to assume they're trying to explain the same thing to me. Otherwise, they're definitely being dicks about this."

"I don't know," Alex said contemplatively. A brace of

flaming arrows whistled by. "We did come into *their* house and start killing them. That seems kind of like a dick move on our part, right?"

"Alex, focus. They're trying to destroy the world." Gracie drove her sword forward and grinned as one of the elementals disappeared into nothingness with a last shriek of anger. "Anyone with plans of killing *everyone* doesn't get to complain about people trying to stop them."

"Sure, sure."

At Gracie's side, Jay slammed his fist into the last elemental, who disappeared in a puff of energy. She could hear him breathing heavily. He nodded at her, all business now, and she looked around.

"Mirra, tell me what's what."

"Nothing unusual for trash mobs so far in terms of DPS," Alan reported, "but most of their damage is actually from DOTs, so if anyone with dispels could cycle through those, it would take a bit off our plates on the healing side."

People nodded.

"Ushanas?" Gracie asked.

"Demon Syndicate had some good intel," Ushanas said. He didn't sound too happy. "I'm not sure how useful I'm gonna be."

"Hang in there," Gracie said. "Don't write yourself off yet. All right, team, let's keep going, and let me know if you think we're going to get random pulls. Any heads-up is useful."

They proceeded across the moonscape quickly, only once winding up with a surprise patrol. Gracie's health dipped dangerously low at one point, prompting a brief flurry of shouted accusations among the others, but a stern talking to kept them on-point, and quick thinking from Jay and Alan kept her alive.

It was an exercise in trust, Gracie thought, to be the tank. You had to go out there and face down the monsters, believing that your team would have your back. Then again, she supposed it took just as much trust to be the healer and know you couldn't take down the mobs on your own, or be the DPS and know that you could neither heal nor soak up the brunt of the damage.

Teamwork wasn't optional here.

Between the moonscape and the floating ruins of the castle, there was a tiny, isolated island from which a beacon of blue-white light seemed to stab into the sky.

And there seemed to be no way to get to it. Gracie stared at the gap between the edge of the moonscape and the floating hunk of rock. Now that she was at the edge, she was very aware that they were on a tiny hunk of rock tumbling in the middle of a nebula.

It made her realize that she didn't know which way was up.

Or if there *was* an up. She gulped.

She edged toward the end of the ground. She could see this going one of two ways: either they could walk just fine on the nothingness, or they were going to lose their tank.

Ushanas must have had the same thought because the fire mage motioned for Gracie to stay back. "I'm clearly the most expendable at this point," he told her. He peered into the void, gave a little shudder that his suit captured quite well, and stepped out onto nothing.

His foot sank a few inches, then seemed to find a surface, and Gracie let out her breath in a whoosh. A few people started laughing, and one or two had their hands pressed over their chests.

"Fuuuuuck," Alex breathed. "Oh, *fuck*, that was scary."

Gracie gave a chortle and edged out to follow Ushanas. Even knowing that the ground was there, it was still insanely hard to force herself to keep going. Every instinct of her very human brain was screaming at her to go back to someplace nice and normal and not do crazy things like walk around in space.

Thankfully, by the time they got to the island, most of the adrenaline had faded and the group was back to joking and laughing. Gracie wondered if they remembered that people might be watching the live stream, but she decided not to remind them.

The last thing they needed was for anyone to get all up in their own head.

They had barely taken a few steps onto the floating island, however, when the beam of light *roared.*

"YOU SEEK TO STOP THE GENERAL?" Light blazed and a figure resolved itself, arms spread, head thrown back in the column of power. "YOU WILL BE THE FIRST TO DIE!"

Ice began to rain down, the ground turning slick with it and shards crashing into the rocky surface.

"Ushanas!" Gracie yelled. "I think you're up!"

"Oh, *shit!*" Ushanas was laughing, but it was barely a moment before a fireball went whizzing over to catch the figure in the chest. There was a scream and the beam of light disappeared, leaving only a white-robed Aosi, his hands raised as he readied another spell. Ushanas settled into a crouch. "Ice versus fire, bitch!"

"Melee!" Gracie yelled. "Get to the squishy! Ranged DPS, any time now!"

The team yelled their agreement, and arrows and bolts of magic began to whizz overhead as Gracie and the others charged. They were halfway there when walls of ice sprang up, making the team flinch instinctively. The surface of the ground, designed to be slick, kept them moving until they skidded into the walls, and they took far more damage than Gracie was comfortable with.

"Fuck!" Alan used his major group heal. "All right, try not to do that again!"

"Aye aye!" Gracie called back. "Sorry, man!"

"No way to know that was coming; totally get it."

Gracie turned back to begin hacking at the ice. It shuddered when magic and weapons hit it and collapsed a few moments later. The group cheered, and Lakhesis signaled to Gracie that she would go ahead, triggering the next walls of ice with only one set of damage.

Gracie and Lakhesis advanced by turns, and it wasn't long before they had reached their target, who had been calling down curses on the whole group. He sneered at them, spreading his hands.

"You want to repeat the mistakes of the past." His face was twisted with fury. "Better the world die in fire quickly than sink once more into warfare. You would bring them suffering, but I will not let you do that. *DIE!*"

He punctuated the shout with a bolt of ice that shot over Gracie's head, Gracie having ducked instinctively as his hands opened to release the spell. Before he could do the same again, she had charged him and was swinging her sword.

"I have to ask," she called as he stumbled back, "does *anyone* ever obey that suggestion?"

"Can't blame the dude for trying, I guess," Jay chimed in, executing a jumping kick that kept their adversary from regaining his footing. "But maybe they've just gotten a little out of touch up here."

Gracie laughed and slammed her sword down like an axe, cheering when the Aosi stumbled, fell, and went still.

"WHOO! Okay." She was panting. "One boss down, probably one to go. And..." She paused. "Didn't Demon Syndicate go in with, like, eight ice mages? Bet they didn't fare too well with this one."

"WHAT THE FUCK?" Thad demanded. He stared around at the island and felt cold disbelief settling into his chest. Three of their mages lay dead, and the gear of the rest of them had taken significant damage.

And apparently, there were no resurrections in this dungeon.

"What the *fuck*?" he said again for emphasis. He looked at Envi. "What the fuck was that?"

Envi said nothing but he could feel the silent reproach.

Thad dropped his head into his hands for a moment. They had to keep going. He had to get hold of himself and keep going. He was beginning to wonder if Envi hadn't been correct, and Demon Syndicate was being set up.

Because what else explained this?

"What the hell was that?" Dhruv demanded. He looked around at the group, his eyes settling on Sam. "Well?"

Sam felt a jolt of adrenaline. He was in it now.

To his surprise, he didn't feel like running and hiding. He understood at last how Jay had felt when he'd faced down Dan and Dhruv the other day. At the time, Sam had wondered in despair why Jay wouldn't just do the smart thing and do what his bosses wanted.

Now he understood.

And he could see where the limits of their power actually were.

"What?" he asked as innocently as he could. He had to be careful not to overplay this. Open mockery wasn't going to get him anywhere.

"We asked you for specifications," Dhruv said dangerously.

Dan cut him off with a gesture. "We understood that this monthly run featured fire, not ice."

"We submitted the full specs," Sam said. "I prepared all of the documents and looked them over myself."

"You said the boss used *fire*," Dhruv said through gritted teeth.

"He does," Sam said, still radiating innocence. *You didn't ask about the* first *boss. Just the last one,* he thought. He didn't say that, though. That would be pushing it.

There was a long pause while the two founders stared at him, then Dhruv swore and slammed out of the room. Dan gave Sam a long look.

"Are there any more surprises?" he asked evenly.

"Everything is to the specifications I sent," Sam said, taking refuge in that one unassailable fact: he had given them a chance to see exactly what he was doing. He hadn't hidden anything from them.

Dan paused, then nodded quietly and followed Dhruv.

When he was gone, the team let out their breath.

"Let me guess," Evan said. He'd sat next to Jay, and had taken it hard when Jay had quit. There was a smile beginning around his mouth. "They don't know about the other part, either, do they?"

Sam gave him an innocent look. "Everything is to the specifications I sent," he repeated with an elaborate shrug.

And, he thought with savage satisfaction, *he* wasn't cheating. He was doing the opposite of cheating. The things he'd built in would level the playing field, not put his team ahead. No one would be able to say that he'd given anyone an advantage.

He'd have to hope that was enough to save his job.

CHAPTER TWENTY-EIGHT

The group waited only as long as they needed to for their health to come up and their cooldowns to finish, then set off again toward the ruins of the castle. This time it was Freon, to general laughter, who decided to go first.

"I can't believe we let Ushanas do this last time," the Ocru rumbled before stepping out onto the nothingness. He paused, his foot still up. "I'm just going to put it out there that I'll be *pissed* if what worked last time doesn't work this time."

"Coward," Ushanas said, chuckling.

Freon stepped out, pretended to fall, and then chortled as everyone gasped and reached out to grab him. Their hands shot through the space where he was standing, and he clasped his hands around his sides as he laughed.

"You're an *ass*," Gracie told him affectionately. "Don't give us a heart attack like that again!"

"Oh, it was worth it." Freon stood up, clearly wiping his

eyes in real life. "So worth it, I tell ya. Okay, let's go get this sumbitch."

"Now you're talking." Gracie walked with him across the second expanse of the void, trying to keep her eyes fixed on the palace and not on the nothing beneath her feet.

She wasn't outstandingly successful, but it helped to focus on the building. She kept her eyes resolutely raised, and as she got closer, picked out the shattered wrecks of towers. Some were floating, their columns destroyed but the vantage points still hovering above, while others had been knocked to the ground to sprawl in scattered heaps of rubble.

Where the castle still stood, magic glittered among the stones, something flickering in the mortar and shining faintly in the gaps of missing stones. Where the castle was broken, the magic sputtered and sparked like a shorted electrical system. Frost sparkled faintly on the ground. The scene was at once telling and utterly surreal.

A battle had happened here; that much was obvious. Unrecoverable damage had been done and lives had been lost, but there was no blood or bones. The bodies here were nothing the human eye could see.

"I love this," Gracie whispered.

They had all made their way onto the last island, and now they could see the line of flames that showed where the final boss fight would be triggered. The boss could be seen prowling around the room, a hulking figure who was half-physical and half-shadow.

"So what do we do, boss?" Jay's voice commanded everyone's attention as he gave Gracie a nod.

Gracie considered. "We plan for the possibility that Demon Syndicate had good intel," she decided, "but also consider what we've seen so far. That means Ushanas and Freon are our top priorities. Swiftbolt, you have ice enchants for your arrows, right?"

"I do indeed," Alex confirmed.

"I made sure to get the ice enchant on my weapon," Lakhesis said, holding up her sword.

"I have an ice elemental," Kevin added, his Piskie now totally dwarfed by the hulking shape of a being fashioned from blue-white ice.

"All right." Gracie swallowed. "I don't think we're ever going to be more ready than we are now, so shall we head straight in?"

"Yeah!" the team chorused.

Gracie grinned at all of them and gave a flex emote. "Then let's go save the world. Team Underdog!"

"Team Underdog!"

Thad had been absolutely certain that they would arrive at the final boss to find another trap. Another ice wielder, perhaps, or some pit on the walkway that would swallow part of the team.

He was more than a little bitter at this point. Everyone was watching them fail, and he had no idea if it was Dragon Soul who had provided bad information or if his team's sponsors were trying to make him look bad.

If so, why? So they could replace him?

With *her*? The thought came to him so suddenly that his

controls went a little wild and his character shuddered to a stop on the final island. No. Surely not. They wouldn't.

They totally would, however. What if, after she turned down his offer, she'd gone to them and said she wanted to be in charge of Demon Syndicate? She was a rags-to-riches story, so she'd play well for all their publicity.

He wanted to scream with rage.

They'd set him up.

Screw them. He was going to take down this boss with seven people instead of ten just to spite them. Then he was going to make it clear to anyone who would listen that his bosses had tried to get rid of him on the sly rather than having the balls to fire him outright.

He looked at the remainder of his team.

"Stay on point," he said. People could hear everything he said in the group channel, so they'd put strict rules in place at the start not to talk about having inside intel. "Here's where we find out if our gamble pays off and the final boss has fire powers."

The part about it being a gamble was truer than he wanted it to be.

The team nodded silently. Envi, who was usually the first one with a quip or a cheer, said nothing at all. The character's arms were crossed over her chest; Thad could practically feel the worry radiating through the air.

Now he was angry. Did they think this was *fun* for him? Did they think he was *enjoying* being made a fool of for the whole internet to see?

"Have we not trained for this?" he snapped at them. "Do we not know how to use our crowd control? Do you not trust me to build threat?" For the love of God, if one of them so much as *suggested* that they wished they'd gone with the guild's other lead tank, he was going to lose it. Louis was lucky, Thad thought resentfully. Just lucky. He wasn't better than Thad.

Anyway, Thad had started this guild. If they didn't like working with him, they could leave.

If he started to look weak now, Brightstar would smell blood in the water and Thad would be out on his ass. No more ranking. No more sponsorship. Back to working a shitty job and living in a shitty apartment.

He wasn't going to do that.

"We're going in," he said, his voice hard. "Envi, ready check."

Envi stirred to life with a faint nod and initiated the ready check. Her silvery face nodded to him when everyone had checked in. They didn't need to do one, of course, but Thad liked to think that it got people engaged and dialed in.

He took off without another word, running for the line of flames that sealed off the final boss fight from the rest of the zone.

They followed him, at least. That was something. Envi caught up, peeling off only as Thad charged into the main room. A quick glance behind him showed that the rest of the team was spreading out, ready to unleash hell in the form of ice storms.

Thad didn't hesitate. He charged the boss at once, skipping the cinematic. He had the impression of height and a flaming color palette, but he didn't waste his time on things that didn't relate to the fight. The boss hefted a two-handed battle axe covered in runes, roaring in ancient

Aosi, and Thad gave a feral grin as he slid under the blade to land a strike.

He danced away immediately, circling around the back of the boss so that he pivoted away from the mages. Letting off a flurry of early strikes, he watched the meter climb.

"Envi, we should be good. Just one— Holy *shit.*"

The ground behind the boss erupted into geysers of flame, each geyser resolving itself into a flame elemental— a wraith with the faint impression of armor. These were clearly fallen soldiers, wounds leaking white-hot flame, and they gave banshee-like shrieks.

"AOE!" Thad yelled.

The mages had already begun, however, with the honed reaction time and planned rotations they had spent months perfecting. Ice began to rain down, cold slithering across the floor, wind blowing, and crystals bursting. A blade of ice sprouted from the boss's chest and he swung with a roar of fury.

Being vulnerable to ice magic, apparently this boss cultivated threat based on who was using ice magic. The boss's attention was now firmly locked on the mages.

"Slow him!" Thad yelled. "Careful of threat!"

"I've got lowest," called Harkness. "I'll slow him first." A snare appeared, ghostly chains covered in frost.

Thad used as many of his abilities as he could, burning his cooldowns with abandon. It was no use waiting to use them at some perfect moment if they were all dead by the time the perfect moment arrived.

"Come on," he muttered to himself as he swung with all his might. Sweat was trickling down his scalp inside the headset and running along his spine, and a knot of anxiety was forming in his chest.

What other surprises were waiting? Could they even *do* this with seven players instead of ten?

"Come on, come on, come on, *come on—*" Every piece of him was focused on the boss.

"Geysers!" Envi yelled. *"Thad!"*

The geysers erupted around him, and the last thing Thad saw was a flare of red. The world cartwheeled crazily and froze, his lifeless body stuck in the middle of the floor.

"Fuck," he breathed.

The team tried. He heard Envi rallying them to keep moving, stay on point, emphasize the rotation, and keep the boss slowed. There were calls about the boss's health, which was beginning to drop and drop—

For a moment, he thought they might make it.

But it wasn't enough. Without a tank, without the extra mages, there was no pulling this off. RUN FAILED announced red text across the center of Thad's screen. TRY AGAIN IN 12:34.

He closed his eyes as the countdown started and tried to banish the sinking feeling in his chest. At least if *they* hadn't pulled it off, he thought, there was no way the other team would.

Gracie jogged toward the line of fire that showed where the final boss fight would occur. She could see him prowling around the room, a hulking figure in armor that was glowing red-hot. Waves of heat skittered across its surface, and his Aosi skin had taken on the hues of fire, only his eyes remaining black.

She shivered.

"Opening cinematic?" Jay asked from beside her.

"I don't want to hold anyone up…" But she wanted to watch it so badly.

"Come on, this was already a long shot, right?" He threw out one elbow and looked at it with a sigh when it passed through her. "I keep forgetting that doesn't work here. Anyway, let's watch. It's only a few seconds."

"Right." Gracie grinned over her shoulder. "We're going to watch the cinematic, okay?"

There were nods and murmurs of agreement, and the next moment, she crossed the line and the world melted away.

"*Betrayed,*" a voice whispered, seeming to come from everywhere at once. Armies clashed around her, ghostly, locked in darkness. "*Forsaken by our allies and forgotten by our leaders. Our bodies left unburied, and our legacy forgotten.*"

The boss appeared: a limping Aosi who was dragging air into his lungs. His commander walked at his side, just as beaten and close to death. Fire and ash rained down around the pair.

"*I could not rest,*" the voice whispered. "*Not while my soldiers lay unavenged. I came here to plead for their souls but found only uncaring darkness, and now my own kin would ally with the ones who struck us down? I will never allow it.*"

The cinematic cleared and the boss stared Gracie down, pits of darkness where his eyes should be.

"All right, motherfucker," Gracie whispered. "Let's do this. Lakhesis!"

"Got it!" Gracie ran slightly to the right and Lakhesis to the left, taking the rest of the melee DPS with her. As Gracie drew close, the boss raised a giant battle axe glowing with heat and magical runes and began to slam it down.

"Shiiiiiit!" She pushed her movement to the limits and prayed, just barely making it out of the way as the axe came down. The haptics in her whole body shuddered and she gave a little gasp.

But there was no time to think. She slammed her fist on the ground for a shock blast and then grabbed her sword and angled it up. This was a video game, of course, but she took a certain satisfaction in knowing that she would have ruined this guy's day completely if it had been a real sword.

Of course, given that it was as tall as she was, she probably couldn't have *lifted* it if it were a real sword.

She swung and danced, waiting for her team to chime in, and it wasn't long before her threat level got high enough for them to start doing damage.

Which was about when it all went to hell.

Jay had leapt in at once with his ice-enchant, and Gracie's threat evaporated. The boss turned and slammed his axe down in one smooth motion, sending Jay scrambling for safety. There were yells as the melee team scattered, and Gracie charged in—only to have Freon's bolt of ice hit a moment later.

Any threat she'd hoped to build up was gone, and the boss started forward with a snarl.

"DPS!" Gracie yelled desperately as the group ran after the boss.

"I'm doing zero damage," Ushanas reported. "Goddammit!"

"Then just stay out of the way," Gracie advised. "DPS, gimme everything you've got. We *need* to kite him away from Freon so that—"

Flame erupted around them. Teef went up in a fireball and Jay yelled as the cat's life bar went to zero, and Lakhesis stumbled away with her health at less than half. A flame elemental swiped for Gracie with fingers made of fire and she jerked back out of the way, only to realize the boss was getting away.

Freon tried to snare him, sending icy chains to bind the boss's feet, but there was only so long he could hold him, especially with flame elementals hemming him in. Gracie ran, despairing, trying every combo she could think of to pull threat, but it was too little and too late. With half their DPS team down, Ushanas useless, and Gracie pulling no threat, there wasn't any way to recover.

By the time the second round of flames erupted, it was almost a relief. Gracie saw her health bar plunge, blew out her breath, and watched the failure text flash up on the screen.

CHAPTER TWENTY-NINE

"Ughhhh." Gracie tipped her head back and bounced back and forth on the balls of her feet, trying to blow off the tension in her shoulders. Easily half her muscles seemed to be burning with exhaustion, and between that, the sweat, and the party wipe, she was feeling more than a bit demoralized.

She hit her Home key and the dungeon dissolved around her, replaced by the ether of the portal system.

"Ughhhh," Alex agreed. "Stop bouncing over there! It's making me tired just hearing it. Young people are the worst."

He managed to startle Gracie into a laugh. She stopped bouncing as her in-game home appeared around her. "Right-o. Well, I hope everyone watching got a good laugh out of that."

"Probably," Jay said. He sounded manifestly unconcerned.

"Do you have a Teflon-coated ego or what?" Gracie

asked suspiciously. "You don't feel the littlest bit stupid that we just wiped in front of however many hundred viewers?"

"Oh, I do," Jay assured her. "I really, really do, don't worry. But I *also* happen to have learned something that's put me in a really good mood."

"Oh? What's that?" Gracie nodded to the others as they all began to appear in the pub as well, each of them with badly damaged armor and weapons. When Jay showed up, she tilted her head to the side curiously.

"It's a *good* story," Jay said. "All right, everyone, let's get a drink. Come on, over to the bar."

"Just *tell* us." But Gracie was laughing as she trailed over to the bar with the others. Everyone got a mug of beer and made their way to the big table in the back corner, trying to coordinate who sat where.

Jay waited as they arranged themselves, then lifted his mug. "A toast."

"Jay, so help me—"

"No, no, it's relevant, I assure you." Jay waited for them to raise their mugs. "A toast...to the team that's *still* in the running to do a month-first clear."

There was a moment of pure silence. In the real world, Gracie's jaw dropped, and she heard Alex give a whoop. A thud on the floor told her he'd literally jumped for joy.

"Are you... How..." She couldn't even form a sentence. When everything had started to go to hell in the dungeon, she'd expected it. She'd known it was a long shot, and on a tactical level, she hadn't even minded. Getting good at something always took iterations. Going up against the unexpected while relying solely on instinct was one of the most fun challenges she could face.

But she'd been disappointed. She had wanted to win; well, she *always* wanted to win. And to be honest, she hadn't liked the Demon Syndicate leader very much. She had been taking special pleasure in the idea of beating *them* for the title.

It had simply never occurred to her that they, with their head start and their inside knowledge, might also wipe.

"They didn't make it," she said finally.

"No, they didn't." Jay wasn't emoting a smile, but she could hear the grin in his voice. "You see, one of this dungeon's rules, I guess, is that anyone who dies along the way *can't* be resurrected."

"Oh, shit," Ushanas said with feeling.

There was a general murmur of agreement and some nods.

"Well, they lost three on the first boss," Jay said. He sounded so satisfied that Gracie found herself laughing silently. "Guess that inside knowledge they got was only for *one* of the two bosses, and I *think* I might know who was behind that."

"I'm the only one who knows about your job," Gracie reminded him.

"Oh, right. Hi, everyone. I'm Jay. I used to work for Dragon Soul Productions." Jay gave a little wave. "Then I quit over them doing…well, basically, stuff like this. Them giving Demon Syndicate a heads-up. I *think* my boss might have had some of the same complaints. He texted me after we wiped to tell us that they also did."

There was a long pause.

"So we're still in the running," Ushanas said finally.

"Hell yeah, we fuckin' are," Lakhesis rejoindered. She looked at Gracie. "And we're gonna go again, right?"

"She might want to switch up the team," Kevin chimed in. "I don't know how useful I was."

"Likewise." Alex sounded glum.

"Whoa! Hey, now." Gracie looked around. "We're a team. \We do this *together* or not at all."

"That's all very good to say," Alex pointed out, "but it means those of us who aren't bringing much to the table are going to hamstring the rest of you. There's no reason for that."

"Why not?" Gracie looked at him. "I'm serious. You're thinking about it all wrong. Really, you are. It's already a long shot, right? And why are we playing this game? Because playing it is fun. Winning it is fun, and winning is better when you earn it. I think it's genuinely possible to beat this dungeon without some super-specialized team, and we're going to find the way to do that.

"They can keep doing whatever the fuck they want with the rankings. They'll be a joke, so whatever. But they made a fun game, and I say we have fun playing it. In a way, doesn't them doing all this manipulation free us up to do whatever we want?"

There was a long silence.

"I like that," Kevin said. "That was really... I feel like my character is getting in the way of this being a serious moment."

A round of snickers said he was absolutely correct. He'd been standing on his chair, but still, only half of his Piskie's face was visible over the edge of the table.

"Look, I'm just saying that it's a really inspiring attitude that makes me want to— Goddammit, people!"

Gracie pressed a hand over her mouth, trying to hold back her laughter. Oh, God, her sides hurt. She was going to explode. She could feel the tremble as Alex rocked back and forth with silent laughter, and the rest turned their faces away...but a squeak escaped Alan's lips, and with that, the dam burst. Everyone dissolved into laughter.

"Oh, God," Freon wheezed. "He's so serious. And so tiny."

"I hate you all," Kevin said, his statement of annoyance delivered in a perky, squeaky voice that did nothing to stop the rest of them from howling with laughter. "*All* of you. I mean it."

"Do you guys hear something?" Gracie asked innocently. "Kinda high-pitched?"

"I will kill you," Kevin muttered, causing the rest of the group to burst out laughing again. "You know what? I give up. It was going to be a sweet moment, but you all ruined it."

"He was going to ask us all to join the Lollipop Guild," Jay guessed.

"Just you try running that dungeon without a summoner! You'll be sorry." Kevin shook one tiny Piskie fist in Jay's direction.

"*Speaking* of which..." Gracie broke in before Jay could retaliate, "we should get ready. Everyone, go get some water, get a snack, whatever. We have," she checked the timer "eighteen minutes on the timer, and Demon Syndicate is going to be able to go again before we do. I don't know if they're going to try..."

Jay met her eyes. "But we have to be ready," he finished. "Callista's right. Everyone meet back here in ten, all right? Go get some food, stretch your legs. Then we're running this again."

"You heard the man. Go, go, go!" Gracie threw him a thumbs-up and took off her headset, then looked over to meet Alex's eyes. "Ready to fail again in front of the whole world?"

"You know it." Alex snatched up his phone. "I'm gonna run to the deli and get us sandwiches, and— Huh."

"What?" Gracie looked at him.

"I have a message," Alex said. "From the waitress where we went to lunch the other day."

Gracie suddenly became very absorbed with taking off her armbands. "Oh, cool. You ask her out?"

"No," Alex said. "No, I didn't. *Wonder how she got my number?*"

"Maybe," Gracie said, "she's a witch." She gave him an innocent look and disappeared into the kitchen to get a glass of water. "Probably best not to think about it too hard," she called over her shoulder.

"Uh-huh." Alex disappeared, trying to look grumpy, but Gracie could hear the smile in his voice.

"Thad." Evan Klein, Brightstar's liaison on the premises, was there as soon as Thad took off his helmet. "We are so, so sorry." He looked around at all of them, shaking his head and running a hand through his sandy brown hair. "*So* sorry," he repeated. "Thad, do you have a moment to talk?"

Thad looked at Jamie, who shrugged. The other man looked as bewildered as Thad felt.

He'd logged out, absolutely sure he was going to lose this sponsorship, and now Brightstar was *apologizing* to him?

"What's up?" he asked cautiously as they got to the other side of the room. The rest of the team was milling around, all of them very obviously *not* looking in the direction of Thad and Evan.

"Long story short?" Evan heaved a sigh. "Heads are rolling at Dragon Soul, I can tell you that much. We got a call from the lead developers after the first boss telling us that there had been some 'miscommunication.'"

Thad raised a single eyebrow.

"Tom had the same response." Evan shook his head. "It was some bullshit. They were trying to cover their asses, but they know they fucked up. In the end, they said it was being 'taken care of.' In the meantime, they'll be sending along a few in-game perks, and they definitely owe us one. *But...*here's the good part."

"Right." Thad gave him a skeptical look. "The good part."

"Seriously." Evan still looked a bit tense, though. "The fact that you wiped dispelled a *lot* of suspicions."

"What?" Thad frowned at him. "What are you talking about?"

"Oh." Evan closed his eyes for a moment. "You don't know. Of course. Shit." He hunched his shoulders and crossed his arms over his chest. "All right, here's the deal. Another team went in right after you, and *one* of them said on live mic that your team going in with that weird configuration suggested that you'd been tipped off."

Thad swallowed. It had been a risk, of course, but Dragon Soul had assured them that the problems would be taken care of.

"Then you reached the first boss and nearly wiped," Evan said, "and clearly weren't prepared for…what do you call it? Where you bring a character back to life."

"Rezzing."

"Right. So the fact that you couldn't…rez? Rez. That caught you off guard, and then you all went down on the final boss." He rubbed his chin. "Honestly, from a PR perspective, it might be the best thing that could have happened. Would have been nice to have a heads-up, though." He shook his head. "We *could* have played it off."

Thad shook his head. He didn't give a damn about the PR ramifications right now. What he wanted was to get back in there and win.

"I'm going to go get a drink of water," he said. "Any other surprises lurking in there that they told you about?"

"They swore there weren't any," Evan said, holding up both hands as if to absolve himself of any responsibility.

The gesture hardly inspired confidence, Thad thought.

He made his way for the door, rolling his eyes in annoyance when Jamie hurried after him. He didn't want to be placating people right now. He wanted to be letting his rage simmer.

"What?" he asked shortly.

"Well?" Jamie asked. "What's going on?"

"What's going on is, Dragon Soul fucked us over," Thad

said with feeling. "Brightstar has them sweating, though." He couldn't keep the satisfaction out of his voice.

"So *you're* okay," Jamie said.

Thad stopped for a moment to look at him. Jamie had been worried about *him*. Now he felt bad for being annoyed. "Yeah. I'm okay. Thanks." He tried to think of something to say. "Oh, we'll be going back in, so tell everyone to take a bathroom break or whatever if they need one, right? Get Porto and Harkness to respec into fire, and replace Lura with Fajj."

"Right." Jamie gave him a nod and hurried away.

Ten minutes later, feeling fresh and filled with a new determination to smash some faces in, Thad adjusted the straps on his hands and put his headset back on.

"All right, team, we gambled last time, and we didn't quite make it." He knew Dragon Soul was listening, and he knew that they heard the accusation in his voice. "But we got damned close, and now we know what we're up against. Let's get back in there and fuck some shit up, okay?"

The team was cheering as Thad put them into the queue and the world dissolved into ether. When they appeared on the desolate moonscape once again, he felt a surge of satisfaction.

"All right, let's—"

"Uh, boss?" Jamie sounded panicked.

"What now?" Thad tossed his character a scornful look, then stopped dead because he could *see* what.

They hadn't been allowed to bring their own gear in this time.

"What the *fuck?*" said the Demon Syndicate tank. "What the hell? Bring up the specs on what everyone's wearing. Jesus Christ."

Sam settled back in his chair with a tiny smile.

As far as he was concerned, he'd given Demon Syndicate their one shot, and it had been more than they deserved.

And, since he was pretty damned certain he was going to be fired in the next hour or so, he was out of fucks to give. He leaned back in his chair, smiled at the screen, and wished he had a beer.

"Guys? Guys. *Guys!*" Jay's voice cut through the hubbub.

"What's up?" Gracie asked him.

"So, Demon Syndicate loaded in again as soon as they could," Jay said.

"Sure." Gracie sighed. She had expected that, after all. Pure stupidity would be too much to ask for.

"Aaaaand it turns out that 'use your own gear' thing was only for a first attempt," Jay said. "The second time you go in, you get preset armor. Which means..."

Gracie felt her heart leap. "We're on an even footing again. *Holy hell.* Okay, everyone, get ready. We are loading in the *second* that counter hits zero."

CHAPTER THIRTY

A spear of ice pierced the center of a fire elemental and it screamed, dissolving in a ripple of magic that shuddered through the air around it. Flaming coals scattered to the ground, its body lying among the ashes of its fellow elementals. The Demon Syndicate team hesitated, gazing solemnly at the corpse.

"*Move*," Thad snapped.

When Demon Syndicate had loaded in again, there had been no one else attempting a run, but it was only a matter of time before someone was on their tail—and they were doing the run in shitty dungeon armor.

That meant Thad didn't have time for them to stand around caring about pixelated elementals. He didn't even have time to savor the fact that Callista's group had wiped spectacularly. They'd barely made it for a minute.

Only now they knew what they were up against, and they had the same gear as Thad's team. He looked at Porto, who was waiting for a cooldown.

"I said *move*," Thad said, deeply annoyed now. "We can't afford to waste time on the trash mobs. Jesus Christ."

Porto tried to stammer out an excuse, but Thad wasn't in the mood to listen to it. He did the pull himself, running toward the next patrol as he felt his heart pound with anger. Evan said that failing in front of everyone last time had been *good*—at least PR-wise—but Thad hated feeling like an idiot. He did not intend to fail again.

He whirled into motion as he reached the elementals, wielding the unfamiliar sword with distaste. It had an elemental enchant, at least, but he missed his own weapon.

Wasn't the whole point of these games that you could be whoever you wanted?

"Thad! *Thad*, watch out for the patrol!" Jamie's yell cut through his internal monologue, but it was too late. Thad heard the hiss as the group aggroed and hurled themselves into the fray. "Fuck," Jamie hissed. "Fuck fuck *fuck*! Kronos, you and Iko slow them. Thad, get *out* of there!"

He had zero interest in looking like a weak idiot who was getting rescued by his healer, but his health bar was dipping so he didn't have much choice at this point. Gritting his teeth, Thad made one last double-handed strike and withdrew with a growl of annoyance.

The elementals followed him with grim determination, and Thad felt the absolute fury of someone losing a fight with an inanimate object. This was a *game*, for fuck's sake. Who couldn't win a simple game?

"Keep running!" Jamie called.

Thad complied, still annoyed. His health bar was climbing, but not as fast as he was used to. That was what they got for running this instance with one healer. It wasn't like it was a surprise.

He still didn't like it.

Nor was he pleased when the mages took down the patrol. Somehow, having other people clean up the mess made it worse.

He had to get his head on straight, or he was going to be responsible for this attempt going down in flames. He paused for a moment, reaching up under his headset to wipe the sweat off his forehead.

In his head, he pictured the glittering screen that announced the month-first run. He'd seen it three times now, and he was hooked. He'd listened to people dissect his play style online, and he'd read the posts about him on the forums. If he did it a fourth time, especially after Dragon Soul had screwed them over like this, he'd be untouchable. Brightstar wouldn't even *think* of getting rid of him.

He looked around at the rest of them. "Let's go."

The elementals clawed at Gracie and shrieked, their mouths stretched wide to show the white-hot cores within. They swarmed her, and it was hard not to think of them as being motivated by vengeance. After all, the corpses of their fellow elementals were scattered across the landscape.

But Gracie told herself that these beings wanted to wipe out life on Elakara. They were carrying a grudge for battles that were long since finished and forgotten. They wanted revenge for those who didn't cling to the old scores.

And she wasn't about to let them destroy the cities she had fallen in love with, seek vengeance on the people within, and let their violence spill out to consume the fae and the kobolds as well.

I protect my own. Her lips moved silently as she fought.

"Gracie! Patrol to your right!" Jay's call cut through her battle haze, and Gracie slid out of the way with practiced ease. She called a thank you as she whirled, redoubling her efforts to take down the group they were fighting before the patrol reached them.

They didn't quite make it, and good-natured groans resounded through the group as the patrol aggroed with a rattling hiss.

"It couldn't just be easy!" Gracie called, mock-annoyed.

"Well, you know, given that you're trying to do the crazy thing and cut across the dangerous part of the zone? Probably not." Lakhesis chuckled, her panting coming over the chat in the background as she cleaned up the last of the first group.

"*We*," Gracie corrected. "*We're* doing the crazy thing."

"I see you're getting accustomed to management," Alex said. He loosed several arrows. "To add to your repertoire, may I suggest, 'Think outside the box,' 'Streamline,' and 'Scrum?'"

"What does 'scrum' mean?" Gracie asked, shooting him a glance as she did a shock blast to make sure all of the new group was firmly focused on her.

"You know, I don't think anyone knows," Alan chimed in. "We all just use it, and no one's sure enough of the meaning to call anyone else on it when we think they're using it wrong."

Gracie snorted with amusement. "Yeah, but is it a noun or a verb?"

"I told you, no one knows. Now, stand still so I can heal you." His character gave an impressive flourish as she did her big heal. "And don't keep pulling like that if you expect me to keep you alive."

"Yessir." Gracie laughed. "All right, everyone, ready for the first boss?"

"Hell yeah, we are." Kevin had summoned his fire elemental and reached almost straight up to fist-bump Alex, whose arrows were flaming worrisomely near his hair. Video-game physics, Gracie thought. By now, with all that ice and fire flying around, they should all be completely hairless.

The thought of everyone without eyebrows made her snicker.

"All right." She eased onto the open void and blew her breath out. "Boy, this just never gets any less terrifying. Come on, people, let's get moving. Demon Syndicate was ahead of us going in, and they probably aren't loitering around."

"They're catching up," Micah murmured to Sam. Tall and lanky, with dark hair and a strong nose, he was one of the Dragon Soul's first employees. Unlike some of the others, he'd always been nice to Sam. He had a way of explaining things that didn't rely too heavily on jargon, and he never complained when he had to clarify a term.

Now he nodded to the two screens. "I've been tracking what time they went past different checkpoints. Demon Syndicate started out about eighteen minutes ahead. Now they're only about ten and a half minutes ahead."

"So it paid off," Sam said quietly. "Her cutting across the bottom of the map like that."

"Yep," Micah said blandly. "Almost like someone designed it to reward risk-takers."

Sam looked at him, but Micah was staring at the screens with only the faintest hint of a smile playing around his mouth. Sam grinned, but as he turned his gaze back to the screens, a flicker of motion caught his eye. He turned to see Dan watching from the back of the room, his gaze unreadable.

Sam waited, hoping Dan would look at him, but the other man disappeared without a word.

Worse, to Sam's mind, was the fact that Dan didn't look the slightest bit worried.

The first boss didn't stand a chance. As he readied the blast of icy magic, Porto and Harkness began raining fire down at once. Thad let them go, creeping forward slowly and waiting for each wall of ice to appear before he advanced. With the fire raining down, the boss was forced into a defensive spell pattern and couldn't spare the casting time to attack Thad.

A few more advances and a few more steps... Thad

made his way carefully up the hill. The boss wasn't going down quickly since they only had two fire mages and the rest were throwing random arcane spells, but they'd tipped the balance enough that the outcome of the fight appeared inevitable.

Good. He felt the savage satisfaction of someone who had cracked a code. Eight mages, two fire and six frost.

He reached the boss and felt his lip curl in a sneer as he leveled his strongest attack. The Aosi staggered, his casting interrupted. Fire was eating away at him and he screamed in fury, turning to throw his spells at Thad.

"I will not let you past me! You will not murder the general!"

Thad rolled his eyes as he attacked. He had no time for the theatrics and the acting. He forced the boss back, his chest heaving with effort and his sword angling up as he slashed, and the boss was driven away, unable to cast his spells or fight back.

As a last stand, despairing, he gave a shriek and threw his arms out as he began to pulse with light. A glowing circle appeared on the ground.

"Thad!" Jamie yelled.

Thad took off, running like hell for the edge of the glowing circle. He had played MMOs since he was a kid and he had always loved the adrenaline rush of a fight, but none of the games had been like this. He was *here*, his world narrowed to the single line on the floor and the knowledge that a spell was cast, inevitable, unstoppable—

He skidded out of range as the boss was consumed in a ball of light. The explosion ripped through the entire hill, sending light shooting skyward and ice crystals flying out.

They thudded harmlessly to the ground mere feet from where Thad was standing.

There was a pause, and then the whole team burst out laughing. It was nervous laughter, but they had made it. They were winning again, and they were making up time.

"Heal up," Thad said, "and let's get going." He gave a contemptuous glance at the smoking wreck of the crater. "Not so difficult this time, was he?"

He gazed across the chasm toward the final boss, and his face broke into a smile.

Everything was finally going right.

"This fight was a little weird," Gracie reminded them as they jogged across the void. Talking kept her from thinking about how there was nothing at all beneath her feet. If she actually had to move her feet to run forward, she didn't think she could do it.

She *hated* heights.

"It's going to start slow," she warned them. "Gary, I need you and Fys to keep your pets with you at the start; we'll bring them through once we've navigated all those ice walls. Do as much ranged damage as you can with Ushanas. Lakhesis, Anders, Chowder, you're with me, there's no need to split the tanking groups. Freon, throw anything you can—and, I guess, keep an eye out for anything weird."

"Right," Freon said. "Sit in the back and look pretty. Got it."

"Just let me carry it all," Ushanas said, flexing under his

flowing robes. "I've got this, guys. Frost mages? We don't need no stinkin' *frost* mages."

"You say that now, but just you wait. That fire boss comes running over with his axe, and all of a sudden it's going to be, 'Oh, Freon, save me! Snare him!'" Freon's falsetto came through the voice filters, and everyone burst out laughing.

"You two want to duel?" Gracie said. "Because that's what I'm hearing. When this is over, we'll meet at the old temple and fight it out. For now, Ushanas, take it away!"

"Yes, ma'am. FIREBOOOOOOLT!" Ushanas sank into a casting crouch and unleashed hell on the figure at the top of the hill. "Rain of FIIIIIIRE!"

"Flaming arrows to the FACE!" Alex yelled.

"Tiny—useless—arcane spells!" Kevin tacked on. "Pew pew pew! Seriously, I feel like I'm shooting at a tank with a BB gun."

"Ha." Gracie advanced, keeping her eyes locked on the boss to see when he was going to cast the walls of ice. "Slow and steady, guys, slow and steady. Wasn't there supposed to be a wall of...oh, there we go. Ushanas?"

"One more rain of fire, coming right up."

"I have to say," Jay admitted, "it's a bit disconcerting to have fire raining down around me. I never really noticed that in other games."

"There definitely is a hellfire vibe," Gracie agreed. "Okay, we're clear. Advance!"

Kevin might be disparaging his own efforts, but the ranged damage dealers *were* making progress. The boss's health was only creeping down, but he wasn't able to spend as much time casting ice spells, which meant that

Alan didn't have to do damage control on the melee group.

They arrived at the top of the hill in a rush, and Lakhesis whipped out a flaming sword. "First you, then your boss, asshole!"

"You know," Gracie commented, "I've never had a boss I cared about enough to do something like this for them. Almost makes me think better of the guy. I mean, Icy Dude's been hanging out here for *centuries,* and he's still devoted to the cause." She hacked her sword down. "That said, you don't get to destroy the world, bitch."

"Gracie's layin' down the law." Jay launched into the fray with a series of kicks and punches. "All *right,* now we're getting somewhere! Look at that health bar go. Whoo!"

"Everybody just keep doing what you're doing," Gracie called. "We'll— What is he doing?"

The boss had shuddered and now began to glow.

"GET OUT!" Freon yelled.

They ran. No one stopped to look back; they just ran. Gracie knew her lips were moving as she went: *come on, come on, come on, shit, shit, shit, shiiiiit!* They could see the glowing line on the floor now, and she was sure she wasn't going to make it.

"Run faster," she pleaded with her character. Her hands ached where she had them clenched. "Oh God, oh God, oh *God…* Oh shit, we made it. Did we make it? Did…" She turned around. "Wait, isn't anything going to— SHIT!"

The entire hill went up in smoke, the boss vanishing and ice raining down where they had all been standing.

"Holy…" Jay muttered. "Okay, so when you take his health down fast, he suicides. *That's* fun."

"Super fun." Gracie's heart was pounding as if she really had run all that way. "Holy shit, guys, that was close. All right, stay on your toes, and let's get moving. If we want to have any shot of catching up with Demon Syndicate, we have to keep going."

In his office, Dan paused, his hand reaching for one of the cables.

Callista's team had gone into the first boss fight about ten minutes behind Demon Syndicate, but they'd lost a few minutes in the fight. If that trend continued, Demon Syndicate would win handily and Dan wouldn't need to intervene.

After a moment's thought, he settled down, his elbows on his knees. He'd wait a little longer.

He was only going to take the servers down if he *absolutely* needed to.

CHAPTER THIRTY-ONE

Thad couldn't remember anything from the trash mob run leading to the second boss. He moved with icy precision, aware of the patrols, pulling groups mechanically so that they advanced almost without stopping.

But he wasn't all there. His mind was focused on the boss fight, still seeing the jets of fire that had come shooting out of the ground to wipe the party last time.

It wasn't going to happen again, he swore to himself.

When they were finally done with the trash pull, he was feeling good. He'd resisted the urge to take short cuts, and as a result, they hadn't put themselves in danger. Games like this punished you when you—

A tap on his shoulder called him back to the real world and he pulled off his helmet, annoyed, to see Evan's face. He covered his mouthpiece. *"What?"*

"The other team cut across the field on a different path," Evan said. He looked pale in the dim light. "They're almost ready to go in. Dragon Soul is asking if they should take the servers down."

"What the— *No.*" Cold certainty settled in Thad's chest. "Like *hell,* we're running from this."

"Frank thinks—" Evan began.

"No. Fuck that." Thad took a deep breath and steadied himself. "No," he repeated. "This is ridiculous. We've been training for months. We have a better team setup, and we're still ahead of them. We're going in, and we're going to wipe the floor with the other group."

Evan looked doubtful, but he wasn't brave enough to assert his opinion right now, and Thad was just fine with that. He gave a brief nod and withdrew, and Thad put his headset back on. After a moment, he decided the rest of them didn't need to know about the development. They were fighting well, and they didn't need the distraction of worrying.

"All right." He bounced lightly on the balls of his feet. "We're going in right now. No way to know who is on our tail, so we're not going to waste any time."

"Everything okay?" Jamie asked over a private channel.

"Yeah, cable came loose," Thad said without hesitation. "Evan noticed. Got it reattached just fine, though."

"Ah, good catch." He could hear Jamie relax.

Thad smiled grimly. "Now, remember where the jets came out. It was in the center of the floor, so spread out and take your sectors for handling the adds. Porto and Harkness, you keep an eye on anyone going for Envi, and call in whichever ice mage is free if you need it. Speak up before you *need* intervention. Everyone good?"

There was a chorus of agreement.

"Good," Thad said shortly, and he spurred his character

to a run, dashing across the line of fire into the final boss battle.

Gracie gritted her teeth as she swung—once, twice, a slash, a downward hack, and then she holstered her blade and lashed back out in one smooth motion to kill the elemental with a punch. She was panting by now. This dungeon was more intense than their usual play, and they were close to two full runs by now.

Alan launched into heals at once, HOTs shimmering in the air around Gracie, Teef, and Fys' current demon. She set off as the heals took effect, swiveling her head back and forth to check for patrols.

"Callista." Jay's voice was quiet, but it got everyone's attention. "Do you want me to check where we are in the timings?"

They had taken another shortcut, and again it had paid off. Gracie hadn't been sure that it would, half-expecting it to be a trap, but they had managed to fight their way through patrols quickly and efficiently, dividing the melee team and alternating so Alan didn't need to spread his heals out as often.

"Nope." Gracie didn't even think about it. "We were behind coming in, and we're probably still behind. There's *no* way we're so far ahead that we can afford to take time checking where other people are."

"Good call," Alan said at once. Gracie could hear Lakhesis and Chowder agreeing as well.

"In fact..." Gracie watched as the next patrol made their

approach, and her mind snapped to a split-second decision. "Run *now*. Everyone go. We'll be able to get past this patrol if we move quickly. We all healed? Mirra, we good to go on heals?"

"Yes. Holy shit, are we just *doing* this?" To her amusement, Alan sounded not at all panicked, and entirely on board. "All *right*. Move, people. Pick it up. Your tank and healer are entirely insane!"

"I say we stage a mutiny," Lakhesis said in a stage whisper to Dathok, but no one took any more time to joke. They were running in an arc to avoid the oncoming patrol, and they stumbled across the line of flames with whoops and cheers.

"Take it away, Callista!" Alex called as the group spread out.

Gracie gave them a grin, and as the rest of the team fanned out, she kept running, lifting her sword and staring down the end boss.

"Surprise, douchebag!" she called. "We're baaaaack."

***

Thad skidded under the boss's feet and rolled into position as the huge battle axe came down on the other side, the shudder running through all of Thad's haptics.

Too slow, bitch, he thought with satisfaction. The boss was swinging around now, but Thad had aced his first interaction. That was just the sort of boost he needed right now.

He spun through his opening rotation with the ease of long practice. How many of these dungeons had he run with his team? Enough that he could do this rotation in his sleep. He'd begun to get a feel for the way Dragon Soul put things together, and the way their rules worked.

Of course, sometimes they threw curveballs like mixing fire and ice, but Brightstar would fix that.

Next time, they'd demand a video run-through before the content dropped.

Thad didn't feel bad, not in the slightest. This was a game. No one was obligated to play it. Anyway, anyone in his position would take the boost if it were offered to them. He just happened to be the one in the way of the good luck.

The first jets of fire shot up from the ground, but he wasn't in the way of them this time, and as the elementals spawned, he heard the mages calling to one another to coordinate their efforts. Thad smiled in satisfaction. *This* was how it was supposed to work; everyone doing their job, responding to the controlled chaos with planned contingencies.

And Dragon Soul had wanted to pull the servers down? He shook his head as he began his rotation again. With the elementals on the board, Envi's healing had spread and she was pulling more threat now, but nothing they couldn't handle easily enough.

That was when the second set of fire jets went off. The set where Thad was standing.

The set he hadn't known about.

Dan's eyes narrowed. From the sound of the yells, the tank

had been unprepared for this development. He looked at the phone, where he was on a conference call with the head of Brightstar's PR team.

"Now?" he asked delicately.

Frank's silence indicated he was wavering, and it stretched for so long that Dan nearly yanked the cord out. But just as his fingers closed around the clasp, Frank said, "No. Our guy said they can pull it off. I don't know about this stuff, so I'll go with his judgment."

Dan sighed. When he'd proposed this deal, a one-time boost to help Demon Syndicate prove the nay-sayers wrong and help Dragon Soul kick Callista out of the top ten, Dan had thought it would be a simple one-and-done. They'd punt the Callista problem down the road enough that they could find a way to fix it before the next content patch dropped.

He hadn't counted on his own team going behind his back, not to mention dealing with the competing egos of Brightstar's executive team and Demon Syndicate's guild leader. Dan had been in the boardroom for ten years and had played MMOs for most of his life. He should have anticipated this, he thought.

The question was, what did he do now?

"Listen up," Gracie said as she sprinted toward the boss. "First thing, Freon will focus entirely on snares. Just snare as often as you can, kiddo."

"Right-o, boss."

"Also…" She watched the boss swing his battle axe up over his head.

One thing she'd say for augmented reality: it was a *lot* easier to give orders on a dedicated voice chat than it would be in an actual battle.

"What's up, boss?" Jay asked, prompting her.

"Right, sorry. I want you all to keep moving," Gracie said, "and we're going to rely on Ushanas to give us directions if we need to. Call the shattered-column side 'stage left,' and the less shattered one 'stage right.' Then there'll be boss-side and — Sec." She dialed in as she swerved around the descending battle axe. "And 'healer side,'" she finished a bit breathlessly.

It all looked so *real* that her body refused to remember sometimes that this was just a game.

"So you want me to be on the lookout for…" Ushanas said.

"*Anything,*" Gracie said. "What happened in the first boss fight with the suicide explosion? They could throw another curveball here too."

"Good call," Jay said.

Gracie started into her rotation, but she knew this was really just her buying time for the rest to get into position. Freon, Alex, and Fys' demon would pull threat away from her almost immediately.

The dungeon designers had really figured out how to get under a tank's skin with this one.

"Everyone is in position," Ushanas relayed a few moments later.

"Good. Freon, go when ready. Gary and Fys, line up all your damage."

"Ready," chorused three voices.

The first snare hit, and the boss swung away from Gracie with a shriek.

"Melee DPS, get in a few good hits and then withdraw back here!" she called. "Don't want you in the way of those jets."

"Aye aye," Jay called back. "Take *that*, you son of a bitch! I don't know about you guys, but I *personally* would not enjoy getting punched in the shins like this."

"He's an undead ghost-thing," Chowder weighed in. "He's been holding a grudge for thousands of years. I don't think he cares about his shins."

"You're a real buzzkill sometimes, you know that?"

"Less smack talk, more getting out of the way of the fire jets," Gracie said with a snicker, and she was pleased to see them scatter. "Actually, you know what? Split into two groups, and head for stage left and stage right. We'll have you pick up the adds as they spawn."

"Cool beans," Lakhesis called. "Teef and Chowder, with me."

"I got the rest," Jay chimed in.

Gracie grinned and gave a satisfied nod as the first jets went off. Within moments, the team was swinging back into action, pulling the adds away from the casters.

"All right, now Freon. I want you to come join me— *Shit!*" Fire jets went off close to her, and Gracie's health bar took a fifty percent hit. "What the fuck?"

"So there's another set of fire jets," Ushanas observed.

"Yes, thank you, Ushanas. Very helpful." She had to laugh. "Mirra, could I—"

"Full heal here in a second. Feel free to pull the adds," Alan told her.

"I think that set of jets is done for now," Freon said, "so I'm still on my way." He started running and the boss, who had been making a beeline for him, howled in protest and tried to follow, dragging its icy chains in a slow arc.

"We need to get these adds cleaned up before he gets back!" Gracie called.

"On it," chorused Kevin and Alex. Teef dashed into the fray as several ice-enchanted arrows came zooming past, and Gracie's shock blast pulled the elementals back to her.

They burned down the group as quickly as they could, and Freon fired off another snare as he looped behind Gracie. "I think it's working!" he called.

"Keep moving," Gracie told him. "Kite him in the center if you can, but stay far to the outside to avoid the jets. Bet you're glad you're not *really* running this much, aren't you?"

"Christ, I hadn't even thought of that." He was laughing.

"*BATTLE AXE!*" Ushanas' voice cut through the chatter. "Stage left, *stat!*"

"Shiiiit!" Gracie and the rest went skidding out of the way, and Alex gave a yell a moment later.

"Fuck! Teef!"

"Oh, no." Gracie knew it wasn't real, but the sight of Alex's pet lying prone on the ground, its body bloodied, made her heart twist. "Alex, I'm sorry."

"Stay focused," was all Alex said. "No battle rezzes means we have *no* margin for error now."

"Yeah," Gracie murmured quietly. "Yeah."

But worry twisted in her gut. They were taking a long

time to get the boss down, and now it would take even longer. What if it was too long? What if—

She'd made the best choices she could, she reminded herself. She couldn't waste any brain space doubting her earlier decisions. They'd gone with the team they had, which was the best decision, and they were using a strategy that was *working.*

She just had to execute it to the best of her ability.

Down the boss's health crept, and further down. Jay got caught in the flames once and barely escaped as Chowder came in for a last-second rescue from the adds, and Lakhesis seemed to be everywhere at once with Fys' ice demon, the two of them making an unsettling but highly capable team.

Gracie, meanwhile, struggled against the sense that all the dice had been rolled at the start of the fight and everything was set in stone already—and still she had to go through it and watch it play out when the conclusion was predetermined.

She was just tired, she told herself, dodging out of the way of a strike she had only caught out of the corner of her eye. She was tired, and she had always known she was going to be the underdog.

"So close," Jay's voice said over the channel, and Gracie felt a surge of energy.

She looked at him with a smile, and although she didn't take the time to emote it, she knew he was smiling, too.

"Ready to finish this?" she asked, speaking just to him.

"Hell, yeah." He understood her, and she could hear the grin in his voice.

Everyone else fell back, and Gracie charged into the

center of the floor. The jets were going to go off in a moment, she knew, but they could *just* make it if they ran. She swung her sword up and Freon pulled the boss toward him with a spear of ice, abandoning the snares as they reached the end.

Gracie's sword came down as Jay launched into a flying kick, and the boss's scream echoed through the room, ripped from its throat, and lost a moment later in the roar of the fire jets.

Gracie laughed even as her health bar plunged to zero. They had done it! They had taken him down, and she didn't even care anymore if they'd done it first. She was just so proud of this team, and so glad to have them on her side—and so exhilarated by the victory.

DUNGEON COMPLETE. The words flashed up on the screen.

"Hey, we did it," Gracie said. "Crispify your tank and you can get anything done."

"Tank kebabs!" Lakhesis added enthusiastically.

"Careful! Now that I'm dead, *you're* the next in line for that," Gracie joked. Disappointment was settling over her like a cloak, but she kept her voice light. "Guys, I think this deserves quite a celebration. We managed to finish a dungeon that—"

"MONTH-FIRST ACHIEVED," a voice announced, and the words burst across the screen in a shower of fireworks.

"WHOOOOOOO!" Gracie couldn't even tell who was yelling. She was pretty sure she was, and she could hear the deafening sound of everyone else screaming. She tore her headset off and launched herself into Alex's arms, laughing as he swung her around and their headsets blared tinny cheers.

In the background, her computer dinged for a video call.

"Just—goddammit—" Alex staggered over that way, still spinning.

Gracie laughed as she pressed the start button for the call, and her heart gave a little sideways leap when she saw Jay's face. "We did it!" she exclaimed incredulously.

"Yeah, we did." Jay was grinning. "One more thing, though. You should check your ranking."

"What?" Gracie pulled her headset back on.

Her jaw dropped. "RANK 1 ACHIEVED," a pleasant female voice was saying. "RANK 1 ACHIEVED."

"Holy shit," she managed.

"Move left," Thad ordered, his voice tight. "No, *my* left, *your* right. Jules, MOVE!"

"Uh, Thad?" Evan's voice was tight.

"Not *now*," Thad snapped. They were so close to taking this boss down, even without him, and he was going to make it work if it killed him.

"No. Thad, it's…it's over. The other team got it."

Thad straightened slowly and turned his head, his eyes focusing on the screens on the other side of the room. In his headphones, Jamie was calling for directions and one of the mages blundered into a set of fire vents, but Thad didn't care anymore.

It was over.

It was over, and they'd lost.

———

Jay leaned close to the screen to watch as Gracie clapped her hands over her mouth. Her eyes were hidden by the headset, but he could see her shock and pleasure in the way she was laughing and bouncing up and down.

Alex gave him a thumbs-up and a wave, and Jay waved back.

"We *did* it," Alex called.

"*She* did it," Jay said. "She made us drill. She saw the way the dungeons worked and took the risks. She learned the spacing and the buffs. We were just along for the ride."

"I heard that." Gracie took her headset off and looked at them both. "And there's no one who's 'just along for the ride' on my team. We have ten people who bring their A-game every time. All the good management in the world won't compensate for people who won't give things their best shot."

Jay grinned at her.

"Well, then," he said to Alex. "*We* did it."

"Hell yeah, we did," Gracie said.

CHAPTER THIRTY-TWO

"What I don't get," Jay said, "is *why*. This is the hour of your—hell, your *triumph*—and you haven't logged in? You're a hero right now, so why not milk it for all it's worth? The team wants to buy you a beer. I know it's pixelated beer, but still…" He gave a little laugh as if to jumpstart her own, then sighed. "Seriously, Gracie, what's up?"

"It's stupid." Gracie groaned and let her head thwump back against the couch. "It's really stupid."

"You keep saying that." He took a bite of Chinese food. "Come on, give me a try. Also, why are you sitting in the dark?"

Gracie considered that. "Fine," she said at last, "but don't judge me. And I have a good reason for sitting in the dark, I promise."

"I doubt that, and I will a hundred percent judge you if you don't tell me what's going on." Jay gave her a meaningful look. "I may also judge you for the fact that I'm out of Chinese food."

Gracie started laughing. "How is that *my* fault?"

"I don't know, but I'm sure you had something to do with it." He settled back in his chair, grinning. "So. Go on."

"Ugh." Gracie heaved a sigh. "All right, here's the deal. I feel like if I log back in, I'll find out I dreamed the whole thing and none of it was real, and…yeah. I've been enjoying the dream." She let her eyes slide sideways. "Also, the money hit my account, and I don't want to give it back."

Jay burst out laughing. "For the last time, you don't have to give the money back. You earned it." He twitched one eyebrow. "*And* a whole bunch of people saw you win and seriously suspect that Demon Syndicate had some help going in, so Dragon Soul can't really get on your case without touching off a firestorm."

"What I *don't* get," Gracie said, annoyed, "is that a Cinderella story should be *good* for them, right? Some unsponsored player coming out of nowhere to storm the rankings? That should draw people in."

"I mean, you're right." Jay bounced his back against the chair as he considered. He blew out a long breath. "I think it's more that they can't control it because of the quest line, and that neither Dan nor Dhruv deals well with things not going to plan. When you started climbing the rankings, they panicked."

Gracie rolled her eyes. Some people, in her opinion, shouldn't be in charge of companies. Still… "I had fun reading their congratulations post," she admitted with a mischievous smile. "You could tell it was written through gritted teeth."

"Oh, it definitely was," Jay agreed. He rubbed the back

of his neck. "Look, I don't want to add more stress to your plate…"

"Uh-oh." Gracie crossed her legs and sat up straighter. "What's going on, man?"

"Well, I got a message." He gave her a meaningful look. "From Harry."

"Yeah, I don't know who that is." Gracie held up a hand as the door to the apartment opened, then grinned and held her finger to her lips. As quiet footsteps made their way into the room, she flipped on the light and crossed her arms. "Just getting home?"

Alex jumped. "Jesus fucking— Goddammit."

"So." Gracie bounced in her seat. "How was the date?"

"How did you even know that was where I was?" Alex waved his hands.

"You were extremely shifty about not wanting to get dinner and disappeared in a cloud of cologne that has lingered for *hours*."

Alex winced. "Oh, God. It's been a while since I dated."

"Yes. I know." Gracie rolled her eyes. "So, how did it go?"

"Better than *your* recent dating efforts." He gave her a look.

"Ouch. Touché." Gracie leaned in to stage whisper to Jay, "He's *grumpy*. Maybe he couldn't close."

"I closed!" Alex said indignantly. He stripped off his dress shirt and narrowed his eyes. "I may not have dated in a while, but I have game, I will let you know. I took her out to a really fucking romantic dinner and got her *flowers*, and we— Ohhhhh, you sneaky bitch."

Gracie gave him a smug grin as Jay burst out laughing.

"Excellent. That was all I needed to know. You can go now."

Alex gave her a long, narrow-eyed glare before disappearing toward his room.

"Mission accomplished," Gracie said with satisfaction. "You ever had one of your friends start to get a little bit sad around the edges?"

"Yeah." Jay took a sip of his soda. "Is he okay?"

"Oh, he's fine." Gracie peered down the hallway to make sure Alex's door was closed. "He was really enjoying the single life for a while. Eat whatever, sleep whenever, spend money however he wanted—all that stuff. You know, it *can* be fun. But he's been starting to get...well, like I said: sad around the edges. A bit aimless. Didn't like his job but wasn't looking. Didn't really like being single anymore but wasn't looking."

"To be fair," Jay weighed in, "dating is the worst."

"No. I mean, yeah." Gracie stared at her feet rather than look at him. "Anyway, so I gave him a little nudge." She took a deep breath to steady herself. "So what were you saying? About Harry?"

Jay gave her a long look, but let the dating topic go. "Harry was one of the three founders of Dragon Soul," he explained. "He was apparently a nightmare to work with, liked to think he was better than everyone else, and threw fits when he didn't get what he wanted. All of that, so Dan and Dhruv kicked him out. The operating theory with your quest line was that Harry built it as a sort of a... Well, we don't really know." He considered. "I suppose that's part of why the Ds were gunning for you. It was personal. Even though *you* hadn't been involved before, Harry had, and they knew he was likely to screw them over in creative ways." He gave a pained smile.

"That makes a lot of sense, actually," Gracie said. "I wish you'd told me all of that sooner. I thought they were just being dicks. But if Harry built the quest, and they thought he was trying to take the whole game down or something..." She rubbed her head. "Now I feel guilty. Maybe I *should* delete my account or reroll or something."

"No! Don't." Jay nearly tipped over.

"Why not?" Gracie gave him a look. "Give me a *good* reason, man."

"I gots to know!" Jay said, shaking both fists. "Gracie, I am *so* curious. And I don't think it's *just* him trying to screw them over, either. You remember the things he was saying to you when you were in the dungeons? Like, he would say that no virtue or cruelty was wasted? I think that's... I think it's *real*."

Gracie frowned at him, tilting her head to the side quizzically.

"Hear me out," Jay said. He paused while he collected his thoughts. "*Metamorphosis Online* is the first game of its type. Ever."

"Sure," Gracie agreed cautiously.

"And you said yourself," Jay continued, "that it's *way* more immersive than D&D. It's intense, okay? In the heat of the moment, you make choices. You can be brave or you can...not. You can stand up for what's right, or just take the XP and the gold and keep your mouth shut, right? And yeah, it's just a game, except...what if he's right? What if it's *not* just a game, and what you do—the choices you make—change who you are and ripple back out?"

Gracie considered this. "I...guess I never would have *doubted* that they did," she said finally with a shrug. "It's important to do the right thing even when it seems stupid and pointless. Who you are—who you *really* are—shows in the small moments more than the big ones."

Jay smiled at her.

"What? Oh, come on, you got philosophical first." She felt obscurely self-conscious.

"It's not that." Jay couldn't seem to stop smiling. "It's just that I don't think it was a coincidence that the quest triggered in the way it did. I think— Okay, look. Harry was an asshole. Probably still is. But I get the sense that this game was important to him, and I think that was part of why he fought so hard to stay involved, and why he got so pissed when they kicked him out. He still had stuff he wanted to do."

"So he reached out to you," Gracie said slowly.

"Yeah. I don't know how he even knew who I was," Jay said. "Well, not a mystery, I suppose; He must still know people. He'll have heard rumors about me being fired, and he'll probably be aware that they were trying to take his quest down."

"So why'd he contact you, then?" Gracie settled back on the couch, pausing only to give Alex a sunny smile as he walked past on the way to the kitchen. He shot her another mock-glare.

"Still hasn't forgiven you, huh?" Jay asked, amused.

"Nope. And that bitch can hold a *grudge*, let me tell you." Gracie pitched her voice to carry and grinned when Alex stuck his head around the door.

"I heard that," he said.

"You were meant to," Gracie deadpanned.

Alex gave an anguished groan and disappeared again.

"So. Harry."

"Yeah." Jay sighed. "He...*found* a back way into the database, and wants me to work on a project with him."

"Jay." Gracie's face fell. "Jay, you *know* that guy is bad news."

"I don't, though! I don't know that." Jay shook his head. "I know that Dan and Dhruv are making some decisions I *definitely* don't agree with, that I think compromise the world, and... Gracie, I'm so curious. *I gots to know.*"

"Oh." Gracie started laughing. "You aren't even sure you want to help him. You just want to know more about how he did it."

Jay gave her a guilty smile. "Busted."

"I didn't bust you, dude. You figured it out on your own." She chewed on a nail. "Look, I'm just worried. You like this world, and you know Harry is pretty vindictive, right? What if he's trying to use you to screw them over and there's nothing honorable about it?"

"I thought of that." Jay held up a finger. "And it's an awful lot of *weird* effort to go to for that, Gracie. Why do this whole dungeon thing and bosses, and why *me*? He didn't know I'd run into you. If it was just to take them down, this was a really weird way to do it. Not to mention, he *must* need me for something."

"What if that something is to be his fall guy?" Gracie asked tartly.

"That's...a better point than I was expecting you to make," Jay grumbled.

"Gracie can be a real buzzkill," Alex agreed, coming

through the door. He spoke through a mouthful of cereal and gave Gracie a look. "What? It's the truth. He should know." He narrowed his eyes at her and went back to the kitchen, but she caught the corner of his mouth twitching.

"I at least want to figure out what he wants," Jay said. "I think it's worth doing that."

Gracie hunched her shoulders. "I think it's a bad idea."

"I think he's not squaring with me," Jay admitted. "But look…if it gets bad, I'll take it to Sam, all right? He didn't get fired, by the way. *Everyone* claimed to be responsible for leaking the wrong info to Demon Syndicate, and they knew better than to fire the whole department."

"I'm glad they didn't fire him," Gracie said soberly. "Look, just be careful, okay?"

"I will," Jay promised. "I'll keep you updated, too."

"Sure." She waved at him and signed off, biting her lip as she stared at the dark screen.

She was being a coward, she knew, avoiding asking him the one question she really wanted to, but the thought of it was terrifying.

"Maybe tomorrow," she told herself. There wasn't a high chance, given that she'd said the same thing for the past two days in a row, but she could at least feel like less of a coward this way. She smiled slightly and went to put on her headset.

"Heyyyy!" Kevin's greeting echoed across the line with an audible smile. "There she is."

"Gracie!" Lakhesis sounded excited. "Where are you? The inn? Don't move, I'm teleporting there."

"Why—" Gracie began, but Lakhesis was already in transit. She grimaced, but she was laughing. When Lakhesis appeared in front of her, Gracie planted her hands on her hips. "It's a magical world. We can hear each other from wherever."

"Yeah, but I wanted to see the 1!" Lakhesis pointed over Gracie's head. "Aw, yeah. That's sexy."

"*That's* what girls find sexy?" Alan teleported in as well, Mirra wearing a shiny new set of robes. "I've been misinformed."

"It's not like we made a secret of it," Gracie joked. "We put it in the minutes from the last meeting. They're all available as PDFs on the website."

Chowder laughed as he teleported in. He gave Gracie a two-finger salute and a nod. "I guess I know what my next research project is going to be, then. Hey, did anyone get hold of Jay to tell him Gracie's here?"

Gracie flushed. "He's, ah— I talked to him. He's handling something, but he'll be here in a bit, maybe. And Alex just got home from a *date*, so everyone needs to give him shit when he logs on. He might not tonight, though."

"Oooooooh." Ushanas had logged in. "Look who's got a *social life*." He made jazz hands for emphasis.

"I know, right?" Gracie shook her head. "Lame. So, what do you say we go do some random-ass questing?"

"Sounds good," Chowder agreed.

"I think we should bat around names for a guild," Kevin objected. "Because we should definitely be a guild now."

"Red Squadron," Alan suggested. When everyone

looked at him, he waved his hands. "You know…'They came from behind!'"

"Ohhhh." Gracie considered. "Wouldn't that make us the TIE Fighters, though?"

"Oh, shit." Alan shrugged. "That was all of my ideas. Who else has one?"

"We'll come up with something," Lakhesis said sagely. "I say we brainstorm while smashing faces."

"*Now* you're talking." Gracie hefted her sword. "Follow me, y'all. We have monsters to kill."

Most of the team had gone home when the phone dinged. The screen lit up, and Dan leaned over to look at the alert. His face didn't change as he read it.

But it didn't need to. Dhruv had known him for a long time, and he knew when Dan was happy about something.

"Well?" Dhruv asked. He'd been slouching in a chair, bouncing a ball off the floor and the wall and back to himself. He threw it again, caught it, and looked over.

Dan settled back in his chair. "They took the bait."

Dhruv raised an eyebrow. "So now…"

"Now we pretend to be Harry." Dan smiled at last, although it wasn't precisely a happy smile. "We have plenty to work with, after all. And they'll lead us right to all the pieces of the quest we couldn't find before." He caught sight of Dhruv's expression. "What?"

"It's risky relying on them to lead us to it," Dhruv said. "In order for him to find more, he'll be playing. Which means *she'll* be playing. Which means—"

"They'll be doing it anyway," Dan said, tight-lipped. "And *you* haven't made any progress, have you?"

Dhruv fell silent, his expression ugly.

Dan sighed and rubbed his forehead. "It's risky," he admitted. "We're driving them right toward the quest line. But chances are that they'd do it anyway, and I want to keep an eye on them."

"You're putting a clock on it," Dhruv said. He kept bouncing the ball, not looking at Dan. "You realize that, don't you? Because we have no idea how many more levels she has, and if she *finishes* the quest—"

"I *know*."

"*Do* you?" Dhruv stood up finally. "Because you're playing around like you don't. If she finishes that quest..." He leaned over the desk. "Odds are we're going to have to nuke the entire game—or let her be whatever Harry's made her into. Which, as far as I can tell, is going to be some sort of fucking demigod. If you don't pull this off, she'll be running *Metamorphosis*."

The story continues in book two, The New Queen Rises, available now at Amazon and through Kindle Unlimited.

Will the creators of *Metamorphosis Online* and their infighting ruin the game for everyone?

Over Gracie's dead avatar.

Others want to learn what is allowing Gracie's team to jump in the ranks, and are willing to go to great and scuzzy lengths to figure it out.

The group has decided to form a guild, but can they hold it together long enough to figure out a team tabard?

Can Gracie hold her team together while her personal life is going nowhere? Will she accept her mom's invite to join the family for her sister's engagement?

Metamorphosis Online is changing lives... Some for the better, some for the worse

The only thing Gracie believes is the power of her family...her digital family. She's learning that the rest of life is just details.

Click here to get your copy today.

AUTHOR NOTES - NATALIE GREY

MARCH 4, 2019

Thank you so much for reading *You Need a Bigger Sword*! I know Michael had been thinking about a GameLit story for quite a while, and I had enjoyed the genre, but hadn't been brave enough to dip a toe in. As per usual with our joint projects, it was Michael who got me to take a running leap off the cliff and build wings on the way down, and I'm so glad he did.

At the start, we didn't know much about the setting of our story. There was one thing, though, that I *knew* had to be involved. No one bats an eye when you talk about how books inspired you, or gave you courage, or made you see the world differently, or even helped you make friends.

But when you say you got those things from video games, people look at you like you're crazy.

And that's bonkers, because I've gotten all that and more from video games. Clear communication, learning what's in my lane and how my role interacts with other people's, thinking on my feet, resource management, absolutely useful skills. And, more than that, I've had both social and non-social testing grounds for exploring conflict, finding my moral boundaries ("Stand amongst the ashes of a trillion dead souls and ask the ghosts if honor matters. Their silence is your answer"), and understanding stories in a completely different way.

Those of you who aren't familiar with my alter ego, Moira, may not realize I've also been *writing* a video game recently - City of the Shroud, a multi-chapter RPG that adapts according to the choices of the player base. That experience, as well as the games I've played and adored, has influenced my part of this story in innumerable ways.

So thank you to Michael for asking me to collaborate on this series. Thank you to J, for introducing me to WoW. Thank you to A, B, K, V, and W for playing with me. Thank you to B, J, K, and A for playing FFXIV with me. Thank you to B for getting me to try Journey, which would help me dip my toe in the console world. Thank you to H and A for geeking out about Dragon Age and pushing me to play Mass Effect (which then ripped my heart out). Thank you to the writers, artists, composers, and game designers on multiple Final Fantasy games, Halo, Hearthstone, and so many more games. There have been times when the courage I found in these stories was what kept me going.

And above all, thank you to the readers. Books are a conversation. What we found in creating this story will not be exactly what you find in reading it. I hope you come out of this appreciating the social aspects of gaming, and the power of being able to learn about your own morality and strength, but I also know you'll come away with thoughts and conclusions we couldn't anticipate, and that's awesome.

To B and L, you make each day wonderful.

-Nat

THANK YOU for not only reading this story but these *Author Notes* **as well.**

(I think I've been good with always opening with "thank you." If not, I need to edit the other *Author Notes*!)

RANDOM (*sometimes***) THOUGHTS?**

Ok, here is where I admit I have been trying to find the right collaborator(s) to work in the GameLit and LitRPG genre for a while. ALSO trying to figure out what the @#%@#% is the difference between the two.

Oh, and crunchy? Yes, that's a thing.

Before I go further, I want to thank:

Dakota Krout—*Divine Dungeon* is what I read first, then *Ritualist* (you owe us the next book - so stop reading and write faster) and for making me appreciate a dungeon core (heart?) story.

James Hunter—*Viridian Gate Online* - (I'm jealous of your narrator's ability) Thank you for being willing to chat to stupid times of the night about this genre and giving me your opinions of what is making fans love these types of books, and what drives them gob-stopping nuts.

Aleron Kong—For taking the time to explain to me what it meant exactly to be LitRPG - and not making me feel completely foolish when I asked you stupid questions

Aaron Crash—For being the physically funniest author I have been around as we chat GameLit. You help me realize I'm ok.

(Yes, Aaron, there is a compliment in there for you.)

Before I get to my collaborator, I want to also think Danielle and Jeanette for supporting their spouses and being ok when I take their time and we geek out on ostensibly stupid stuff for incredibly reasonable reasons or reasonable stuff for incredibly stupid reasons.

Whether it is with scorpion stories (SHEILA!) or whatever bullshit we get up to.

I'd like to sincerely thank Natalie Grey for allowing me to argue, cajole, and encourage her as we created our first GameLit series. When we discussed this story, I wanted to capture something (we both I believe) have an interest, and we wanted to express for our generations (she is younger than I am) that...

Games, especially MMORPG and similar ones are a way for normally shy or introverted people to get a chance to meet others from around the world.

Games are a way to escape the stress and pressure that today's society brings us, and they allow us to release our frustrations upon the hapless kobolds or orcs (or humans, you Horde people), since carrying around a twenty-pound chunk of steel is usually frowned upon in polite society.

Games allow us to socialize with someone next to you, next door, some other state, or in even a country across the world.

And kill them for loot and plunder. Hopefully, they don't camp on your spawn point and grief the hell out of you.

Looking at you *FarCry001Zedbot*.

Further, one thing I wanted to convey in our story is that we (gamers) have been helped by people we've never met, at an emotional level through this powerful medium known as gaming.

So, all of those who decry gaming as evil (*should they ever read our books*) might see how gaming has changed lives, and often for the better.

I know it's changed mine.

I'm reminded of the Friday nights we system-linked our XBOX consoles together and sniped the hell out of each other playing *Halo: Combat Evolved*....

Damn, good times.

Until my then-eight-year-old sons kicked my ass at *Starcraft II*. It was at *that* moment I figured out it was time to (perhaps) hang up my XBOX Duke controller and mouse.

Or ground him from playing video games until he lost his preternaturally quick hand-eye coordination.

I couldn't do that, so I've stayed farther and farther away from video games and taken on writing (eventually) as a career.

I don't live in a home with enough room right now, but when I do, I'm buying that 75" or larger flat screen, a Microsoft XBOX, Sony Playstation, and a sound system to upset my neighbors and get back into it.

Until then, I have to enjoy living vicariously through stories that bring my early love of games back into my life.

Like right now I'm reading Eric Ugland's *One More Last Time* and it has brought a smile to my face.

For those who love game-integrated stories, I raise my flagon of root beer in your direction and yell a hearty *GAME ON!*

You might take the games out of my life for a time, but gaming is in my blood, and I'm happy as hell to be creating stories where games are a part of the character's life.

Like they have been to me since *PONG.*

Yes, I am that old, don't judge me ;-)

So, To Natalie Grey, I raise my virtual game controller in your direction. You built a story beyond my hopes, and I'm damned proud to have my name on this cover with you.

FAN PRICING

$0.99 Saturdays (new LMBPN stuff) and $0.99 Wednesday (both LMBPN books and friends of LMBPN books.) Get great stuff from us and others at tantalizing prices.

Go ahead. I bet you can't read just one.

Sign up here: http://lmbpn.com/email/.

HOW TO MARKET FOR BOOKS YOU LOVE

Review them so others have your thoughts, and tell

friends and the dogs of your enemies (because who wants to talk to enemies?)... *Enough said ;-)*

Ad Aeternitatem,

Michael Anderle

Mahalia

BOOKS BY MICHAEL ANDERLE

For a complete list of books by Michael Anderle, please visit

www.lmbpn.com/ma-books/

All LMBPN Audiobooks are Available at Audible.com and
iTunes. For a complete list of audiobooks visit:

www.lmbpn.com/audible

CONNECT WITH THE AUTHORS

Natalie Grey Social

Email List

https://landing.mailerlite.com/webforms/landing/w0k9j4

Follow Natalie on Amazon

https://www.amazon.com/Natalie-Grey/e/B01MYG7K8P/

Facebook

https://www.facebook.com/Natalie-Grey-393234677682987/

Michael Anderle Social

Website: http://lmbpn.com

Email List: http://lmbpn.com/email/

Facebook:
www.facebook.com/TheKurtherianGambitBooks